PIG IRON

Benjamin Myers

BLOOMSBURY PUBLISHING

LONDON · OXFORD · NEW YORK · NEW DELHI · SYDNEY

BLOOMSBURY PUBLISHING
Bloomsbury Publishing Plc
50 Bedford Square, London, WC1B 3DP, UK

BLOOMSBURY, BLOOMSBURY PUBLISHING and the Diana logo
are trademarks of Bloomsbury Publishing Plc

First published in Great Britain by Bluemoose Books 2012
This edition published 2019

A catalogue record for this book is available from the British Library.

ISBN: PB: 978-1-5266-1118-5; eBook: 978-1-5266-1119-2

2 4 6 8 10 9 7 5 3 1

Typeset by Short Run Press

Printed and bound in Great Britain by
CPI Group (UK) Ltd, Croydon CR0 4YY

To find out more about our authors and books visit
www.bloomsbury.com and sign up for our newsletters

For Adelle Stripe

"Even within the most beautiful landscape, in the trees, under the leaves the insects are eating each other; violence is a part of life."

~ Francis Bacon

This is a work of fiction.

Part I
Beasts of the Field

The green cathedral sleeps. Soon it will throw open its doors and let the light in. Shades of amber will creep across the forest floor, the shadows will shrink away, and the daily service of life and growth and death and decay will go on.

For now the night is still fuzzy around the edges. Blurred. It's not dark and it's not light. The sun hasn't risen. The sane world is sleeping. It's that strange inbetween stage that belongs to the creatures.

Beneath the stained-glass canopy the beasts and the creatures daren't really nod off, for the closing of eyes can be fatal.

Unlike me they only intuitively understand that a fate awaits them, summat that's a threat to them, and that life is but an attempt to prolong the whatsit. Aye. The inevitable.

The air is grainy and dream-like. It's like watching an auld film. One of them silent ones. Not black and white, but a sort of washed-out brown. A silent brown film about the dawning of a new English summer's day in this green cathedral of mine.

Mebbes one with a happy ending though.

There are shadows down there in the trees. They emerge for a moment, then disappear silently. The shadows are beasts and the beasts are shaped like humans.

Between me and them the grass is rustling and the daisies are stretching and yawning and the insects pupating and the rodents scurrying unseen. But it is happening. Life is happening all around us; it always does.

I feel like I always feel, an outsider. I'm laid out up here, flat on me belly at the top of this sort of quarried cliff face high up in

1

the green cathedral of the great outdoors, me clothes wet with the dew from the long grass and me eyes trained to that gap in the trees where I last saw them. I'm used to it, mind. Being on the outside looking in. It's funny though because just over a month ago, and for five year before that, I was on the inside looking out. Craning me neck to see half a tree or a patch of grass or the jackdaw coming in to roost on the roof. I'd have done owt for a few breaths of good clean fresh air, and now I've got bloody hods of it I still don't feel free.

Some might say that's whatsit. Aye. Ironic.

I'm gasping for a bine but I cannot spark one up. They might see the glow of it in this crooked pre-dawn light, or the smoke rising from this little quarry cliff top.

Summat's digging into me thigh an all. It's the eye in me pocket. The glass eye that I've carried around with us for five year. The unlucky charm. It takes some quiet tugging but I carefully pull it out and stick it in me zip-up side coat pocket instead. That's better.

The woods are more like a dream now. Like it could all disappear at any minute.

I've not moved for ages. I daren't even blink.

Me cammo army coat is sopping.

I swear down. I never asked for none of this.

I've been squinting at the same view for hours but only now is it becoming clearer.

I'm perched where the western moorlands give way to the woods that roll down to the flatter eastern plane, which then ripples all the way to the sea. I reckon I can just about see a fuzzy grey band of water where the sky meets the horizon however many miles away. Eight or ten mebbes. Probably more.

The land is laid out here before us. My land. The turf that birthed us. And it'd be picture bloody perfect if it wasn't for the beasts that I know are down there, waiting. Them that's after us.

2

The shapes. Them that's tucked in the trees like terriers round a rat hole. Just waiting for a movement, a moment.

Bloody pack animals, them lot. Beasts of the field. Povvy little gets.

I don't want none of this shite. Alls I've ever wanted was to get me head down and crack on. It's a load of bloody bollards, the lot of it. Alls I've ever wanted is to be left alone to work and wander and breathe the same air as everyone else.

But no. There's always summat or someone sticking their nebby nose in. There's always new enemies lining up left, right and bloody centre, and all for what. All for being born under a queer moon into the wrong family, that's what. Cursed from birth and that. Shat out like a bloody turd and treated like one ever since.

I tell you what though. I'll do what ever it takes to get out of the green cathedral alive because nee-one's laying their hands on us again. I've had enough of all that. I'll not stop at battering them either.

I'm sick of it all, me. Sick of running, sick of the guilt that's like a hand round your throat in the night, when you're all alone and exposed in the darkness, and there's just you and the knowledge of what you've done.

You carry it inside you, this fear of your own dark potential. You carry it in your chest. And you carry it in your blood.

Mebbes it was always there, right from the beginning. From the moment circumstance grabbed us.

*

There was the sound of a grave crying in my ear that night, and that's when I knew he wasn't going to make it.

You took that ash-coloured poker and you raised it one more time and you brought it down right on his head again.

3

Metal on bone makes an awful noise and his skull cracked like an eggshell. You could see the skin split to show the squirming redness beneath it and I did go to scream but nowt came out save a backwards hiccup that stuck in me throat like half a wishbone. I'd not wish this on me worst cursed enemy.

His eyelids were fluttering then, and his right leg went dead straight like a mouse that's just had its back flattened in a trap. It shot out, then it twitched and I knew that blow had him done for.

There was a dent in his head and in the bottom of the poker-shaped hollow I could see the brain inside him. It was pink and white and blue and brown and many other colours besides and I swear on the Virgin Mary's name I could smell it an all. It was the one muscle that was never much use to him, bless him.

And the poker – it was in your hand. It was hanging there by your side, and there was blood everywhere. Little spots all over the van walls. Droplets. A thousand of them. In that moment I could see that death was crawling over him. Crawling all over my husband. And he was wrestling it, and he was losing. Losing the will, like. His body was a grey beach and the tide was going out, out, all the way out, never to return.

He was a twisted heap at your feet and his bones were all broke up and he was barely breathing. He was like a little bird that had fallen from his nest or summat. I'd not seen him so small. Such a big man when he was upright an all.

It might be that his insides were all ruptured and it might be that his head was tapped in like a scrap-heap kettle pot. It might be that his last breath was working its way up through his chest and all that anger and energy and violence and madness was working its way out of him like a poison that only death himsel can release and it might be that you'd flogged the life out of him. Bashed and battered him, as he had bashed and battered others with nowt but coiled fists swung like mallets.

Flesh and blood. You took that flesh and blood and you reduced it down to the dying gasps, the little bird, the sea-less beach.

And he was smiling. His top lip had curled back into a sneer. When he had the drink in him he had this look about him — you'd have recognised it no doubt, you more than most. It was like even in the death throes he was laughing at you. Even when you'd broke up his bones and caved his face in, he was grinning. The grin said that even in death he was winning.

I've seen nowt so grim as the way he looked in that moment, his lip curled back and his gums turning blue like bits of horse meat going off in the knacker's yard drain.

It was a queer moon that night an all. That's the other thing I remember. Another odd moon, just like the one the night you were born. There's only twice have I ever seen the sun block the moon in such a way, and both times it cast its strange light on you.

And you — you were just stood there with that poker in your hand, breathing heavy, with sweat on your brow and this sort of devilish glow about you. Like the moon had turned you strange.

It was like Satan himsel was in the room, like you were wearing his eyes, and I says to mesel, Oh Lord what is it that I have done to you to get dealt a hand like this? But the Lord didn't answer because if He were watching down upon us He'd a struck you down there and then in the van. Smited you good and proper for the wicked thing what ye done that day. Or mebbe he'd have given me the strength to take that poker from your shaking hand and bash you senseless mesel.

But you're flesh and blood an all, and where would that have got us. What would that have made me, then?

And the breath was rattling in his chest. Oh yes, I did hear it and so did you.

Him that could shift a ton of scrap in half a day or run a mile through the woodland in four minute flat or pull out fence posts four feet deep; him that even bulls a feart on account of his bare-handed yoking; him who carried the fighting crown for all *them years, whose name was known on every site on this island of ours – he was finally slipping away. Bleeding like a river he was, from all his holes, and his head was turned at an angle something queer, like.*

And all the while he were rattling and you were just stood there and it was only then I saw, for the very first time, that you had the look of your father about you, and that did chill my bones to icicles.

I had a mind to run and fetch one of the others, but it were too late for that. Time was running out as he lay there, his skin turning white and yellow and blue and a bubble of blood on his lips, and when that bubble did burst and the rattle did stop, his spirit lifted out of him – what was left of him anyway – off into the heavens, because when all is said and done, and even after all them beatings and cruelty and everything else that happened, he was after all a man, my man, and I believe that was where he was going.

And that was when I got the weakness on me and I did faint.

*

They reckon that elephants can detect the presence of a dead relative. Like they can tell if a random skull in the wild belongs to a brother, or a mother or summat.

I saw a programme on it inside. This camera crew tracked a herd of elephants for weeks and then one day they walked through the trees and into this clearing – a clearing a bit like this one, come to think of it – and suddenly all these great creatures slowed their pace and fell silent. They bowed their heads and this sense of quiet agitation fluttered through them. The camera crew knew summat was up because they'd followed them day and night, knew their eating habits and their toilet routines but they had never seen them acting like this before.

The gadgie talking over it all in this sort of hushed voice then telt us that the reason they were acting weird was because they knew the bones of one of their own were laid nearby.

And sure enough a minute or two later they came across the bleached-white remains of another elephant, its flesh long since rotted and removed by the scavengers of the savannah. Then the gadgie tells us the bones belonged to the mother of one of the calves in the herd, and she'd disappeared six month earlier during the early days of them making their fillum.

The elephants crowded round the skeleton, unsure at first. They started sniffing the bones, then pushing them about with their trunks. And as they did they had this look about them – all sad eyes and bowed heads and one or two of them letting out the odd gentle wail of pain. But they were graceful and all. Dignified. It was like they were all whatsit together. Aye – mourning.

They reckoned elephants are the only creatures that grieve like that, except mebbes for humans.

Well, even the maddest cold-blooded nutter would have felt summat watching them creatures like that.

Then one of the older elephants picked up the skull and carefully moved it a few metres away into this shaded part on the edge of the clearing. Somewhere more peaceful and secluded. Like it was laying its relative to rest.

"A common practice for the elephants is to move the skull of a loved one," the gadgie whispered.

Me, I can relate to the lingering presence of the dead an all. Only I'm not mourning, just remembering and never forgetting. If I could dig up that skull I reckon I'd be inclined to boot it around in the dirt for a bit first because though I've got a heart, a beating heart, a git biggen, until I've got free of the past and free of this bloody town it'll always ache in me chest summat rotten.

*

They never much cared for Mackie Wisdom, didn't your Gran and Granda. Auld Cooper and Pearl Dunne. Even before they met him, even before he turned up that day with his whitest

7

white shirt starched stiff across his chest and his free-range face scrubbed clean, their minds were made up.

Because betimes history does cast a shadow over everything and never before had these two particular bloodlines had cause to mingle.

They knew of the Wisdoms. Of course they did. Everyone did. Travellers and country folk alike. Some said they'd been cursed with the wickedness since the days of Cromwell.

Said it had made them all crooked and wiley, and they weren't to be trusted. Said they had the violence running through those Wisdom generations like a coal seam in the northern soil. Toughest of the tough that lot.

Because we were good folk, the Dunnes. Good honest workers. Land people. Field people. You'd not hear a bad word breathed about us from any mouth. Because any Dunne would give any man his only mattress or his last morsel; it's the way we are. The goodness was bred into us, just like that wickedness ran through the Wisdoms all the way back to days of wattle and daub.

It didn't stop us from falling for the one they said was the rottenest of the lot though, did it. Mac Wisdom. Big Mac to all that knew and feart him. The oldest of seven boys; some born daft, some born sneaky, but all of them surly and tough as pig iron.

I never did think to find out what Mac stood for. Macdonald or Mackenzie, perhaps. Or mebbes MacHenry.

Too late to ask now.

So the day I fetched up with him your Gran and Granda Dunne's eyes did tell their own tales. They saw a bully and a braggard, an uncouth youth who would spell no good for their little Vancy.

It was a condemnation of silent eyes and whispers though, for it was bad doings to be vocal about another family. That way vendettas started. The Wisdoms were not a brood to engage in a blood feud with, nor were the Dunnes the type to seek one out.

He was handsome alright, was your Dad, a good looking man, born swarthy, but my Ma and Da thought everything about the way he was put together was wrong for their Vancy, a snip of a child at barely fifteen year old. He was salt to my sugar, they said; overbearing and unwieldy, as if no room could contain him. Too big for his body, they said. Too big for anywhere but the outdoors, like.

He had meaty arms and large knotted hands, thick lips, a strong jaw and a landslide brow that cast his squinting black eyes into a permanent state of shadow. Where others saw menace I saw the face of a matinee idol.

My Da called him Desperate Dan on account of the black stubble that looked like he'd just rubbed mud into his cheeks instead of aftershave.

"Is Desperate Dan coming round with his face fungus?" he'd say because he knew how to wind us up like a spinning top, your Granda. "Shall your Ma get a cow pie on the go?"

"Why don't you ask him, Dad?" I'd say, and that'd have him muttering because by the time Mac had turned twenty, all them years of smashing and lifting, wandering and fighting had built Mac Wisdom up into a straight six feet of muscle. Nature's gymnasium – that's what he called the great outdoors that had shaped him; the outdoors through which he'd run as a feral creature of the fields and woods, the boy who couldn't read or write but could tickle trout at ten, or poach a brace of pheasants or a branch of rabbits or take down an engine and put it back together again blindfolded.

There was no need for school and its book learning. And that's where the Dunnes and Wisdoms were similar, you see. We all of us lived in caravans and proudly called oursels traveller folk and we all of us regarded them classrooms as prisons. But that's where the similarities ended.

The Wisdom name whispered its way across the corn and the coalfields and round the villages long before your Dad ever even went on the cobbles.

Me Mam and Dad knew this. It's every traveller's business to know the way of the clans. What lines run where. Who's married who. It's the travelling way and the key to keeping the bloodline. Because once the bloodlines start getting too mixed up – or not mixed up enough – things start turning in on themsels and things get bent and then you do be getting bother.

And in the long run bother it was that came to our doorstep, right enough.

*

Fresh air. That's all I was after. A bit of bloody fresh air and the freedom to walk without having to turn corners. A bit of sun an all, I thought. That'd do nicely. Aye. The sun on me face and mebbe a bit of a breeze blowing through me hair. Blue cloudless skies above and nowt but fields and trees and streams in all directions as far as the eye can see. That was all. It's not that much to ask, is it.

And if it rained I'd not even be arsed. I'd still be bloody happy just to be out in it getting soaked to the skin. It could hoy it down and the sky could be alive with lightning and that and I'd still have a git big bloody grin on me face. I'd be out in it probably, running through the fields billy bollocks and laughing me mouth off.

Because I'd be free for the first time in five years. Free for the first time in me life actually, come to think of it. Nee-one pushing us there or pulling us here; nee-one prodding or piss-taking or wanting to have a go. Sweet relief. What I'd do for a bit of bloody peace and quiet.

It's hard to believe that was only a month ago. Time grinds when you're all alone.

There was nee fanfare when the moment came. Nee popping corks either, mind, and nee-one to tell that I'm not coming back to this shite hole. Just a kick up the scut and me bus fare home, and then there's just me and me thoughts and then the world suddenly pouring in like the walls I've built around us have just sprung a leak. Loads of bloody leaks. The world streaming into us.

I'm walking out through the foyer across the car park out the front, past the trimmed little hedge and the turning circle for the mini-buses that'll soon be bringing in the next lot of gobshites, and then left out into the road by which point I'm going Adios gimlets. Adios the bloody lot of you.

And that's it. Five years is ower and gone in the time it takes to draw breath and I'm stood there facing forward, thinking about nowt much but putting one foot in front of the other.

Smalls steps towards a brighter future, all being well.

It's warm out, proper warm, full summer an that, and the air is so fresh I can taste it. I can bite crunchy chunks out of it. The fresh air tastes lush. Luxurious. I suck it in and feel it blowing away the lingering smells of stale farts, cheap hash, buckets of bleach and steaming bowls of liver and bloody onions.

It cleans us from the inside out, this fresh air. The world smells good. Smells of freedom.

It's quiet out here an all. It's not like how you've read about, where cons on the street are bombarded by the noise and speed of the outside world so much that they want to turn and run back inside, cowering. Na. No way. It's inside where you're bombarded. All that bang and clatter. All them braggarts and blowhards whose howls and bellows merge into ghostly echoes at night, the echoes of scared little boys rebounding in the corridors and rec rooms and disinfected dining halls.

Fresh air and silence. Bloody lovely.

I get to moving, glad to finally be left alone at last.

I walk.

I walk without my shoes squeaking and without feeling edgy or para.

I take deep breaths and I walk in a straight line along an empty road that leads back into town. I've not walked this far in a straight line without some hand at me elbow or breath down me neck for bloody yonks.

I could get a bus but I'm not going to. I never got them before and I'm not about to start now. If you can't fetch yersel somewhere by foot, then it's not worth fetching to. Or you're a lazy get, in which case you should get out more, like.

And these boots are made for walking, marrer.

It's not long before I've got a nice sweat on. I could walk for miles without tiring, me. Always have done. It's in me blood.

I take me top off and drape it round me neck to give me pits an airing.

I just want to keep walking past it all, keep on ganning down the streets, across the cobbles and through the town and out the other bloody side, out into the dark dense woodlands, just get mesel away from this bloody place and on up to far-flung fields and hills and moors, keep on walking all the way up to the sky.

Because this town's not for me. Never was really. I prefer to be on me tod and that's hard to do when there's nebby nose gadgies everywhere.

Aye. It's not like in the fillums. There's nee words of wisdom and clip round the ear-hole from the friendly screw. There's nee greeting party out here. Not for me, anyway. Nee lasses to snog us, nee new born bairns with leering Winston whatsit faces and heads to wet; nee fat cigars or slaps on the back.

Neebody's missed this lad.

But there's somewhere to gan though. They've got us in this place so they can keep an eye on us. It's one of me parole conditions. I signed a bit of paper. A contract. I made promises. All that blether.

The estate where me new flat is, is through the town and up the hill to a jumble of red bricks and dog shit.

I've been here already mind, up on day release with the case worker, then after that with the re-assimilation worker and then with the social worker and then finally with Dickhead Derek my probation coordinator, a right tit of a man with nostril hairs like spider's legs and a proper bad case of dandruff. It's like, do you not have mirrors in your house or summat. Sort it out, you bell-end.

Aye, cos they've been easing us back in slowly. Or easing us out. Really it's like going from one prison to another, a big one to a small one, but at least I can come and go now. At least I'm away from all them povvy gimlets inside.

So there's been tests to do and forms to fill in just to get us to here. Hods of them. Bloody hundreds actually. It's a good job I've been working on me reading and writing otherwise they could have had us signing owt they fancied. And there's been one-to-ones and head to heads an all; assessments and interviews and medicals.

Because there are channels to go through, they say.

Processes and protocols, they say.

Conditions and that.

Mebbes they just want to keep their conscience clean when they unleash us into this town. This town of bloody ghosts and shite and nightmares. Putting us back in the past like this. Well, it can't be good can it. I'd rather they sent us somewhere else like, where me family name wasn't known. Switzerland or summat. Or Middlesbrough mebbe.

The flat they've put us in is an insult to humans and pigs alike, but I'm not arsed, me. At least I get to lock the doors mesel for once. Got me own key an everything. And anyroad, I'm not stopping long. This is the thought I cling to: I'm not stopping long.

So it's up the hill I go. Up the hill and into the estate where broken windows watch us, and eyeballs blink from darkened doorways and footsteps disappear down grubby little snickets. It's a right rabbit warren, this place.

Aye. This flat is a proper insult, and that's exactly what I telt them when they brought us here a month or two back, all of them cooing like pigeons, gannin ooh look at this John you can see the dual carriageway from your bedroom window, and me going, big wow – and by the way it's John-John not John. Take that name and double it.

Still though. It's better than that povvy half-way house in town that they had us in at weekends. Just about.

Christ almighty – what a place that was though. Worse than being in prison. Mould and damp and more locks than the big house. Full of winderlickers too. Proper nutty, some of that lot. Proper pervs.

So four year into the sentence and they get us out on the day release. One day a week for starters. Then after a bit it's alternate weekends, stopping at the half-way house with the jalkies.

Then after that it's every weekend. Then it's every weekend and Wednesday nights. So, three nights a week. And that's been going on for the past however long.

Easing us out. Easing us back in.

Nice and easy, John-John lad, they telt us. Keep a cool head. Nee-one's out to get you no more. We're here to help you lad. Got a nice little flat for you to help you find your feet.

Help you whatsit. Aye – assimilate.

So now they've got us up in this flat on the estate with its broken fences, the kiddies on bikes and mingers loitering in skirts that only just cover their barely hairy fannys. There are always lads kicking about, with this helmet hair they never used to have when I went in, and everyone talking on mobile phones, looking like they're yapping into thin air like proper numpties. They all look the same as they ever did but yet different somehow. Like they're one step removed from the place I remember. Like they've fast forwarded themsels into the future and left me behind to try and make sense of it all.

Cars flash by and I finger the key in my pocket. I've got me bag on my back, with me books and baccy in there.

Mind, for all this estate's faults I'm glad to be away from the case workers and all them nebs in suits. They're nee better than the screws in Deerbolt, Low Newton, Hassockfield or any of them places. Worse sometimes. At least the screws make no bones about not giving a shit about us. Them social workers have to pretend to care and that fake sincerity proper boils my piss.

I gan through the arch and up the stairwell. Put the key in the door.

Live here, they telt us. Live here, it's lovely. Your own place. Look – you can see the dual carriageway from your window.

I can't live here, I telt them.

Why not?

It's not my way. It's not what we do.

You'll be fine.

And though it pains us to say it, I say it anyway: looker, I've never lived in a bloody house before.

Well beggars can't be choosers, John.

I'm nee beggar, like. And it's bloody John-John. I telt you already. Take that name and double it.

Sorry. *John-John.* We didn't mean you were a beggar.

I should have telt them I was sick of being kept in smelly boxes. I should have telt them how I'd rather be anywhere but here, how confinement is even worse for us than it is for everyone else and I'd rather kip in a ditch. How despite the way I talk and what me file says and what they already think about us, I'm not one of them charver kids that spent his life indoors eating crisps and watching telly while mummy sucked off podgy truckers for money upstairs. I should have let them know how I spent me years in the fields in the fresh air, just as nature intended, just as generations did before us, and if that makes us an animal, then so be it. Then I'm an animal.

But I didn't say that. I just sucked it up and took the key and signed the forms and nodded in all the right places. Yes sir, no sir, kiss me rusty sheriff's badge sir.

The stairwell is dark and dank and acidic in me nostrils.

Indoors it's nee better. The flat is shadowy and sparse and fusty, barely fit for vermin. It's exactly the type of place me Mam

15

would screw her nose up at, shaking her head and gannin look at them poor bastards stuck in them brick boxes like bloody hamsters. It's not right, that.

Because Mam was a woman of the fields and woods, and a lady of the road an all, a proper traveller from good travelling stock, and she always kept the vans spotless, whatever was gannin on. Whatever me Dad done. Whatever he'd been up to she'd always be there behind him, sweeping up the broken glass and mopping up the stains.

I turn on the light and the wall crackles. Dodgy electrics.

There's a halo of flies around the bare light bulb and some weird stain on the carpet. A faint smell of shite in the air makes us feel right at home. There's nowt much else to see. Just an armchair and a crappy MDF unit in the living room, a bedroom with a mattress and some blankets on it, and a kitchen with a fridge and a cooker and a microwave with nee door on it. Mouse winnets on the floor.

Oh aye, and a view of the dual carriageway.

I chuck down my stuff and do a rollie. I get up again and light it off the blue flame from the hob in the kitchen, then sit down and inhale.

Well, I think.

I'm out, I think.

Finally out.

Then I exhale.

*

We've always been short and stout, the Dunnes. Built like bullets, me Dad always said. It's in the breeding, he reckoned. In the bloodline.

Land-grafters, most of us. The men and the women. Agriculturalists and farm labourers. Scythers and bailers. Wood cutters and pail-fetchers.

Good people; strong and stoic people, our bodies compacted from the years of stooping and planting; compressed from generations of being near to the ground that fed and clothed us.

There was no duckering or chorring amongst our ancestors. No. The Dunnes could be trusted. Country folk knew us. Knew we were different.

Your Gran and Granda moved around for seven or eight or more months a year following the seasonal work. They'd pick apples down in Somerset and hops over in Kent. They'd help with the harvest in Hampshire and when the going was good they bought and sold horses at the fairs of Cambridgeshire and Cumbria. And when it was bad they knocked on farmhouse doors offering labour for bait, milk and somewhere to stop.

These were the travellers that the farmers who are old enough to remember speak of fondly: them that wafted in with the first warm breeze of spring and hitched up and out with the turning of the leaves, leaving no trace except for a stale patch or two of grass where the kids had put up a couple of makeshift hazelwood bender tents.

It was the coal that brought us to the north-east. Before they had me the Dunnes tried their hands at sea-coaling up in Northumberland. Lynemouth Bay, I believe. They worked the tide with nowt but a rented horse and a rotten auld salty cart, knee-deep in the swell day after day. They lived on steamed kelp and limpets and the blackness did stay in their skin and under their fingernails for a long time after. This was when coal washed up on the beach of course. Back before it all changed.

Me Dad – your Granda – Cooper had not long married your Grandma Pearl of the Smith lot. There were gypsy Smiths all ower the place so I'd not bother trying to track down that side of your family if you value your time. There's a Tinker Smith or a Tommy Smith or a John Smith on any site you'd care to name, and they'd all lay claim to be your relative if they thought there was summat in it for them.

17

Well then. Fate must have brought them together because they were married that winter and by the next summer they were working the eastern shoreline, from Teesside to the crumbling coasts of County Durham, up past Wearmouth and the Tyne and on to the black beaches up as far as Lynemouth. Back-breaking times.

It was the fields and meadows of the land of the Prince Bishops that they liked best though, and that was where they decided to stop for a while, labouring patchwork land that was waiting to be ploughed and turned and tilled. From then on they were Cooper and Pearl Dunne: no fixed abode, but plenty of places to stay.

And stay they did.

And that's where a part of you comes from, my son.

*

I get mesel a job the second day I'm out. Piece of piss. It's no thanks to the spanners down at the parole board mind, who tell us I'm a special case. Those are the words that they use: special case.

A special case that they're monitoring closely on account of all that happened. Load of bloody bollards, the lot of it. I can't wipe me scut without being assessed first. And according to them I can't get a bloody job without their say-so either.

Your reputation precedes you John-John, they go.

I said nowt to this. Just let them speak, like.

Finding work may not be easy, they said. You're known around the town. And beyond the town too. People know your name, John-John. They remember you. They remember what happened. And if they don't remember what happened they still remember the Wisdoms.

So I stood up.

What are you saying, like.

It's alright John-John. There's no need to get upset. It's just going to take time that's all. Time to readjust and slowly re-integrate you back into mainstream society.

The silly twats. They knew fine well I'd not been a part of any of that in the first place. Or they would if they'd bothered to have read my case notes and not just them newspaper clippings they've got filed away. It was circumstance that put us away – they know that. They even telt us as much.

It's not your fault John-John, they said. It was your domestic situation. The abuse. Mac.

Aye. Well.

You know, your case was quite well publicised they said, their voices all greasy in their throats.

Folk have heard of you John-John, they said. You and your father.

Oh, you're off your heads you lot are, I telt them. One minute you're telling us I need to get me head down and get a job to keep on the bloody whatsit – straight and narrer – the next you're telling us to do nowt. Well, listen to this: I'll get a job mesel. And it'll be a good one and all. And I'll keep me bloody head down and I'll pay hods of bloody taxes and you can mark it down as repayment for the rent up in the big house. And don't be bringing me auld man into it neither. He's got nowt to do with this.

OK John-John.

OK John-John, I mimicked, the dumpling-arsed, grey-faced numpties.

Off your bloody heads.

Then I got up and left.

And it's me that's laughing now because here I am, a couple of days out, and I've already got mesel a job selling bloody ice creams for Arty Vicari to the bairns around the town.

So just to re-cap in case any one is monitoring us even more closely than I thought: I've got a flat, a job and I've got big plans.

Git big bloody plans to get as far away from here as possible. So far away you'll never see us again.

So what do you lot think of that then?

Aye – just what I thought. Stunned into silence.

*

We were stopping on a site a few miles out of town, up on the side of a valley flooded with bluebells when I met your Dad in the beer garden of The Shoulder Of Mutton during the earliest days of summer.

I'm no good with dates. It was the year that England won at the football, I remember that much, a long summer of endless possibility. For three long golden months it did feel like the sun was shining down on our own green corner of the world.

The only travelling we did that season was by foot. It was a time of cook-outs and long walks over the auld viaduct and along the meandering river bank paths down into town.

Mac showed me new places. He brought the landscape alive. He could do that just by pointing out something other people wouldn't notice. Animal tracks funnelling their way through the long grass, the fallen limb of a tree scratched to pieces by a passing badger.

Betimes we'd take all day strolling through the buttercup patches and freshly-shorn fields, clouds of dust ballet-dancing over the stubble and the hum of distant hay-balers hanging heavy in the air as we followed the Wear down into the city. We'd stop off at The Shakespeare or The Dun Cow for a drink or two before getting chips or a roast pork sandwich from the indoor market that we'd eat on the long slow walk back, me arm looped through Mac's, his thick muscles pressing against my thin crook.

It was adoration. He just had a way. A way of holding himsel. A look. You could see it in the way people acted around him an all. They never looked at him square on, always sideways, after he'd passed.

Mebbe they recognised him, I thought. Mebbe they had seen him scrapping down at the Big Meeting that spring, when all the collieries had paraded their flags and the knuckle men went behind the big tops and tents and stalls to settle some scores.

I was just a wee slip of a thing. Just gone fifteen and green as spring corn cobs. I knew nowt about the world, nowt about anything much but how to get the logs in and how to polish brass pots so bright you're the envy of all the magpies to fifty mile and back.

*

You ever worked with ice cream before, Johnno?

What do you think, I want to say. Course I bloody haven't. And you can stop calling us bloody Johnno an all, daft get.

But I bite my lip and keep quiet because I need this job. I need to get some money together to get away. Away from the town of ghosts before they suck us back in.

I've eaten a few, like.

Funny says Arty. But he's not smiling.

Arty is Tony's Dad. Arty Vicari.

Arty and Tony Vicari.

Tony was in Deerbolt with us. He was this smackhead lad who had somehow ended up getting three year for accidentally kidnapping some bloke. If that makes him sound tough he wasn't; he was just another daft knacker in hot water thanks to a hankering for the brown powder, like most of the herberts in there. It was summat to do with tying up a dealer that he owed money to, or owed him, or shagged his girlfriend. It didn't really matter. I heard similar stories every other week from someone or other in there. Knobheads, the lot of them.

He was nowt to look at, Tony. A proper streak of piss he was. All ribs and elbows and wide eyes like a little spuggie waiting for a worm. He was taller than me but he just had the look about him. Textbook soft touch. It's not how big you are, it's how you hold yersel. That's one thing me dad learnt us. One of the only

21

things he said that made sense. And the way Tony Vicari held himself advertised his vulnerability like a roadside billboard.

It wasn't long before the lads moved in. That trial period where they'll leave you be until they've sussed out whether you're a nutter or not had passed and Tony V had failed with flying colours. He was nee nutter. Neither am I mind, but at least I can pretend. Tony trying to act hard only made it worse. Lads already knew that Mr Whippy was his dad.

The lads. Them half dozen dribblers, knuckleheads and underfed nerks who had got this far on brute force and brainless stupidity, already institutionalised by the time they were old enough to tax. They were real medieval merchants this lot, proper old fashioned in their approach to antagonism. Ambushes, shanks in the arse and pans of boiling water were their idea of fun. Sexual assaults and imaginative humiliations. Bum business; all that stuff you probably read about. Like I say, soft as shite on their own. But they were rarely on their own.

Well they had young Tony pinned as another soppy victim, quicksticks. And they wouldn't leave the lad alone, always mithering him and niggling him, making life hell for a bit of fun.

We all of us got it; it's how you first handle it that matters.

It started subtle – just enough to crush him slowly: piss in his tea, skids on his pillow, snapped phonecards. Anything to keep themsels amused. Grabbing his cock all the time, joking that they were going to tear his hole. It was all hot air to anyone with a bit of summat about them, but unfortunately for him Tony had nowt about him, and nee-one looking out for him neither, so it took him all of five minutes before he started to crumble.

That's when I stepped in with a bit of baccy and a few friendly words after his daily fleecing in the rec room left him on the floor clutching a sore jaw and balls and his kecks round his ankles.

Listen, I telt him. Low-key is the way in here. Mystery and that.

Aye, I telt him. You don't want to go about pretending you're summat you're not because nee-one'll believe you. You talk too much; you need to keep it on the down-low. Be mysterious. Freak them out. And don't be blubbing into your pillow for your mam neither.

I helped him up.

Because if I were you I'd occupy the middle ground, always try and remain whatsit. Aye, impartial. Blend in. Don't scare and don't be scared. Be subtle. A few words. The odd favour. Nee shit-stirring. Be low-key. That's all it takes.

That's all I said to him. Owt that anybody with half a brain would tell you, but you'd think I'd just saved his bloody life or summat. After that he stuck to us like glue, like a bloody shadow, all thanks-John-John this anything-you-need-John-John that.

I had to tell him to cool it right down.

See, you're trying too hard again, I telt him. You don't need to be up me ringpiece all the time. Find your own way. The lads'll be bored of you soon enough. Any day now, you'll see.

He perked up after that. Perked up and opened up. Telt us his Dad ran the vans and did good business selling ices to the charvers and the pit-yackers and the touroids around the town and down at the Miner's Gala when the sun was shining. Telt us he'd repay the favour one day; telt us he'd already put in the word with his Dad Arty.

He's not bothered about you being a gyppo, he said. Reckons he likes you lot.

All I had to do, he went on, was call up his auld man when I got out and tell him I was a marrer of his flapping-mouthed feckless junkie kidnapper of a son.

You know what us Italians are like, he said. Family orientated and that. Any friend of mine and all that. You know – just like the Corleones.

The what?

You know, The Godfather?

Na. Don't know that gadge.

Well, we always return favours.

OK Tony, I said, thinking to mesel: aye, right. OK.

But it turned out that unlike most of the yarn-spinning workie tickets inside, Tony Vicari has been true to his word because here I am, months later, talking to his auld man Arty, who sounds reluctant but says to us, aye come and see us first thing tomorrow, early like, and I'll try and fix you up with summat. Nee promises.

And five on the dot mind, he says.

Aye.

That's five in the morning, he says like he's not expecting us to turn up.

Aye.

Is that a problem for you?

Nor.

You'll not be sleeping through the alarm because you've been doing bongs all night.

Na.

Or chasing blinge.

Na.

Or out on the rob.

What ye saying, like?

Good. See you then.

Bingo, I'm thinking. Have that, you gimlets.

*

When them three months were up and the hay bales were in the barns and the leaves were curling we did get married.

It's too soon, said your Granda, though there was nowt much he could do about it once them Wisdoms started planning a party. He said nee good'll come of it. You'll see.

But marry him I did, and the wedding lasted all weekend as Wisdoms and Dunnes and many more travelling families besides gathered from across the north and far beyond to join the holy

*communion – or drunken commotion as your Granda Dunne
called it.*

*It were a church wedding and then later when the formalities
were over we did throw a git big party down the road at the
Edenside site where we were to live as husband and wife, just
up the hill and cross the fields from Godric's Abbey.*

*A fire was built, songs were sung, new marrers made and some
auld scores were settled too. I barely knew people there, the most
of them coming from the Wisdom side. There was drinking and
there was gambling on the cards and the spinning coin game they
called headinams, and it went on long into the night and right
through to the next day. Money was made and money was lost
and bottles were drained past dawn.*

*And when dawn came we got out the skillets and fried bacon
and eggs on the open fire then the carousing started all over
again. Those that wanted sleep crawled into caravans until the
heat and their headaches woke them, and those that didn't,
didn't.*

*For once Mac kept out of the fighting. It would be a foolish
man that stepped up to a Wisdom, on his wedding night, but
more than that he seemed fit to bursting with the happiness.*

*And I was happy too. Happy to be wed to this big man; happy
to be enjoying the good times as the endless summer drew to a
close and we all of us used the same sky as our blanket and used
our smiles for umbrellas when it threatened to spit.*

*And that fire did burn for three days without ever once
dying out, and when it was finally down to its last embers, and
the men were too drunk to gather more wood, and the orange
pulse was turning ashen, we crawled into our van and slept the
sleep of princes and princesses, our cheeks glowing and our hair
raggedy, and me making a memory in my mind that I'd find
meself clinging to in all them dark days that were to come.*

*

Eyes on sticks. There's loads of them. Git big ugly things on the top of poles sat on street corners and in the middle of traffic islands, watching ower everything. Big robotic eyes up in the corners of the rooms and on the stairways, prying eyes at every turn.

And now there's bloody more of them outside than in, glegging into every nook and cranny, up the closes and down the alleyways. Unbelievable. A lot can happen when you're indoors for five year.

It's worse than prison this, I say to Arty.

What is?

All this, I say. Them bloody cameras and that.

It's the "in-security" business Johnno, he says. They watch ower everything these days, you know.

Why's that then?

You have been away a long while haven't you, lad. Because it's just the way it is.

Aye, well. What are they watching out for?

For owt. Crime and that. It's this estate. It's full of wrong uns.

Looks alreet to me I say, and it does. Or it's certainly nee better or worse than most places. There's that cladding stuff on some of the houses, for starters. Double glazing and that. Decent tarmac roads. Play areas. All that shite.

Looks can be deceptive, he says. Two years ago this place was a nee-gan area.

Looks alreet to me. What about now?

It's not much better.

I'm halfway through shadowing Arty in his van for a week and so far it's a piece of piss. Alls I have to do is keep him company while he talks us through the drill: how to do the ices, how to clean the pumps, where the float bides, how to crank up that funny music these vans always play.

And the route. He talks about the route a lot. Mind, he talks about everything a lot.

While he drives and blethers ower his shoulder to us I lean against the counter and eat so many ice creams slathered in the sticky sweet bright red shite they call monkey's blood it's enough to put us off for life.

You've got to stick to the route, he says for the third time today. At all times. Never veer from the route, because if you do you might end up on someone else's route.

Aye.

I'm not messing, he says. The route is everything. If you end up on one of our other boys' patches it's hassle, but if you end up on a rival's it's bloody turf warfare. The Manfredis from Washington mebbe. Or the Granellis from Gateshead. Either way, stray from the route and it's all fucked. You'll not remember the ice cream wars, I expect.

Nor.

Good. Cos it was messy and I wouldn't want to gan through all that again.

Aye, I say, trying not to smile.

It's nee laughing matter, mind.

Aye.

And that's how the day goes – him yacking about the route and me with me ice cream nosebag on, ganning aye Arty, no Arty, every now and again.

When he parks up and does the cones for the bairns, I climb into the front seat and do a rollie for each of us.

He doesn't seem such a bad gadgie though, Arty. He's one of them third or fourth generation Italians and his north-east accent is thicker than mine. And, aye, he's a bit of a knob and he yacks too much and he keeps calling us Johnno like he's off bloody *Neighbour*s or summat but I reckon he's got a decent head on him, and at least his endless blethering saves me having to say owt. That's good.

Our Tony reckons you helped him out, he says when we stop for a brew break.

I have a drag on my tab, then exhale, making sure to blow the smoke out the hatch because Arty says the smoke gets in the pipes or summat and then the ices taste of tabs, and that's bad for business.

I was just looking out for him, I say from beneath a big shrug. It was nowt much though.

Well, I appreciate it, son. We all do. I know it's not easy being in there with all them nutters and nonces and that. I know you need marrers to get you by. People to look out for you.

Fact is Johnno, he says, our Tony should never have been inside in the first place. He's just a daft young bugger, that's all. It was the smack that done it, you know. There's nee use complaining about it now, mind, but if I could turn back time and find out who got him on it in the first place I'd break their fucking legs. Then I'd break his for being such a daft little shite.

I squint out the hatch and flick out some ash. Gob on the ground. A greener. A proper oyster.

Aye well, I say. He'll be alreet.

Arty drains his mug then leans forward and clicks the switch that sets the music playing. Music that's already doing me nut in after only a couple of days. The same jangling and parping day in and day out. It's not music, it's bloody torture is what it is.

I'm glad you came to us actually John-John.

He shouts this over the din.

Our Tony says you're not scared of owt, he goes. Says you're a bit of a one-off. I can see that you take after your Dad.

This gives us a bit of a jolt.

Me Dad? I go.

Aye. I knew him a bit, like. What a fella he was, eh. I remember this one time –

I'm nowt like me Dad.

I say this all surly like and my tone seems to register with him because his eyes sort of flick away, and I instantly feel bad. Arty's alreet, but I don't hardly know him and when people are being friendly like he is it makes us nervous, and him mentioning me Dad takes us out of the present moment. Pushes us back to where I divvent want to be.

It's not his fault, the daft twat. He's not to know.

Then it's as if Arty has just remembered the full story with what happened and that because his eyes widen in remembrance and then he looks a bit embarrassed.

Sorry lad, Arty said softly. I was just saying, like.

Aye, I mumble. Well.

I don't have the heart to tell Arty that just because me Dad had been known to throw a few good right-handers and the odd knockout bullhammer and had a name about town for being bananas, and just because every traveller in England knew the Wisdom name, and probably still does, and just because of what he did and what I did and all the shite that followed, it doesn't mean I'm owt like him at all. The only thing we share is a name and it seems like nee-one will let us forget that in a hurry.

I feel like telling Arty all this. I want to tell him this but I don't. I don't because I know he'd not understand. So I button it. Like I always do.

Then we're turning a corner, then another and we're crossing the main road and entering the other estate further on down the way. We drive in with the music jangling and clinking just above our heads like a bleeding migraine, then we follow the road round into a long crescent of houses. There's some scrubland in the middle with a burnt out car sat on display like it's meant to be summat else, like a fountain or a statue or a piece of over-priced abstract art, only somebody's nicked the gallery brick by brick from around it. It looks like it's got delusions of whatsits.

The car's paint has been stripped by the heat of the fire. It's left a sort of dirty grey shell. There's nee wheels on it neither.

It marks the exact centre of the Nook estate.

Some kids are clambering on top of the car as Arty pulls ower and parks up. They're treating it like a climbing frame.

29

Oh, right shit hole this place, he sniffs. The Nook.

Yeah, why come here then?

Because if I don't, someone else will. Once you give up your patch, that's it – you'd have to kill to get it back. Anyroad, it's still summer and even if the little skidmarks round here have nee money one or two of them can still afford a cone or an eighth. Make hay while the sun shines and all that.

An eighth, I say.

Aye.

Of what.

What do you think? Pollen. Tack. Whatever's in.

Weed and that? You never said owt about you dealing, Arty. Bloody hell, I've only been out a week.

Come on, it's only a bit of puff kiddo. It's practically legal these days.

Is it? Nee one telt me.

Practically. They're not going to lock you up for a bit of puff, not these days. Nee-one's arsed any more man.

Easy for you to say, I gan, pissed-off and feeling like I've been hoodwinked. Bloody typical. I get mesel a job – me first proper job – and it turns out to be doing deals on wheels. And here's Arty going on about breaking the legs of those numpties that sold his Tony gear when he's selling stuff himself. Hypocrite.

The trick is to be discreet, he gans, totally oblivious to the darkening of me face to match me mood. Don't offer it around – just sell to those that ask. And don't make enemies because they'll end up being the downfall of you. There's a lot of grasses about, you know. That pun was intended, by the way.

I'm not really listening to Arty. I'm feeling too anxious now. Anxious because I'm sitting on a pile of summat illegal and I bet there's enough of it to send us straight back inside. And if there's tack there's probably other stuff too. There's the fact I've not even got a bloody driving licence neither. One more blot on me copybook.

I'm anxious about this place an all. The Nook. You get your senses sharpened when you're inside and there's summat about it that I don't like. I can feel it. It's a red brick maze with nasty surprises round the corners and eyes on you all the time. Bloody hell, I'm thinking. Pissing bloody bollards.

I appreciate the job you've given us Arty, I say. But I'm not your man.

What ye gobbing on about?

I'm not into drugs. They turn you daft. You of all people should know that. I don't touch them mesel. Never have.

What, not even a puff?

Na.

Bloody hell, you're a rarity, you are. But divvent worry, lad. I'll see you right. Like I say, I've been waiting for someone like you.

Eyes, I think. On sticks.

Watching us.

*

The wedding was the best of it. The happiest memory. The golden time.

Mebbes it rained that summer but if it did I don't remember. I was drunk on the amber light of the summer – and the love for this dark man whose eyes said more than his mouth ever would.

But now the season was over and we were living in a van on Edenside. The wind was getting shifty like a weasel and the burning of the leaves was in the air. Autumn was in the post.

There was never any chance of moving into a house. Your Dad would not have that. We're no chickens, he'd say, so why would we want to live like them, all caged up like that, pecking oursels to death?

They said at the time the council in the town had a list, and on that list was names, and to have a house your name had to be one of them – and the less work you did and the more bairns you had, the better the house they gave you. Well now, I thought.

Where's the sense in that. A house is nowt but the payment of rents, with nowt left at the end to show for it. It might be as well you spend what little you have on something you can own.

Travellers look down on others that stop and settle, think they've gone loopy or summat. Think they're giving up the ghosts of them ancestors that lived in the hedgerows. We'd have sooner slept in a damp stable or in a shed with the cattle than a house that belonged to the council. Anything other than being called a settler.

The gifted money was gone. New china cups had been broken and the pans already had dents in them, but I knew we'd not go hungry, not when Mac could pull a fish out the river with a piece of grass or take a chicken from the jaws of a stoat. But we still wanted for fuel and clothes and a future we'd given no thought to. And money didn't grow on trees no more than turnips fall from the sky. Beer didn't flow from hill-top streams either and Mac Wisdom had quite a taste for it, all told.

Quite a taste for it.

He would have to go to work if we were to get through the coming winter. Then come the spring we'd get to moving.

So he got himsel a job sorting scrap. He went out and got it just like that, and was I proud. He was to work at a yard that belonged to a friend of his cousin's just off the A690. An alcoholic gorger owned it. A big fat drinker called Wally Milburn; a real scrap man through and through, and a right tight one at that. No piece of copper wire or lead piping was too small for Milburn to scavenge and sell on if there was a pound note or a drink in it. And if he could short-change you along the way then alls the better.

And so Mac was up with the spuggies for a cold water wash and a cup of tea, then he'd walk the three miles or so through woods and fields to the yard with his baitpoke on his back, then he'd work all day on the auld bangers that Milburn and his boys brought in, stopping only for lunch and brew breaks and the odd tab. Then around about five he'd walk the hour back through the woods and fields and down the lanes.

Oh, he could work then, could Mac. He was the strongest of the lot, and strength was what was needed to haul those tatty wrecks up onto flat-bed trucks to strip them of their salvageable valuables – tyres, windscreens, bumpers and mirrors – then take what was left and crush it down into compact cubes of metal that they stacked in piles that shone in the moonlight all watched over by two underfed German Shepherds. Mac was the best worker. Milburn said so.

The crushing down was what he liked best. Seeing those big cars reduced to gleaming shapes like that. A whole car shrunk down to the size of a washing machine. He reckoned it was magical.

Betimes he'd loop up some fishing wire and set off early to string up a half dozen snares by a warren that he'd have spotted out on the edge of an open field, then he would stop off to check them on the way back. More often than not he'd find at least one rabbit, strangulated and stiff in the slipknot, wide eyes staring up at him, glassy marbles not yet taken by the birds.

Then he'd skin and gut them and pass them to me to stew the auld way, on an open fire, with plenty of carrots and onions in there, and served with spuds. Joey Grey, we call it. Mac gave me the recipe himself. Told me to cook it the Wisdom way, like his Ma did, with flour dumplings sat on top.

We had a wood burning stove in the van and a fresh water tap nearby. A pile of newly-split logs drying nicely under a tarp.

And after he'd eaten Mac would go have a few drinks with some of his brothers and the lads and whoever else was stopping nearby, at one of the two pubs down in Edenside village or on the nicer nights sat outside the van on upturned crates around the fire. But Mac made sure he was up at five, hangover or not.

These were the times of plenty.

Then Milburn started to take the piss. One Friday evening your Dad's pay packet was down from the previous week. A lot down.

"What gives Wally?" says Mac.

"We've had a quiet spell. It's the best I can do."

"I've been breaking sweat all week for youse. I'm not on commission you know."

"Sorry, but times are tight. You're going to have to like it or lump it, lad."

"I'll lump it then," said Mac, and knocked Milburn sparko with one punch.

Your man did fall like a sack of King Eddies and before some of the lads could help him up, Mac had got his bait bag and was striding off through the fields, steaming and cursing as he kicked the heads off daisies all the way home.

*

Nowt's changed on the Nook.

I remember coming here as a kid on me wanderings and even then I knew it was a bad place. There were always stories about robberies and stabbings and prossies doing business in the bottom flats. Stories of teen gang bangs and wild methadone parties. Dark gatherings; a place of retribution and revenge. It's where they put all the scumbags in the sixties. Then them scumbags bred. And the bairns of them scumbags bred with each other. And on it goes.

Divvent gan up there, they'd say around town. They divvent like strangers.

Even travellers avoided it. Nee-one ever bothered us though. My Dad knew half the gadgies up here. All the crooks and hard auld povvy bastards who had somehow stayed alive despite the years of tough living. The Nook was full of them and their tired wives, their battered girlfriends and bruised mistresses and their whatsit families – aye, dysfunctional.

And now they've got all these eyes on sticks up here and they've cleaned up the outsides of the houses, scrubbed off the sooty blackness to reveal the red brick beneath and tarted up the pointing. They've given them all new winders and filled in the pot-holes, stuck grills on the ground floors and put these concrete posts in the entrances to all the alleys to stop the joyriders.

But it still feels all wrong. As wrong as it ever did, like. All the eyes looking in.

They've spruced it up, but they've not got rid of all the povvy little gets that have grown up here. Five year on it's still not a place you'd go on your holidays.

Arty's yacking like the clappers as we drive. He's just like everyone else: he talks too much. There's enough hot air coming out of him to float a balloon to the sun.

*

We sell a few cones and then leave the Nook, turning out past where they've built a massive new supermarket on what I remember as being nowt but scrubland ten years ago, and we take the country road up to the villages, then beyond that up to the auld coal fields that bleed on down all the way to the sea. We're sticking to the route. Always the route.

And all the while Arty is talking out the side of his neck as he fills us in on the complete history of the family empire.

It's a proper source of pride to him is this ice cream business. He's telling us how it was his great-great granda who first left Italy ower a hundred and twenty years ago to move up to Glasgow, to the West End – where they're so hard they shit girders, he reckons – to open up the first ice cream parlour north of the border: Vicari's Ices.

Just imagine the vision and balls it took to open an ice cream parlour in bloody Scotland during the industrial age, he laughs.

Ice cream, he says again, shaking his napper. In bloody Glasgow. In the *winter*.

He tells us how later on his granda was working the pumps before he could kick a football, and then when he got a bit older he was such a promising opera singer that his Dad paid for him to gan ower to Naples for voice training and schooling, what with there not being much opportunity for opera in Govan and the Gorbals and all that, and how he got himself a few small singing parts but really it was too late to get into it all by then.

Why, I ask.

Because ice cream was in his blood son, Arty says all serious and sombre. In his blood. It happens that way. You'll see.

Will I shite, I think, but I keep quiet and let him carry on with his blethering. I can't keep up with all the grandas, great-grandas and all the other old-timers but I listen anyway because Arty has a good way with words and it's better than hearing about the route and the cones and where to store the hundreds and thousands for the millionth bloody time.

Aye, he gave up the singing and went into the family business soon after, says Arty. More parlours were opened, but it was *his* son – my auld man and our Antony's granda – who decided to seek out lucrative new territories by moving his young family south of the border, to England, to the north-east, where he built up a small fleet of vans. Proper entrepreneurial, he was.

Aye, I grunt.

Aye. Well that was forty years ago and here we are today, heading up a winning franchise of frozen confectionery that's spread right across the county and north up to Tyneside, south to Teesside and North Yorkshire and trickling all the way down the East Riding too. Fourth generation Italian ice cream empire, still going strong.

As he says this I can't help but wonder what the original auld man Vicari would make of his descendents knocking out teenths and eights of crappy black leb on the side, or his great, great grandson Tony's brief and unsuccessful career in kidnapping, but I'm not daft me, I know when to keep quiet. I've been doing it all my life and I've got proper good at it.

Then as if he's reading my mind Arty's off talking about knocking out gear. It's as if he feels the need to explain himsel to us, but I don't want to know. Because the more I know the more I'll be involved. Ignorance is whatsit.

Things have changed while you've been away you know, he says. I'm just following the laws of supply and demand, that's all. Rolling a spliff is like making a brew these days. They're all at it. The twenty-first century will all be about diversification, specialisation and convenience, kidder. You'll see. If Muhammad won't gan to the mountain then the mountain must gan to Muhammad. We're on the cusp of a new era.

I don't know what to say to that so I tell him, I knew a Muhammad inside.

Arty laughs.

Oh aye.

Aye.

Muslim was he?

Eh?

Was he a Muslim lad?

I don't know. He was from Chester-le-Street.

Arty laughs again, harder this time. Then he leans ower and switches the grinding ice cream music back on and even though it's a right bloody din I'm glad of the break from him mithering and yacking like an auld biddy.

Then he climbs out of the driver's seat

Howay then, he says. Your turn.

He gives me a map too, as if I need it. The entire route is already seared on me retinas.

It is imperative that you stick to the route he says, tapping the map. At all times.

He's even drawn the route on in fresh red pen for my benefit, the silly sod.

Right, I say. The route.

At all times.

Yip.

Don't get tempted to stray from it. This is a highly thought-out route. It's tried and tested lad, and if you deviate from it I can't even begin to explain the amount of shit it could cause.

OK Arty. I get the idea.

You *can* drive can't you?

Aye. Since I was eight.

*

The stork must have been up Edenside or the moon must have looked me sharp in the eye because the next thing we know I did fall pregnant.

"How did that happen, like?" says your Dad.

"How do yer think you daft bugger?"

Mac said nowt. He stared at the floor for a while, then he stared into the fire, then he spoke.

"We'll need a bigger van."

Then he stood up and went to the pub.

There was summat else that happened around that time that sent our lives off in a different direction. Your Dad fetches up saying he's been offered a fight by a travelling man by the name of Lovell. Barker Lovell.

"Well, what does he want to fight you for?" I says.

"Not him. With some other gadgie, for money like."

Turns out this Lovell one was a friend of Mac's cousin John Wisdom – one of many cousins he called John Wisdom – and a good man with it. Staunch as they come, your Dad said. He was what you'd call a gambler, a fixer and a middle man. A traveller all the way.

Barker already knew all about Mac. He knew about him before he even heard the story about him mullering Wally the scrap man. Things like that have a habit of getting about. They get passed around the sites and spoken about over pints. Because the travelling vine is far-reaching.

"He wants us to fight up Consett way," your Dad said. "Something just for the travellers."

38

I didn't like the sound of it one bit. What good God-fearing wife would?

And I saw the future that day. A future of black blood and broken bones; of bandages and broken hearts. Because no good can come of the fighting, no matter what anyone says – traveller or house-dweller or the holy Mary herself.

But the seed was already planted, and it did take root in Mac, for he was never one to shy away from any challenge no matter how big or small.

"The fight's in two weeks time," said Barker. "There's two ton in it for you, and owt you make on side bets is your lookout. You reckon ye can handle it?"

"Handle it? I'll bloody murder it."

Then as an afterthought: "Wait a minute – who am I fighting?"

"Henry Bradley."

"Our Henry Bradley?"

"The one and only."

"Bloody hell, Barker."

Henry Bradley was your Dad's uncle. Your Great Uncle. Family. And he was near enough twice Mac's age with it, a good traveller with a brood of kids, all made in his image. Henry was the man who used to give Mac little brown paper twists of sour pips or cinder toffees when he was a nipper. He was the man who brought something for their pot when their Dad had disappeared off for days on his wanderings. He had even taught Mac a few boxing moves.

"You can always say no," I said.

"Don't be so bloody stupid, woman," said your Dad. "You can never so no to nothing."

*

As soon as I get me first day off I gan into town to get some bits for me flat. I'm near enough twenty year old and I'm in me

39

first proper home that doesn't have wheels or bars on it. I might as well make a bit of a bloody effort.

Mind, I'm not intending on stopping in that little hole long. I telt the parole bods that, and I telt Arty that too. Aye, as well as telling him I wouldn't be knocking out gear for him I says, here boss I appreciate the job and that, but just so's you know, in the long run like, I plan on moving away from the town, a fresh break and that. Arty nodded, but I could see by the way he raised his eyebrows like an opening drawbridge he was thinking aye that's what they all say, which just made us all the more determined not to end up still following the route when I'm sixty-bloody-five-year-old.

Town's rammed when I get there. Proper chocker.

All these people make us nervous after so long away. Edgy and that. I'm waiting to be recognised an all. Waiting to see hands raised up to mouths and hear the whispers – looker, it's that John-John Wisdom – as people turn to get a proper gleg at us and muttering just loud enough for us to hear summat like are you sure that's *him*, he's bloody tiny?

So I get me head down and concentrate on getting me bits and bats for the flat.

Up at Cash Converters I get mesel this mint telly that has a built-in video player that the lad in the shop reckons can record stuff that's on when you're out. He tries to sell us a DVD player an all but I've nee need for one of them. I've not even seen one before, but I divvent let on.

Nor, I say. I'll stick with the video, ta.

They'll soon be obsolete, them, he says.

Aye.

He pauses.

What I mean is, he says, pretty soon they'll be non-existent.

I know what obsolete means you gleaming bloody bell-end, I snap back.

Bloody students, I'm thinking. Reckon they know everything. But he doesn't know I've been reading two books a week for five year though, does he. Do the maths. That's a lot of books. Daft sod.

What about a Sony Walkman then, he says.

A what?

A Sony Walkman, he says, with this little smirk that I'd dearly love to wipe off his mush with a bullhammer. It's a CD player, he says.

Aye, I know that. What a-bloody-bout it.

It's portable. Perhaps you'd like one.

Nah, I sniff. They'll soon be obsolete, them.

He says nowt to this because the look I give him is enough to get him to shut his flapping cake-hole.

I count out the money for the little telly then head down to the Army & Navy to get mesel some bits and pieces. Clothes and that. It's five year since I've been in a clothes shop and I spend a good while picking things up and feeling and sniffing them, then having a gleg at the price tags.

The shop's the same as it always was and they've got some good cheap clothes in there. Army clobber. Tough stuff. Made to last. For soldiers and that. War clothes. Your body'll wear out before some of that stuff does.

So I kit mesel out with the cash Arty has advanced us. I get some trousers, cammo T-shirts, a couple of jumpers because even though it's the height of summer it's not going to last forever, a check shirt, a khaki jacket, socks and some boots. Proper clod-hoppers. When I've got the gear on I feel brand new and ready for owt. I mebbes look a bit odd wearing it all together but I'll take me chances.

On the way out I see this proper good insulated sleeping bag with this hood thing that pulls ower the top, so I end up buying that an all, and some blankets. Then I realise I'm brassic and have got about a bloody quid to live off until the next pay day, but at least there's tins in the cupboard and there's always the ice cream. Can man live off ice cream alone? Aye, mebbes. I'll give it a bloody good go. Anyroad – at least I won't have to worry about gannin shopping again any time soon.

Because this place makes us nervous. All them crowds surging around us. People coming at us from all directions. Makes us wonder what they're all up to, dashing about like mad uns or stood round blocking the street and talking shite, smoking tabs, ogling each other, groping each other, shopping, spending, haggling, cackling, yakking. And everyone's on them bloody mobiles. You'll see two people stood together, like a lad and a lass or summat, and when you get closer you'll see that they're both on bloody mobiles, each talking to someone else.

Me, I like to see who's in front of us and who's sneaking up behind us because it's when there's people all around us like this that I start feeling hemmed in. Me heart starts jumping and me head starts humming and it's like I cannot breathe.

That's how I'm feeling today. The crowds are making me proper shaky and there's hods of touroids an all, especially by the statue of the horse in the market place. Americans and Japanese and that. All clicking their little cameras and that. Smiling and drooling and talking shite.

I have to sit mesel down and have a tab to catch up with mesel and take it all in and the funny thing is, after a few puffs and a couple of minutes, I start to see the town through their eyes. I see it as a tourist. Like I've never seen it before. And in a way I haven't – not as an adult anyway.

It's been that long since I mooched about town like this, doing anything to avoid gannin home for fear of what me Dad had in store for us.

Bloody years it's been. Years of confinement. It does your head in if you think about it too much. All that time locked away just up the road with nowt so much as a bloody postcard or visit from anyone.

And after the judge said his bit they just packed up and moved on and that was that. Nee messages, visits or nowt, from neebody. Dis-bloody-owned, man. Can you imagine? Cut off from the vine. Cast out.

I might as well have been sent off to another planet, me.

Might as well have been dead.

And here I am, the only Wisdom left in the town, and it's me that's the alien in my home land. Nowt but a bloody touroid.

It's hard to explain. I mean, the buildings look the same. The same rain-beaten stone, the same wonky slabs smoothed flat by generations of feet. The monument in the market place is still here an all, and the town hall and the statue of Neptune with his git big fork. Even the worn-away steps at the bottom of the monument that holds the horse and the cobbles down Silver Street all look the same.

And that's before you've even gone up past Bimbi's chippy and up to the old part of town, up to The Bailey and Palace Green where the cathedral sits all tall and proud and ancient and that, and the castle nestles up next to it, the two of them sat there with the river coiling around their feet like a big wet snake; the proper historic bit with all them listed buildings and snot-nosed students in their stupid bloody scarves thinking they're about summat.

But it all still looks different. Feels different.

I can't quite put my finger on it. It's like a dream of the town. I recognise it, but mebbe it doesn't recognise me. Mebbe the place hasn't changed at all. Mebbe it's me that's different. Mebbe it's me I don't recognise.

*

For the next fortnight Mac was up with the cock for an hour's training each morning.

The night was still bottle blue when he put on his pumps and trackie bottoms that were too tight and took off down the lanes with only the dawn birdsong and the occasional stoat returning home from a night's hunting for company.

43

The sound of rubber on the wet road, his own breath in his ears.

Sometimes I'd wake up and wrap the blankets around us and watch him from the window as he did a lap of the field as a warm up. Shivering and yawning I'd watch him run round the circumference fence, behind the vans, along past the two taps and the drain that the council put in, past the pile of blue gas canisters ready for collecting, past the chicken coop then a quick hurdle over the stack of pallets they put down when it was muddy. Then it was over to the corner where we dumped the ash into a hole, along the paddock fence to say morning to the tethered horse and down past the edge of the woods where he'd unleash a quick combination on a punchbag that was hanging there like a sheep's tagnut, slowly going mouldy green from the morning dew. A quick splash and sluice of water and he was off again.

Some mornings he ran all the way over to the Lord's country estate, chasing the day-break as the sun slowly rose and the sky shifted through a thousand shades of blue, the mist stalking the fields.

He laid off the booze and the tabs and the only thing he didn't give up was that which marriage allows between a husband and wife. I was plump with pregnancy then, and he said I had a special glow that prevented him from keeping his hands off us.

And he turned his mind to violence. Focused it. Trained it to thoughts of ripped cheeks and broken bones, busted knuckles and ruptured eyeballs.

I didn't want him to fight. But I'd not say so. Instead I'd knock up a six egg omelette and bite me tongue.

It's nowt to worry about, said your Dad.

I'll not break sweat, he said.

*

I set out at five each morning because I want this job and I don't mind Arty but most of all I like the three mile dawn walks to the industrial estate to pick up the van.

I get up early and quickly get mesel a whore's bath in the sink. Pits, bits, knackers and that. Sometimes when I least expect it I catch mesel off-guard in the mirror and see mesel for what I really am – how everyone else sees us, like: git big lugs and hair that sticks out at angles no matter how short I keep it or how much I try and smooth it down. I see wonky teeth that have never met a dentist except for the once when I was locked up, and a brow that looks like it's pushing down on me face. A permanent frown, me Mam used to call it. Like a bloody colliery landslide, me Dad said.

And them dark eyes I got off him. The part of us that always reminds us of him. Dark eyes that pull us back to dark places.

It's this time of the day I enjoy the most – stepping out the door in the early morning just when the sky is changing colour through pinks and peaches, and the birds are chatting each other up from their branch tops and there's nee-one else about, except mebbe the odd pisshead staggering home sideways and arguing with lamp-posts. I walk and I breathe and I'm still surprised I'm out. I can't help but think of some of the lads inside waking up to the same bowls of cereal, the stale fug of dead air.

When I get to the lock-up I let mesel in with the key Arty's given us.

Guard it with your life, he said. Don't let nee fucker get his hands on it. *Capeesh?*

Aye, I tell him. What ye said.

I'm always the first of the drivers up there so I make mesel a cup of tea with water from the dripping tap outside and while it's mashing I bun up a rollie and spark it.

By now it's six or mebbe half six at the latest, depending on how fast I done the walk, and me stomach is usually stirring so I stub out me fag and gan and empty me back in the one bog that serves the entire industrial estate. It sees more logs per person than the crappers inside. Disgusting.

And that's the other thing about being locked up: your body becomes programmed to routine. If they tell you to shit at six,

45

soon enough you'll be shitting at six on the dot. They don't just own your time, they own your bowel movements an all. I'm still as regular as clockwork now.

The industrial estate is silent and still and I like it that way. At this time of the morning, before vans start pulling up and people start opening their shutters, it's like being on another planet. All the buildings are made from chrome and corrugate and they twinkle as the sun comes up. Future World I call it, because it feels like I've stepped into the future: a future where there's nee fugger trying to start summat with us. Instead there's just silence. Silence, stillness and calm.

I stand there with my re-lit tab, smoking and watching the buildings shine like ships in the flat sea of tarmac, feeling content in the perfect stillness of the morning. There's just me and the sun and the tarmac and the ribbons of smoke coming out me nostrils like a bull's steaming breath.

In one of the other units they make frozen curries and you can smell the spices a mile off, even when they're shut as they are now. It's proper good. Well exotic. It always gets me belly rumbling: another prison reminder that I'm due some scran any minute now. That can wait though.

There's a place that does electrical goods down here an all, and there's a builder's merchant and an MOT garage. All that type of stuff. Most of them won't be open until half eight, nine, by which time I'll be long gone, out in the lanes and the estates and the B-roads.

Oh aye, and there's this place that makes Christmas decorations an all. All year round they're at it. It's weird being sat there and looking at plastic Christmas trees stacked up in August and fake snow blowing across the forecourt. Bits of silver tinsel on the breeze. It's the closest to the whistles and bells of the festive season that I get.

And now's the time to take a few minutes to sit and read a book for a bit while I run the engine of the van to get the freezers and the ice machine working before I stock them.

I lean against the wall outside, reading and basking like a cat in the sun, the engine chugging and purring.

I'll read owt, me. Any book will do. It was reading that got us through that five year. I went in hardly knowing me ABCs and came out after having read right the way through the prison library and whatever else one of the screws, a likeable bell-end called Palmer, would lend us. Palmer was alright. He wasn't a fat lump like most of them key janglers. He reckoned he had a degree or summat. Reckoned he cycled three hundred miles a week.

Anyroad. Thanks to him and the fact that nee-one else used the library, I got through hods of books and a fair few crusted porn mags that circulated an all.

It's adventure stories I like best. Books about men surviving and that. They give you a bit of perspective. Hope and that. Books that make you realise that though you might feel it, you're not always alone in life. Like, you're not the first person to experience what it is you're feeling. The fact there's others that have gone before and there's others that'll come after you.

I read a lot of a gadge called Jack London inside. *The Call of The Wild*, the one about the dog in the wilderness. Then I done *Huckleberry Finn*. The lad on the raft with the slave and that. That was mint. Tom Sawyer an all. Mint. Done them in about a week each. Caned them. And the one about the pigs and that. That's a good one an all. It reminded us of prison a bit, all them animals scrapping each other to be in charge. Then *1984*. Bit of a tough one to get into that. I read some Dickens too. I knew how *Oliver Twist* felt. We'd have probably been marrers, me and him. Eating gruel and that. Surviving, despite our parents. The Artful Dodger an all. Proper little character, that one. And Bill Sykes. A bit like me Dad, he was. All big and growling and obvious. Your man Dickens knew a thing or two about the wickedness we do to one another.

That was just some of the good books, the auld ones – the ones you'll know about – but I'll read owt, me. The life stories of actors and footballers and that. Books about lasses on horses shagging blokes in the stables. Detective stuff. Books about bloody goblins and hobbits and wizards. There was always plenty to choose from an all, because most of the lads were too thick to bother; they'd rather sit there with their hands down their kecks turning their eggs all day than being called a puff for reading.

I touch the glass eye in me pocket. I rub me finger round it, then take it out and hold it to the sun. It's not eye-shaped like you'd think it would be. It's not whatsit – oval shaped – it's perfectly round. Because it's only the eye hole that's oval, isn't it. The eyes themsels are orbs.

I turn it and let the sun bounce off it. It's a smoky white colour, with the dark brown bit at the front, then the black bit in the middle of it. The pupil. I gently hoy it up and down in me hand. It's solid like a marble. Heavy and all. It's beautiful in one way, but ugly in another. Ugly if you know the story behind it, like.

After a couple more pages of the reading I flick away me tab, stick the eye back in me pocket, fold down the corner of the page then give the van a quick rub down before heading off to the wholesalers to pick up the big tubs of cream, the lollies, tubes of cones and the boxes of flakes and sprinkles. All that shite the kiddies love.

*

The morning of the fight your Uncle Eddie came knocking at dawn. He was your Dad's driver and corner man, there to help his big brother if a miracle befell Henry Bradley and he somehow mullered him.

Even at seventeen Eddie was the same then as he is now. Boisterous like all them Wisdoms but crafty with it. If Mac was the fighter, Eddie was the hustler. He was thin as a whippet, sly as a fox and full of shite at all times. They said he was born smiling, Eddie. They said that smile could sell owt. They reckoned he could have the watch off your wrist, and you'd still be nodding and listening. And then he'd sell it back to you and be down the track before you knew it.

The scrap was happening early to avoid attention from the muskers and it was still dark when they left in Ed's latest banger. He changed his car every couple of weeks, swapping one auld rust bucket for another. It was a running joke in the family: only the paintwork held his cars together. When they stopped working he'd dump them and walk home from wherever he was. Abandoned cars littered the county wherever he went. Where other people left footprints, Eddie left cars. Half of them probably ended up cubed at Milburn's yard.

They took the long way round the city. They kept the river to their left and avoided the main roads. It was better this way; better to be out in the countryside with the winders down, away from all the house folk driving to work.

"Have you got a gameplan?" Eddie asked.

"Aye. I'm gonna batter him like a haddock."

*

The route lasts five days and takes us all ower the shop. It runs round the city in a massive circle taking us through all the estates, villages, hamlets and holes of the county.

I start at different parts of the circle each day, but always pass through the housing estates of Belmont, Carrville, Shincliffe. They're not bad little places. There's usually plenty of business and most of the kids are as good as gold. Polite and that.

Then it's on to Bowburn and Cassop and up to Littletown, Pittington and the Raintons – East and West. That's one side of the city. Two days at least.

Then it's over to the private housing estate at Newton Hall – the biggest in Europe they telt us when I were a kid – then through there to Pity Me and Framwellgate Moor, and out to Witton Gilbert and Sacriston – Witton Giblets and Segga to the locals – Bearpark, Ushaw Moor and all them places up there, and on and on and on, the music playing at all times, except when I stop to work the ice pump for snot-nosed kids who take ten minutes deciding whether they want a 99, a Screwball or a white chocolate Magnum.

And that's just the nicer estates, where the bairns have more money to spend. The route also takes us through the dark-hearted backwaters where my Dad used to go get mortal and fight farmhands and drunks for pints and pennies. Those places miles out of the city, nowhere holes with one road in and the same road out, and family names going back donkey's. Wee places with their own rules, where the people gape at the sight of a wheel and where all the bairns can afford is a mini-milk or some kets from the penny box I keep under the counter.

I'm out all day, dawn to sundown. That means nine or ten hours minimum. Dropping the van off then the long walk home adds another hour. It's no wonder Arty's got a good few bob tucked away, the way he works us. He might blether a load of shite, but there's nee flies on him.

I pull over every few hours for a slash and a stretch and a couple of minutes of peace and quiet. Then it's back on with the music, the engine growling, the hatch open, the breeze blowing. Back to business. Roll up lads and lasses, Vicari's is here. The nicest ices in the north and beyond.

Often licked, but never beaten.

Thursday is different though. Thursday is probation day. The worst day; another pull back into the past. Hours of grunting and scowling at Dickhead Derek the dandruff wonder with his face like a derelict bungalow, and having to fanny around with forms and questions and cups of crappy coffee in that bloody building that's just a bit too close to the courts for comfort. Always with one eye on me watch, the other wandering out the window.

Half a day I waste, sat in a chair in a stuffy office being prodded and feeling like a numpty. Then another half day to do me errands, wash me smalls and sit there doing nowt but smoking and reading. And that's my day off.

How are you coping? Derek asks us.

How do you avoid confrontation?

What about money? Your flat? Your feelings?

Oh, get fugged the lot of you.

That's what I want to say.

Get fugged and shove it up your fudge tunnel while you're at it.

That's what I want to say, but as usual I don't, because inside was full of mouthy little povs who telt the screws and the social workers and their psychologists to shove it up their scabby scuts, and look where that got them. Neewhere. Divs. I'm not like that. I'm not a dribbler or a drooler; my priority is making sure these probation gadgies put ticks in all the right boxes so they can sleep well at night thinking, yes, what we're doing is saving lives here and yes, society does work after all and OK, it's hard work, but it is immensely satisfying to be able to help *real* people with *real* problems.

I can just see Dickhead Del with his beak in a glass of wine at some dinner party: well, we've got one lad in at the moment, a gypsy you know, a right little character...

So I tell them what I know they want to hear and they nod and grunt and give us forms that take hours to fill in, and they only give us five minutes break to drink that crap coffee and smoke a bine in the little courtyard round the side.

I see a few lads I recognise from inside and they're talking the same auld shite now as they were then, a lot of nonsense about scams they've got gannin on and dodgy deals they've been doing, or girls they've been shagging and money they've been making. They don't know it but they're just enjoying a little holiday before being sent back inside, or mebbes up to the big house where it's a whole other thing if you're a bit green or pink around the hole as it were. I'm glad to leave them stood there, their mouths opening and closing like goldfish.

When I'm finally done I gan up to Lidl and get me shopping in. The same stuff I always buy. Tins of chilli and tuna and packets of rice and bread and apples and tea and cereal. Milk and crackers and custard in a packet. Broken biscuits and bog roll.

Toothpaste.

Definitely nee ice cream.

*

They passed through the villages of Kimblesworth and Plawsworth then dropped down into Sacriston, sped through Witton Gilbert and turned right onto the A691 main road to take them all the way up the Deerness Valley to Consett.

Where one valley gives way to another and the villages and hamlets that circle the city become fewer and far between, the countryside really opens up. The landscape is a green carpet unrolling on either side of them.

They drove in silence, Mac lighting his first tab in a fortnight. They passed Langley Park down at the bottom of the valley, then went through the old Roman village of Lanchester and on up to Leadgate, and then to Consett. They skirted the town along Delves Lane and drove down more lanes that took them back out into the country.

Then suddenly the hedgerows gave way to a gap where a track lead to Buttermilk Lane. It was invisible to all but those who knew it, a closed off little world behind nature's walls.

"What a shit hole," said Mac, though the site was much like the one we were stopping on: a field with a dozen or so trailers and not much else.

The men were already there, milling about. There were about twelve or fifteen of them, smoking and spitting and talking in clipped whispers suitable for an early morning,

Your Dad recognised some of them – Minty Green, Ben Brown, Levy Riley and his son Levy Jr. Others were unfamiliar. They were travelling men one an all. Men who had a day's work ahead of them, or a night's behind them; men in work overalls and boots and thick jumpers against the slight chill of the morning. Ben Brown was wearing a greasy poacher's coat, with its deep side pockets for storing chorred rabbits and pheasants in. All of them had the long hair and thick sideburns that were the style of the day. Or the style of five year before that. Only the former safe cracker and now successful haulier Minty Green was well dressed in an expensive wool suit.

Your Dad and Eddie pulled up. The car coughed, then stalled.

"Here comes the champ!" said Eddie, leading the way. "Make way for the champ!"

"Stow it," said Mackie, though he couldn't help smiling at the hide of his brother, coming here to this site and announcing their presence. Your Dad had had many a fight, but none of them official enough to warrant a nickname like the champ.

Mac peeled off his sweater so that he was bare-chested in his trackies and trainers.

As he did, one of the trailer doors opened and out stepped Henry Bradley. He was wearing a white vest and the same tatty suit trousers he always wore. He had stout work boots on his feet.

Bradley had a barrel chest and an even bigger belly.

"Christ, look at the size of his purr," said Eddie out of the side of his mouth. "He looks like he'd rather eat you than fight you."

*

It's the hottest day since I got out.

There's pure golden sunlight beaming down into all the darkened crannies, and the blue sky looks naked without any clouds covering it up. It's one of them days where if you just stand still you can hear nowt much except mebbes the odd lawnmower or the faint sound of the motorway traffic. Because it seems like wherever you gan these days you're always near a bloody motorway.

I'm wearing me new togs: lightweight combats and a vest with the word BUNDESWEHR written across the front of it. I think mebbe BUNDESWEHR is a beer or summat.

It's hot in the van even with the air con blowing a good un and I'm proper sweating when I switch on the overhead music and turn into the Nook.

As usual there's loads of kids hanging around. On days like this there's grubby little grommits everywhere you gleg, but not much money to be made from ices. It never feels right here. The bairns are never laughing and skipping and singing like other kids do. They're arranged about the place like crows. Hoying things. Smashing things. Hanging off things. Tough adult faces on wee bairns' bodies.

I'd skip this hole altogether but Arty would have my balls for baubles if he found out.

Stick to the route, he says.

Always the route, he says.

Even over the Nook the sky is proper beautiful today though, and you can smell the tarmac. It smells good. It's one of them nice smells from your childhood, like creosote or firelighters or a spent sparkler.

I drive on round the git big crescent that runs round the edge of the estate then towards the green in the middle. I pull up.

As usual there's a few little scrotes about. They're crowded round summat on the ground. One of them is on a bike with nee seat on it and is perched over an exposed metal spike. He's leaning forward on his handlebars, watching as one of them bends over and pokes at whatever it is that's on the ground with a stick.

The lad's got a lighter in his other hand. The thing on the ground looks like a ratty old jumper or summat but then one of the kids jumps back and howls and the others all laugh and I see the jumper is in fact a cat that has just run off. It has something tied to its tail. Something long and straight. Its tail is wobbling about like a broken antenna. It looks like mebbes it's a firework. A rocket.

The kid who jumped and howled hoys his stick away and picks up half a brick instead, then runs after the cat with the lighter still in his other hand. He doesn't need it though because now there's a trail of fizzing sparks shooting from the tail of the cat as it darts under a hedge. All the little charver kids are squealing with excitement. They're hopping from foot to foot and pushing each other out the way to get to the hedge. Then there's a hiss and a boom as a shower of pink stars explodes from beneath the hedge and the kids jump backwards, their squealing turning to hysterical delight.

The poor cat's nowhere to be seen. It's business as usual on the Nook.

Across the green, some crappy dance music is pumping loudly out of speakers that are balanced in the downstairs front window. Happy house, they call it – the music, I mean. I divvent know about the actual house. It's the same headbanger crap the charvers used to play all the time inside. Toytown music, I call it. All bleeps and farts and cartoon voices.

Joyrider music.

Wanker music.

Outside the house there's a couple of lads sat on the garden wall with their tops off. Two more come from inside and join them. They're wearing trackie bottoms and jeans with words printed on them. They're swigging their beer and burning their biffters and looking my way.

Then the kids are at my hatch all talking at once. There's five of them. They can't be older than nine or ten. They're ugly little gets. Proper mirror breakers.

Give us an ice cream.

I'll pay you next time, says one of them.

Give us some tack on tick, mister.

I want a can of pop. Giz a can of pop.

I hold my palms up.

You know the rules lads, I say. Nee money, nee kets.

Just give us an ice cream you tight cunt.

Money first, I tell them.

One of them slaps down a 50p bit.

The others laugh. Their laughter is hollow and as cold as the ice cream machine. There's bile in that laughter. Nee joy. Just bile and bitterness. They've got worse manners than half the lads in prison.

Without taking me eyes off them I reach for a cone and draw a swirl of ice onto it. You've got to watch these little squirts. They're like them coyotes I saw on this BBC programme; they'll take on owt if there's enough of them. Even if it's a buffalo or summat, they'll still attack it and overwhelm it. Tear it apart, "increment by increment" the gadgie on the programme said, which I reckoned to mean limb by limb, like. This rabble are just like them. They've got the same mentality because they're always hungry. Safety in numbers and that. Half of them'll be inside within five years, mark my words.

Here, says one of the kids to his marrers, crouching down and swinging his arse about. Who's this?

Ah dinnar.

The lad points at me.

Mr. Whippy having a shit.

The little coyotes cackle. I stick a flake in the cone and pass it to the lad, but as I do, one of the others grabs it and legs it, then they're all off, hooting and cackling as they chase him across the green, only five short years away from smack habits and their suppers slid under their cell doors.

The 50p is gone.

Way overhead I can see a plane flying, its vapour trail fattening then fading behind it like the tail of a tiny white kite that's broken free of its strings.

I reach into the fridge to re-stack some of the lollies that fell over when I went ower a speed bump coming into the estate. Then there's a voice talking at us.

Christ. Where's the war at?

I turn back to the hatch and there's a couple of lasses stood there in vests and cut-off jeans, smoking a spliff. At a guess I'd say they're in their late teens. A year or two younger than me mebbes. One of them's this proper boiler packed in tight to clothes a couple of sizes too small for her. She looks like one of them Spice Girls after she's been sucking on a tyre pump. Michelin Spice. There's little rolls of flab popping out over the top of her shorts, out the side of her bra, rippling under her pits. It reminds us of those bubble-necked frogs in the rainforests.

She's got too much make-up on and all, and even I can see that it's not been put on right because there's a change in colour on her neck where one layer ends and the rest of her flabby face begins. She's a right butterball.

I've never understood why lasses have to trowel on so much make-up. It's like they're trying to hide from summat all the time, but sooner or later the slap has to come off.

The other lass is nicer looking though. She's got this jet black hair pulled back into a pony-tail. There's a narrowness to her eyes that makes her look a bit oriental but a bit mean an all. Or mebbes she's just got her hair pulled too tight.

You can sort of imagine her being proper mental when she's pissed. But she's pretty fit at the same time. She's got nee rolls of flab rippling all over the shop for starters, though from where I'm stood I can see the top of her tits. They're dead white and though they're not massive or owt she's still managed to make them look like they're on display, like football trophies or summat. Like badges of honour.

She could be in the Spice Girls on her own merits. I'm not even taking the piss.

Eh? I say.

You, the sexy one with the ponytail says. You look like you're dressed like a bloody soldier or summat.

They laugh like drains at this. Proper gurglers, the pair of them.

Hey – are you having a gleg at her tits, says the fat one. He's looking at your tits, he is.

They laugh again. Piss off you fat get, I'm thinking. I bet you could make cottage cheese under all them rolls of blubber. But I just blush and say nowt.

What happened to the other fella, says Ponytail.

What fella?

The one who's usually here.

Arty?

The bald fella.

I don't know any bald fellas, I say. I've just started, me.

Shame. Kell fancied him.

No, I never, the fat lass snaps back.

Aye you did. You said he looked like Bruce Willis. Then to me: Do you have any Slushes.

I don't know. What's a Slush?

You know: a Slush Puppy and that.

What's a Slush Puppy?

'What's a Slush Puppy?'

Aye.

Fucking hell. Have you come from another planet or summat?

They look at each other, smirking. Near enough I'm thinking, and I feel mesel gannin red. I feel like a plum. A right big tit.

Ponytail takes a draw on the spliff and then passes it to Butterball who blows smoke in through the hatch. It's sweet and muddy and sickly, like a slurry run-off that's gone stagnant. The smell takes us straight back. Back inside. Crap hash. Tack and that.

Nor, I say a little too defensively.

Alright, keep your wig on, she says. I thought everyone knew what a Slush was.

Well I don't.

It's made from crushed up ice she says, more breezily this time, as if she's letting us know that even though she's taking the piss she's only trying to be friendly. That's what people are like round here. They take the piss out of you if they like you. And if they don't, they take the piss as well. It's bloody confusing. Travellers don't do that. Travellers'll just blank you if they think you're a knob.

You can get pina colada or grape or raspberry ones. They turn your tongue blue, she gans. I never understand how a raspberry could be blue.

They do a coconut one an all, says the fat lass. Then she leans back to look round the van, across the green to where the lads with the music are sat on the garden wall.

Piss off she shouts, and gives them the finger.

They sound minging, I say.

Na, they're dead nice, says Ponytail. I can't believe you've never had one.

Mebbes I have, I say. I'm not going to tell this lass that they don't give you Slushy whatsits when you're locked up.

Everyone's had a Slush, she says vaguely, already losing interest. Then mumbling to herself, like she's drifting away and already thinking about summat else, she says, they come out of a machine and that.

Sorry.

Oh. Well you should sell them. You'd make more money. Specially on a hot day like this, innit Kelly.

Eh, her mate says while doing a wanker sign to the lads.

Do you want some of this?

Ponytail waves the biffter in front of us. It trails silky blue smoke into the van. The smell of prison.

No ta.

Mebbes you can give us a 69 then.

Butterball turns back to us and laughs when she hears this and I feel like saying summat about her dodgy make-up and her ripples of flesh because I know they're taking the piss but I keep quiet and anyroad, Ponytail keeps a straight face so maybe she's not. Maybe she's just being friendly. A smile means nowt these days and like I said, it's hard to tell if people want to be your marrer, suck your bell-end or stove your head in.

Aye, says Kell. And can you stick a nice big flake in it.

I'd be hard pushed to find the hole in you is what I want to say to this worky ticket, but I button it. I stick me head out and look up and down the road. Then at the sky. Anywhere but them nice white tits.

Then there's a bleep and Kell pulls one of them mobile phones from her pocket and answers it by going yeah? – no hello or Butterball speaking or nothing, mind – then wanders off towards the boys. I can see her white thighs rubbing together. It must be hot down there. Sore. Chafed to all buggery, probably. And the stink...

I reach for a cone. One of the single ones.

Do you mean a 99?

Aye mebbes, she says. Give us an eighth of tack an all.

Sorry. I've not got any tack.

Nee tack?

No.

How come?

I don't know. Just don't.

Fuck. I'm nearly out.

Soz.

The other lad gives us it on tick an all. Cos of Kyle and that.

She draws on the spliff. It's nearly down to the roach now. It's turning brown. It crackles. I don't know what she's on about.

She offers it to us. I shake me head again and try not to gleg at her tits. She says nothing. Neither of us say owt. Then I clear me throat.

Do you still want this ice cream then?

Mebbe.

I just stand there like a plum with a cone in my hand, not sure what to do.

Have you not got any skunk or owt, she says.

Nor. Nee skunk neither.

'Kin ell. Have you got *anything* illegal?

I have to think about this.

Nor, I say. I don't think so. Not unless Cider Quenches or Twisters are against the law these days.

Well you're nee bloody fun are you, she smiles. What's the point in an ice cream man who only sells ice creams?

I say nowt to this.

You're properly missing out, she says then: you don't say much do you?

I shrug.

Sometimes. I mean – not always.

She drops the roach on the ground, grinds it out, then leans on the hatch counter, looking in.

Do you come from round here? She says this without looking at us. Only cos I don't recognise you.

No, not here, I say, clearing my throat at the same time. Not the Nook.

Where then?

Around the town. A few places, growing up. But then I moved away.

Where?

Where did I move to?

Aye.

Just around.

What was it like?

What was what like?

Where you moved to.

It was alreet. Depends.

I pause for a moment, then I say: the food was terrible.

She laughs at this. It's a genuine laugh and it makes her face look different. Like a different person. Her face really comes alive when she laughs and her eyes go all squinty. Her tits wobble an all but I try not to notice them, and I realise that I've not been this close to a pair of tits for many years. Probably ever, actually.

The food was terrible, she says, mimicking us. Like food do you?

Some of it I say, wondering what sort of a question that is to ask.

What about drink? I bet you like a good drink don't you.

As it happens I don't like to drink. I never touch it. But I'm not going to tell her this either.

I shrug.

I love to get pallatic me, she says. I fucking love getting mortal. There's nowt else to do is there.

I still say nothing because I don't know what to say. I'm not used to this. My mind is racing but it's also completely blank. I want to speak but I've got nowt to say. Absolutely fug all. Because I'm not used to talking to lasses like this. Or any lasses at all. Bloody useless twat, I'm thinking. Just talk to her, man. But me mind is blank and all I can think about is them tits. And how my mouth is dry. I'm so busy trying not to panic that I miss what she says to us.

Eh?

I said, do you like knocking about with girls an that?

I feel mesel turning into a plum again. A git big plum. A big plum that's blank inside. Blank and hollow. A shell of plum. A plum with a dry mouth and nee clue about owt in life.

Some of them, I say. I mean it depends.

Aye, I bet you do you dirty get, she says, but she's smiling when she says this. There's no need to be shy about it. All lads like you like lasses. Then as if she's talking about the same thing she says here, have you got any Soleros?

Aye.

What about an Ice-cream Sandwich. I'm dead hungry, me. Proper got the munchies.

Aye, I think so. I glance into the freezer. Aye, I have.

What about Callipos?

Christ, I'm thinking, make your mind up, though I'm not actually bothered because I'm enjoying just chatting to her, even if she is just listing different varieties of ice lolly and asking daft questions. It's still a conversation isn't it. The best I've had with a lass in yonks.

I look into the freezer again.

Aye.

Orange?

I've only got the Tropical Fruit.

She scowls.

I divvent like them.

Then she scrunches her nose up, thinking. When she does she looks a lot younger. I thought maybe she was about eighteen, but now I'm thinking mebbe she's about sixteen. It's hard to tell. I'm crap at guessing how old people are. Especially girls because they always act older than they are. And them tits are misleading an all.

Just give us that 69 then.

99, I say.

Aye.

She smiles as I pull the handle and swirl the ice cream onto the cone.

Do you want a flake?

Aye.

I stick two flakes into the cream then hand if to her.

She takes it from us and slaps 50p on the counter.

Divvent worry about it I say, and push the coin back towards her.

Ta she says, then takes a lick and walks off backwards as I try not to cadge a final look at her tits.

I'm Maria by the way, she says, squinting, her head cocked to one side.

I just stand there.

See you then soldier, she says. Then she turns and gans before I've said owt.

When she's left I realise I'm still stood there with one of my hands raised up by my shoulder in a sort of half-wave. Like a

63

comic book Red Indian or summat. Like a knobber. I climb into the front and when I sit down I see I've got a semi-on.

I put the stick in gear and when I have a look in the rear view mirror two of the shirtless lads from the garden wall are walking ower towards the van but I turn on the music and drive off.

*

Barker was right behind Henry Bradley when he stepped out of the van. He stopped to talk to a couple of the men on the way. Money was peeled from rolls, bets laid.

Your Dad walked over to Henry Bradley.

"Now then Unc."

"Alreet lad," nodded Bradley. "So you've come for your tannin."

Mac laughed at this.

"Well, one of us has, Unc."

As fair play man, Barker stepped forward to lay down the rules. Everyone knew them already: it was a square go, which meant it was a stand up scrap. No biting, gouging, kicking, butting, grappling or kneeing. It was fists and elbows only and they'd fight until one of them called best or couldn't get up. There was to be no corner men or breaks. No cold compresses, stools to sit on or bottles of water. Just pumping blood and stinking guts. Bone on bone.

"Uncle, you're a good man so for you and your family's sake, and them kets you used to give us as a bairn, I'll gan as easy as I can," said Mac. "And after I've panelled you we'll shake hands and say no more about it. Agreed?"

Bradley shrugged.

"Good," said Barker. "Your good name's at stake so let's keep it nice and clean and we'll have nee bother."

As he said this Bradley stepped up and lamped Mac in the eye. Not on his brow or his cheekbone but the eyeball.

"Howay," yelled your Uncle Eddie. "That's not fucken fair."

The punch forced your Dad to take a step back as his eye took to watering and swelling. It came up like an Autumn dawn mushroom.

He shuffled forward and threw two short arm jabs and the fight was on. One landed in Bradley's eye and the second split his bottom lip. Mac followed through with an elbow that caught Bradley flush on the cheek, then before he could compose himself moved in and swivelled his hips to send a piledriver into Bradley's rib cage. He felt something crack. Heard it too.

They all heard it.

They heard the fracturing of a rib and the air whooshing out of Henry Bradley's mouth in one long animalistic groan, like an accordion being dropped into a horse trough.

Bradley went to butt Mackie but age had slowed him. Your Dad took a side step and threw a left and a right to Bradley's chin then pulled back his arm and threw another good right straight into the centre of his screwed up mush. Bradley's nose gave way. His whole face was coming up like a blind cobbler's thumb. Everything fell silent. There was only the breathing of the two men to be heard. No blood either; just distortion and diagonals.

Henry Bradley turned his shoulder away and gave best. He bent over, wheezing and retching, one hand held over his broken rib. Mac spat on the ground then extended a hand to Bradley, who shook it limply without looking up.

"Well," said your father. "You've all seen it: the better man has won here."

Some of the men muttered but some of them smiled too. Only a fool would have bet against Mac Wisdom in this fight and there was clearly a couple of fools amongst them.

Mac though – he felt cheated that it had ended so quickly. But that's your father. When he gets in the fighting he wants to see blood. All that training for a minute's work-out. Well. It was hardly worth bothering with.

So he stepped back and swung his arms out, loosening up his shoulders and rolling his neck.

"Right, then. Who else wants a slice while I'm here?"

No one stepped forward.

"Come on, you shower. Double or quits with this ton I've just won mesel."

The men scratched their heads and looked at the ground and smoked their cigarettes and glanced at one another with raised eyebrows. But there were no takers.

"What about you Ben Brown? I know you can mix it."

Ben Brown said nothing.

"Howay, you git big bloody nightshirt. I'll fight you one-handed if you like."

The men shook their heads.

Mac picked up his sweater and without putting it on began to back away.

"Let it be known. I'll fight any man."

He turned and left. His brother followed. It was not yet eight in the morning.

And that's how your Dad did start out as a knuckle man.

*

I'm up at one of them farms about six or seven miles out of town. It's about as far out as the route takes us, up to this little hamlet whose name I divvent even know. It wouldn't be worth bothering with except Arty telt us that every August the farmer gets a bunch of lads in for the month to help with the baling and the bagging and the picking and three times a week he buys them all ice creams and pop and kets, so it's always worth a detour.

It's a big sprawling place down this track in the arse-end of nowhere, full of junk and jumble.

Disused agricultural equipment litters the yard out front. There's a disc harrow with blunted spikes and once-sharp spiral blades that have rusted in the rain and an auld red chisel plough with its tyres missing. A classic John Dere tractor that looks like it has seen better days and has no front wheels sits hunched nose first into the ground. Over across the other side there's a couple of barely-standing barns that are more daylight than corrugate and even though it's hardly rained since I got out there's pools of something murky in the divots across the yard, and there's a strong smell of pig shite in the air.

I turn the migraine music on to let them know I'm about, light a tab and wait for the ten minutes it usually takes one of the lads to come ower from the fields with a little list of things they're after.

But today it's the farmer himsel, a big auld boy called Snowball. He's got his sleeves rolled up and there's a collie at his heels.

Now then young Mr Wisdom.

Alreet Mr Snowball.

We always talk like this, the two of us – mister this and mister that. It's part of our crack.

Aye canny, he says. Canny.

Keeping busy?

Aye. It's a hot one int it? We're on our third cycle of baling and it's only August. What do you think of that?

I don't think owt about that so I just say, reckon you'll get another one in then?

Oh aye. I hope so. I hope so.

Thirsty work and that.

Aye, says Snowball. Here – you divvent want a puppy do you?

A dog?

Aye.

Nor, I don't think so. Why?

Our Molly's had pups. Eight little buggers. The missus wants rid but we're having a job shifting them all. Actually, she'd as soon keep them but you can have one if you want.

What are they?

67

Terriers. Jack Russells. Lovely little things, they are. Proper good ratters an all. They've been wormed so they're good to gan. You can have one for free if you like.

I'm not sure. I'm out working all the time.

They're good as gold. Here – let us show you them anyway.

Snowball leads us ower to a small stone building that looks like it used to be the outside bogs or summat. We walk in and it takes a moment for me eyes to adjust to the darkness, then I see the pups in a pen. They're all black and shiny with bits of white patches dotted about and they bounce ower to us, yapping and scratching at the MDF he's used to wall them in. Snowball's right, mind. They're lovely little things. Wide eyed and tiny.

I says to him, What'll you do if you cannot sell them?

The usual, I suppose.

How do you mean?

You know. Stick em in a bucket.

What for?

Snowball looks at us.

To drown the poor little blighters.

Really?

Aye. Eight terriers'll take some training otherwise they'll run riot with me sheep. That's why they're called terriers – because they terrorise. You cannot get sentimental. Me sheeps me livelihood.

Can you not set them loose, like?

He shakes his head.

That'd be cruel. They'd not last. And you cannot have feral dogs wandering the country can you?

You'd really drown them though?

Aye, John-John. There's a couple reserved, but the rest'll be for the bucket.

I'll take one then, I find mesel saying without even thinking about it.

They'll need minding for the first few weeks. Are you sure you can take one John-John?

Yeah, I'll manage. I'll bring him out on the van if needs be.

That's up to you. Pick yersel one out then.

I gan into the pen and the pups scratch and nip at me boots. All but one of them, who's sat off to one side. He's the smallest in the litter. A little shadow of a pup with a smudge of white on his breast.

I'll have him, I say. That one.

The little runt?

Aye.

He's not as strong as his brothers and sisters, mind.

I'm not bothered, me.

He'll not be as fierce with vermin.

You never know – he might be.

Aye, well. True. You never know. Depends how he's raised dunnit.

You're right there.

What ye ganner call him?

I dinnar.

I reach down and pick him up. He lets out a little strangulated cough.

Reckon I'll have to call him Coughdrop.

Coughdrop's a good a name as any, says Snowball.

Coughdrop it is then.

Coughdrop Snowball has a ring to it.

He winks at us.

Coughdrop Wisdom you mean.

Aye, he smiles. That works an all.

I bring him up to me face so that we're eye to eye. As I do, the dog does a piss. A nervous yellow trickle on my boots.

Hallo little Coughdrop, I say. Hallo mate.

*

In the smoky wood-panelled snug of a pub in town that had stood on the same spot for eight hundred years, Mac did fetch him and his brother a couple more pints.

"That eye's coming up summat big," said Eddie. "Mebbe we can get you a steak for it."

"Bollards to that. I'm not wasting a good steak on that feeble punch. You can get us another drink though."

They had two more pints each, then moved on down to the student end of town, stopping in The Swan & Three Cygnets, The County, The Half Moon and then finally The Dun Cow, where they started on the whisky.

Evening became night and everything was a blur. Your Dad turned up swaying in the darkness, banging about demanding scran and growling summat about Henry Bradley. There was nee need for him to scratch me ears out with his midnight goings on like that.

I cooked him eggs and fixed him a brew but he must have had the devil in him because when a yolk broke before I served him, he lunged across the table and lamped me square across the cheek. Said The Champ deserved more.

He threw some money down at me feet. Then he curled up and went to sleep.

*

It's hot all week. Proper sticky and that.

After I've dropped the van off, cleaned up, disinfected the pumps and wiped everything down then walked back home I'm banjaxed. Totally knackered.

Coughdrop's there yapping in the pen I've made for him from a couple of palettes leaned over against the kitchen cupboards to make a right good den for him. There's shit and piss on the newspaper I laid down but he's pleased to see us.

I open the window, lift him out the pen and clean out the jobbies, put down fresh paper, scran and water for him and then take him through to the living room for a wrestle and a play with the squeaky rubber rat I bought him.

I strip off and sit there billy bollards in me armchair, drinking water and smoking a bine while Coughdrop flips his rat in the air, then settles down to gnaw at it.

Even in full summer, the flat is dark. It's like they've designed it so it's full of shadows. They do that with cheap houses. At least growing up in caravans you could turn and face the sun wherever it was at. It's hard to get a breeze blowing through an all. It's a hot little airless box this place, a bit like prison, but I'm knackered and I've been out all day so I just sit there, naked, and a bit hungry but too shagged to do owt about any of it.

It's noisy too.

The dual carriageway is only a minute's walk across a footbridge from the flats and there's cars and lorries gannin past all hours, or someone is playing music, or there's kids shouting outside, or there's sirens wailing at 3am as the polis chase another twocked car swerving round the estate with its doors open, some short-arsed, pubeless pov behind the wheel.

I feel anxiety stirring in my stomach. It's this place. It proper does my nut in and the only thing to stop that feeling of unease is to get out and about. The early mornings are the best, when it's barely light and I take Coughdrop out for a shite and a run around the houses to let off some steam when there's nee-one about, before I gan off to work.

The sunny afternoons aren't bad either, driving through the country roads with the wind in me hair, the fields flashing by and the smell of pollen and rapeseed hanging heavy in the air. Nature's scent.

These are the times that remind us of them few moments from me childhood when things felt good, when the world was me oyster, the fields me theme parks and the woodlands me beautiful green cathedral. Those brief moments when owt seemed possible. When things hadn't yet entirely gone to shite.

It's this anxiety that stops us from sleeping at night. There's nee fresh air and there's shadows creeping about.

I just lie there knackered but awake, a sheet snaked around me restless legs, smoking tabs and reading books and stroking Little Coughdrop.

And then I'm up with the birds.

And then I'm gone.

*

I woke with a black eye, and a bairn in us belly.

That Wisdom tree had gained another branch.

Your Dad Mac smiled when I telt him the stork had been. It was a smile I'd not seen before and I divvent mind telling you it scared us. It was like a wild dog smiling.

And both of us with our black eyes like that.

Your Dad celebrated by having a two day drink with the lads. They drank and they sang and they did fight one another; they visited marrers and relatives on other sites and Mac Wisdom did joke that he was glad to know his knackers were in full working order, telling everyone that he was going have another twenty nippers "just like me", and then they drank and sang some more.

And all the while I sat there alone, only eighteen, the Wisdom seed in us, wondering where me husband was and whether it would always be this way.

*

The street corner queues get longer as the days get hotter. And they do get hot. Hot as hell.

Some days I have to gan back to the wholesalers halfway through the route just to pick up more tubs of cream and flakes and that. And with everyone after ices and kets the route takes much longer to get round. I'm hardly sleeping and out even longer so I take to smuggling little Coughdrop in the van with us. As long as I let him out to shit and piss and he has a pig's ear to chew on he's happy.

I'm not back up at the Nook for a bit but when I do make it there's this proper heaviness in the air that I notice as soon as I turn off the main road and into the estate.

The road splits the Nook from the new build estate ower the other side where the middle-class kids live. It's only a hundred yard away but it's a world apart – there's nee CCTV cameras in metal cages on big metal poles for starters; and nee speed bumps or road blocks down every alleyway neither; nee fences missing posts snapped off during running gang fights, or stray dogs, or scowling squinting lads who hold their tabs inverted in their cupped hands, or crescent streaks from tyre tracks across the communal patches of grass, or cars on bricks, or bricks on cars, or spliff-eyed pre-teens with scars from falls and fights and bungled burglaries across long latchkey weekends.

The new estate dunt have scorch marks up the sides of half-burnt electricity sub-stations whose roofing lead was long since twocked either; or fridges flopped open in green spaces, or houses without carpets where the lights are never off, the front door never closed, the stereo and the TV always on, and a passing cast of rat-nosed characters crossing the doorstep.

It's a different world driving into the Nook where the air is tight. High tensile. Mega-para.

There's summat about this place I divvent like; summat that makes us want to accelerate right on through it. It's like when you stand close to an electricity pylon and you can feel a crackle or a charge, or the times inside when I've walked into the dining room for some scran and it's so quiet that you know you're seconds away from a proper old school Borstal-style kick-off. It's your senses doing what they're supposed to do: warning you to cover your whatsit. Cover your scut.

And today the Nook is proper humming and crackling with a demented energy.

I've not been up there five minutes and she's out again. That lass. That Maria. She waves us ower from down the road. She's wearing proper tight jeans this time, and a T-shirt with sleeves torn off at the shoulder and she's got a tiny band of belly showing at the waist. Her hair's in a pony-tail again. Proper tight.

Hiya soldier, she says.

Hello.

How's it gannin?

Aye, canny.

We stand there for a moment.

Can I get you owt, I say after a bit.

No ta.

It's on the house, I go, like I'm charlie big potato all of a sudden.

Whose house? Where?

No, like I mean it's free.

I know what you mean you daft bugger, she goes. I'm just joshin you. What you been up to?

Nowt.

Nowt?

Aye.

Well that's sounds exciting.

I suddenly remember about little Coughdrop. Lasses love stuff like that.

Oh aye, I go. I got mesel a dog.

Did you? I love dogs, me.

Aye. Me an all.

What type is he?

What type of dog?

Aye.

A small black un.

I meant what breed.

I dinnar. A terrier I think. I'm not very good with that stuff.

What's his name?

Coughdrop.

That's a funny name.

Aye.

Where did you get him?

Up at Snowball's place.

You what?

Snowball. He's this farmer up the back of beyond. Out in the sticks.

So where's he at now then?

Snowball?

No, you knobber. The pup.

Oh, he's at mine. Sometimes I bring him with us but I've left him at home today. He's mebbes just sleeping or chowing a pig's ear or summat.

Pig's ear? That's minging.

Not to him it's not. He bloody loves them.

I'd like to see him sometime. I'm great with dogs, me.

Aye well. You can if you like.

When, she says, and this takes us off guard a bit. I thought she was just being polite and that. I didn't expect her to actually want to see the wee fella.

Whenever you like, I say. Dead casual, like.

I need an invite.

Aye.

Well?

Well what?

Are you going to invite us?

Oh aye. Well, mebbe. I mean, if you like. Or I could bring him out with us on the round.

Are you not going to invite us to your place? I'd rather see him there, me.

I shrug and start to turn plum red again. I'm hesitating because it feels weird letting someone know where I live, even this lass. It's always been that way. Growing up I'd not even tell anyone what site we were on. It was summat me Mam and Dad always taught us: don't tell nee fugger where you're at unless you need to. Them that wants to proper find you will find you right enough.

Aye, I hear me big plum mush stammering. Aye mebbes.

Why only mebbes?

I hesitate, me mouth proper floppy like it's got a life of its own. It always bloody does this. Gives up on us right when I need it to work the most.

It's just a bit of a shit-hole that's all. A proper toilet, like. I've not had much chance to get anything nice yet. It's just somewhere to sleep really.

Just sleep?

Aye. And eat.

And nowt else?

Nor. Not really. I spend all me time working and when I'm not working I'm walking the pup.

And there's just you is there, Maria says.

Aye.

Nee-one else?

Why're you asking, like?

Nee reason. I'm just asking. Divvent worry I'm not the social or owt. You're bloody para, you are.

I'm not on the social.

You don't sign on?

Na. Never.

And you just get by doing this, do you?

Aye.

Maria shakes her head.

Bloody hell, you're a one-off you are. I've never met anyone who's not on the dole before.

I divvent know if this is a compliment or she's taking the piss so I say nowt.

Here, she gans. You've not answered me question.

Which one?

About whether you live with anyone.

It's just me and our Coughdrop I say, and though I'm trying to play it cool inside me heart is a butterfly trapped in me jam jar chest and I'm thinking – *Christ, I'd love to jump your bloody bones.*

76

Tell you what, she gans. Why don't you text us sometime. When your Coughdrop is ready for a bit of company, like.

Shite, I think. No bloody phone.

OK.

What's your mobile number, she says. I'll call it now so you've got mine stored.

Hellfire, I'm thinking. Bloody mobiles. I'd not heard of them when I went in five year ago, now they're bloody everywhere. They're just another reminder of how out of step I am with the rest of the world. I come out and it's all bloody Britney this and Tony whatsit that. Everyone gannin on about this bloody internet game on the computer like it's important or summat. And what's everyone got to say to each other that's so important that they cannot say in person anyway? Nowt, I bet.

Then I'm frowning and mumbling. Um, I've not got one.

You've not got a mobile?

Not yet, like.

How come? Everyone's got a mobile.

I've just not had a chance to get to the shop.

I'm proper stumbling over me words now. Me mouth feels like it's got ten pieces of chutty in it. I cannot even talk proper.

I've been busy like.

You're proper mental, you are.

Well, I lie. I did have one, like. Someone twocked it though.

Oh aye, she says, like she's knows I'm pulling her leg. What type?

One of them what-do-you-call-it?

How the bloody hell should I know, she smiles at us.

You know...

Nor.

I blush.

So who nicked it? she asks us.

Well, if I knew that I'd get it back wouldn't I?

Would you though?

Aye, mebbe.

77

Is that what you'd do then? Find out who chorred it and gan round and break their legs.

I say nowt to this.

Hard fucker are you? she says. Proper radge?

I shrug and try not to blush mesel any redder than I already am.

Not really, I say.

I telt you you're weird, you. You sound weird an all.

How's that, like?

I don't know. It's your accent isn't it. It's just dead funny. You don't sound like you're from round here. But at the same time you sort of do.

Aye, it's probablys because I've lived all over, me. Moved about a bit and that.

Maria's leaning on the sill of my hatch now. She's pretty close. So close I can smell her. The natural smell of her.

I'll tell you why else you're weird, she gans. You're weird because every lad round here reckons they're dead hard, thinks they're about summat, but you just stand there and shrug and say nowt. And you're not on the dole. You're a bloody ice cream man.

What's wrong with that, like?

There's nowt wrong with that, it's just most of the lads round here wouldn't be seen dead selling ice lollies to kiddies.

Why's that?

They'd be worried what people'd think.

How do you mean?

They'd worry that people would think they're a paedo or summat.

I just look at her for a moment, then I say, is that what ye think, like?

What – that you bribe kids with the promise of a free Mini Milk then take them off and bum them somewhere? Don't worry, she laughs. I can tell you're not like that.

How?

78

I just can.

She falls silent and there's an awkward moment where we both just stand there, and I'm wondering how the hell you tell if someone diddles kids just by looking at them.

Then Maria gans, so how you going to text us if you've got nee mobile?

I dunno. Smoke signals?

You can phone us if you like she says, missing me joke. Or I can phone you.

Shite, I think. Bloody great skipfuls of sloppy shite.

Aye.

Give us your number then and mebbe I'll ring you up sometime.

Shite.

I shift from foot to foot, then scratch my elbow. Thing is, I've not got a phone either.

He's got nee phone either, she says, as if to an imaginary friend or summat. How do you talk to people then?

Like this.

Like what?

Like we're talking now. The auld-fashioned way.

And he reckons he's not weird, she says, her eyes widening with exaggeration. I can't help smiling at this an all.

Aye well, I grin. Mebbes a bit weird.

Aye, mebbe just a bit she says. Then turning away, sighing she says: well, perhaps we'll not bother then eh.

Had on, I say, surprising mesel and suddenly feeling like summat good and new and different and scary could happen here. Or it could happen if it wasn't slipping away. But then I think: I don't want it to slip away, even if it is different and scary and she's always taking the piss out of us. Had on a minute.

Aye? she says, stopping.

She's got one eyebrow raised like she's waiting to hear what I have to say next, like she's waiting to be impressed, and I know in this moment that I have to say summat good, summat that will surprise her and make her heart pump and her fanny tingle, and I know I have to get it right because I've never even been with a lass before, never felt a lass's tits or owt like that, I know that if I say the right thing I might be able to change all that, and I might stop feeling so alone in the world, even just for ten minutes, or I might stop living in the past, even just for ten minutes, and things might even change and get better and I might end up becoming an upstanding, functioning member of society and that; a reformed character and that. No longer a slave to my animal DNA and bad family name. Even just for ten minutes.

I can give you a ride in me van if you like, I say, me face darker than beetroot.

She screws up her face, as if she's having a big hard think. She's holding her chin and her mouth is sort of crooked and her hip is cocked and she's having a gleg at the sky with one eye closed.

Then she gans, Christ. I thought you'd never fucking ask.

*

I was beached, me arm wrapped around me stomach, an itchy wool blanket pulled tight across my back, the rattle of the rain on the roof like tambourines as the glow of the fire's embers cast the van in a haunting orange hue. Winter was on its way; it was in the air. There was a cruel front coming. You could feel it.

And there was a right devilish pain inside us.

"What's wrong with you, girl?"

Your Dad was at the table supping milky tea and excavating his nose. I said nowt, knew it wasn't worth it; words wouldn't cover this dull fiery roar in me abdomen. There were no words to describe it. Only moans and groans and wet eyes.

He leaned over, opened the door of the wood-burning stove and jabbed at the logs with the poker. Embers rose then he flicked a bogey in there and closed the door.

"Well?"

"I want me Mam."

"Well your Mam's not here."

"You need to go and find her."

Mac snorted.

"I reckon she's up Northumberland way," I said. "Mebbe you could ask around."

He slurped his tea like a hog. I watched his Adam's apple throb as he swallowed then slurped again.

"Or mebbes a pig'll fly right into that frying pan, sliced and salted," he said.

I reached round for the blanket and wrapped mesel tighter in it.

"I want her here."

"You'll not be needing her."

"But she's me Mam."

"You're a Wisdom now and all Wisdom bairns are born strong as an ox and stubborn as a donkey. We're famous for it. You're worrying about nowt. You're just soft, is all."

The burning in me middle had us bending double. Someone had lit a fire there, then put it out with bleach and now they were scraping us clean with a blunt tatty peeler. My thighs were slick with blood. Blood as black as you'd ever see.

Mac rolled a tab, lit it, then smoked while staring into the flames. The smoke came through his nostrils. The crackle of the burning logs and his breathing were the only sounds cutting through the tambourine rain.

"I'm not soft," I finally said. "And anyroad it's gone."

"What ye yacking on about now?"

"The bairn. It's gone."

"Eh?"

"It's miscarried."

He turned to look at us.

"It's miscarried an I want you to fetch me Mam."

Then I added, "And you're a heartless bastard, Mac Wisdom."

81

I said this as soft as a could, and for once he didn't raise an eyebrow, much less a hand. It was the one time I could get away with calling him like that. The one and only time.

He just sat there staring into the fire, the dimp between his fingers and smoke wafting from his flared bull nostrils.

"Well," he finally said, his voice thick and flat. "We'll just have to put another one in there then, won't we."

*

I divvent even know your name.

We're out of the estate and riding down the country roads. It's starting to rain a bit but I don't even care because it's warm and the window is open and it proper smells of a pungent summer and this lass Maria is eating a white chocolate Magnum, the most expensive thing on the menu. I'm behind the wheel with a fag between my fingers, the breeze blowing in my sweaty pits. I'm just just hoping I'm not stinking too much.

We've got the radio on top whack. It's playing this song she seems to know but I've never heard before. It's sung by some lad. The chorus gans *Upside inside out, she's livin' la vida loca* or summat like that.

Eh?

I divvent even know your name, she says again.

It's John-John.

It's what?

John-John.

That's a daft name isn't it. Blatantly. Here, turn it up. This song's proper dopper, this is.

I turn up the radio and look in the rear view mirror because she's sat just behind us clapping her hands, the Magnum wedged in her gob, doing a funny little dance, where she's making a circle with her hips and her bare arms are up in the air, and her shoulders are tanned except for the white bit where you can see where her bra strap has been. The breeze is in her hair and there's the faintest smattering of drizzle tapping at the window, but it's summer drizzle so it doesn't matter, and she looks so free and so into the music that I feel a bit weird, like I just want to grab a hold of her and wrap my arms around her and kiss her all ower. Kiss her tits, her belly, her feet, her eyes, her fanny, her arse – everything.

Upside inside out, living la vida loca.

Have another Magnum if you like I say, drawing on me tailor-made and shouting over the music and the noise of the breeze and the engine. Have two if you like – I'm not arsed, me. Arty says I can scran what I like.

Does he?

Aye. Perk of the job.

One's enough, ta.

We gan on like this for a while, laughing and messing about, and me ganning *Cha-cha-cha* and her ganning *La Vida Loca!* and pissing oursels, and it feels so good driving down the lanes that I stray from the route and I don't even care. I take us down roads I've never driven before and think to mesel that this just might be the happiest I've ever felt in me whole stupid life.

As we drive on a back road that takes us to the peak of a hill I've never seen before, the whole of the north-east opens up in front of us. It's a new view to me and it's so breathtaking and unexpected that I pull over sharply into this little lay-by that's full of pot-holes but has a view that's pure nectar.

Inland to the west you can make out the industrial estates then, past them, a bit of space then the city and the spires of the cathedral poking up from its sunken position in the ground, all mystical and ancient, like. To the north there's Penshaw Monument up on a hill, a mini Greek whatsit – aye, temple – and past that you can see all the way to Team Valley and Gateshead and somewhere in the distance beyond them a smudge of Newcastle; looking east there's nowt much to see because there's more hills and undulations rising up to the skyline but I know that the North Sea is out there somewhere, a grey swash about ten mile away, but to the south it's greener and more rural-looking except for a haze in the very distance which I reckon to be the huffing, stinking power stations of Teesside. I've never been down to Teesside before. Or up the Toon, come to think of it. It's a bit ridiculous. I mean, who's ever heard of a traveller who's never bloody travelled?

Hell, Maria murmurs. You can see for miles. How come it looks so beautiful from up here but is so fucking ugly down there?

Not all of it is ugly. In fact, most of it's beautiful.

Not where I live, it isn't.

I say nowt.

Maria has climbed ower the front seat and is squeezed next to us in a seat that's not made for two. I can feel her bare arm against mine. There's a prickle, a hot tingle between us, and I'm wondering if she can feel it too. Even when her arm moves away from mine I can still feel it, like there's pins or wires or summat connecting us.

Do you reckon that's it ower there she says, pointing back towards the town where you can see what looks like an over-sized pylon painted blue but which is actually part of some industrial power planet.

What?

The Nook.

Aye, probably. I reckon.

Show us where you grew up, she says.

The van is pointing out across the land and we're looking through the windscreen at the north-east of England, the only place we know.

Though it's raining ower the town if you look further north, up towards Newcastle, the clouds are spread so thin they fade away to nowt but pure blue, and the light is shining down in magical looking shafts. Heavenly almost. And there's that smell in the air an all. That special smell; the scent of wet roads and dandelions and warm gravel; ragwort and mulch.

I get a whiff of Maria too. Her shampoo. And her skin. It's salty, like. Fusty. A nice fusty though.

As it happens my sense of smell is very sharp. After five years indoors me nose only ever seemed to experience the same odours but now I'm out it's like I'm experiencing some scents for the first time. I have a very finely tuned sneck.

I've definitely not smelled a girl this close up before either. It's a proper headrush.

I clear me throat and then I point vaguely to the countryside a couple of miles outside of the city.

Ower there, I say.

Then I slowly move my finger across to beyond the other side of the city where things open out again.

There.

I point south.

And there.

I point to the space this side of Chester-le-Street.

A month there.

I point south.

A month or two there.

Then I point back towards the city and keep going. She follows my finger as I arc round way past the city and point off into the hazy distance towards where I think Deerbolt might be, beyond the skyline ower Barnard Castle way.

And five years there, with good behaviour.

Maria smiles but she looks a bit confused.

You've lived in a lot of houses.

I don't say owt at first, like always when people quiz us about me past and me family and that but then summat comes ower us and I think fug it, you have to open up some time, to someone.

Not houses, I say.

Not houses? What then?

Caravans.

Caravans? Here, are you a —

I interrupt her to save the embarrassment of saying the wrong thing. To save us both.

Aye. Me family were travellers.

She goes quiet for a moment.

Is that the same thing as a gypsy?

More or less.

And is that the same as a pikey?

Even though I've had the word spat in me mush a thousand times by a thousand horrible dirty mouths, and each time it's like a slap in the face or a knee in the nadgers, the way she says it so innocently and inquisitively I can't help but smile this time. This one time. Because Maria's so sweet she makes an insult sound like a kiss. It rolls off her tongue like honey. The way she says it so timidly I actually feel like laughing.

Well, pikey's an insult to travellers, I say. A pikey is someone who chors stuff and never washes their bollocks and does fug-all for a living. A pikey is them that dumps broken fridges by the road-side. Pikeys don't work like I work. Really a pikey's not a traveller at all; he's a figment of you lot's imaginations.

And do you wash your bollocks?

Oh aye, I grin. Twice daily. Soap and water, then talc and a nice perfume.

She smiles at us again, then reaches for my baccy pouch to knock up a rollie. When she's done it she sparks it up, inhales and slowly blows out a perfect smoke ring.

Cool. I've never met a traveller before. Not a proper one. Only pikeys.

She grins again, then she puts her hand on my knee. It's dead casual, but my knee nearly explodes. That's what it feels like anyroad. There's fire in me knee and it's running right up me thigh and into me un-perfumed knackers.

I pretend not to notice but I feel mesel gannin red again and burning up with blazing embarrassment.

So where's your family at now then? she asks us, but I barely even hear her say this because her hand is moving up my leg and it's making us dizzy. Then it's up on me thigh. Oh Jesus. Now my junk's stirring underneath me combats, and in a minute she's probably going to notice it and she's going to think I'm a weirdo who can't control his dander or – worse – see us for the virgin I am, and then it'll all be ower.

Er.

I'm stammering. Stalling. Fog-headed.

They're off somewhere, I croak. Fug knows.

You don't know where?

They're travelling and that, you know. That's how it is with us.

She actually believes this and I sort of feel bad even though I'm not really lying. I could just tell her the truth: that me Dad's in the ground and the rest of them are a bunch of bloody bastards that have rejected us, how me Mam took off somewhere and cast us out like a whatsit, and so much for bloody family ties. Thinking about all that again makes us feel sick. So we just sit there like that for a moment, her smoking with one hand and the other resting on my thigh, and me with my dander pulsing. Me face plum red like, and me bell-end lit up like a bloody lighthouse.

Maria breaks the silence.

Here – how come you say fug instead of fuck?

Eh?

It's weird though isn't it.

I don't know. Aye, mebbes.

It sounds daft. It's not proper swearing.

Nor, I say. I suppose not. I'm not a big fan of swearing.

How come?

I dinnar. I suppose I've just heard that much of it over the years. It's vulgar isn't it.

Vulgar! Christ. Whoever met a lad who worries about being vulgar? You're a proper oddball, you are John-John. Proper confusing.

As she says this she gives me leg a squeeze and me dander jumps in me kecks so hard I reckon she can't fail to have noticed it. I'm tingling all ower an all, like there's electricity in the van. Fug, I'm thinking, me cock's going to explode in a minute. It's ganna gan off in me kecks like a Roman fugging candle. Good job we've pulled ower or I'd probably have crashed by now, and the pair of us would be a mess of ice cream, flakes and nearly two decades worth of sploodge.

I touch the glass eye in me pocket. Me knob's pressed up against it now. It's been with us everywhere that thing. Even up me scut for safe keeping, though that's not an experience I'd like to go through again. It was like summat off a horror fillum getting that thing out.

What ye doing down there, she goes. Having a wank or summat.

Nor, I go. It's not that.

Well, what's in there that's so interesting?

I wrap me fingers round the eye.

Are you sure you want to see it?

Aye, well I do now you've got us so curious, John-John.

Close your eyes and put out your hand. She does. She lets out a nervous little giggle.

There you go. She opens her eyes then flinches.

Urr – that's *minging*. What is it?

What do you reckon it is. It's a bloody glass eye, isn't it.

Where did you get it?

I shrug.

Around. Then I laugh. Do you get it, I go. *A round.*

You're mental, you are.

We sit for a bit more and she looks at the eye then she goes so you said you lived ower there for five years, and nods in the direction of the city. Does that mean you stopped in the same place all that time?

Shite. Here we go.

Aye, I say.

88

Was that in a caravan an all?

Not quite.

A house?

I could just lie. I could just lie and say aye and then we can move onto to whatever comes next. Probably me junk exploding in me kecks, at this rate.

I can almost hear the cogs and wheels of her mind whirring as she tries to work us out: he didn't live in a house and he didn't live in a caravan so he was either homeless or he was somewhere else. And he did mention summat about time off for good behaviour...

She's a bright lass though because she works it out soon enough.

Have you been inside then, she finally says like it's nowt, and as she does I feel a sense of relief wash ower us and I even stop worrying about me untouched cock shooting spaff all over the shop.

I turn to Maria and we're facing each other now, dead close, and I'm looking into her exotic eyes that seem sharpened by the tightness of her ponytail and for a moment it's like we're looking right inside each other, properly inside each other, to the core, and it feels like mebbes we don't even need to talk, and it's a bit like all that shite you see in films – but better, and with *La Vida Loca* ringing in our ears rather than some slushy cobblers on a tinkling pianner.

Aye I say, my voice all hoarse. Aye, I have actually.

And then we're kissing, proper snogging like, and her lips are dead soft and wet, and she's the first girl I've ever kissed and one of her tits is pressed up against us, and she tastes of smoke and white chocolate Magnum and it feels mint, top drawer, and me dander is twitching like a mouse in a trap, and it's all so mental and new and alien that I want to swallow her up and keep her inside us where it's warm and safe and quiet and she'll not have to worry about owt ever again, and I'll carry her everywhere, and we'll always be together, and she'll just sit there inside, warm and safe and happy as Larry, with me feeding her Magnums and singing *cha-cha-cha, living la vida loca,* over and over. Proper dopper, that.

Her tongue's working overtime in me mouth, then she pulls back and looks at us for a moment and her dark eyes are wild like those of a tiger or summat. Squinting and hungry and on fire. Dead serious, like she's searching for something in my eye. Then she pulls back and draws on her tab.

That was nice.

Aye, I say, my voice breaking like I'm thirteen again.

She looks at us all wild still, then she sort of licks her lips.

I start to say summat, summat stupid probably, but before I can she flicks the butt out of the window, leans ower and moves her head down to my crotch, to me stiff dander, and I close me eyes and exhale to stop mesel exploding into a thousand little pieces of me.

*

Barker Lovell pulled up on the site a few days later.

He was dressed up the old travelling way, like how you see in the books or in them photos your Gran kept in a biscuit tin under her bed. He had on trousers held up high by braces, a beige check shirt, brown cardigan and matching trilby, with a red silk scarf knotted around his neck to give him a flash of colour. And he had the narrowed eyes of a man who had spent years squinting into the sunlight.

There was six vans on the Edenside site that day and Barker knew travellers in each one of them. But it was your Dad that he was here to see.

He knocked on the door. Mac answered in his shirt sleeves and invited him in for a brew,

"Social visit is it?" asked Mac.

"Not entirely. I've got us a bit of work coming up."

Their conversation was a series of nonchalant sniffs and grunts and statements. Swollen pauses hung between them. I mashed the tea.

"I knew you'd muller Henry Bradley, but I needed to be sure. It was a test, like. I knew you wouldn't bottle it but I needed to see if you'd put the work in."

Barker took out his cigarette case and lighter. He made a great show of laying the polished pewter case and matching zippo lighter on the table before him; made sure we both noticed. He would have known we were still using matches. I decided there and then I didn't like this Lovell one.

"Go on."

"Everyone in town knows you're a brawler Mac, but there's a big difference between clumping some lummox on the cobbles when you've had a skin full, and fighting someone bare knuckle in front of the lads, for money – for git big bets, like."

Mac sniffed.

"If you're going to fight regular, you've got to pace yersel," said Barker. "Learn control. And you've got to win. A bare knuckle man is only as good as his reputation and if you're a one-punch Mary then nee-one is going to put up any prize money worth fighting for, are they?"

"Spose not."

"Well then."

"Well then."

Barker stopped talking, opened his case and lit a cigarette without offering Mac one.

"So you're going to have to keep in shape if you're fighting for me."

Mac helped himself to one of the cigarettes and lit it with his own matches. He took a couple of drags.

"What I mean is, I could use a radgey bastard like you," went Barker. "I reckon between my brain and your fists and big heart we can make a pretty penny for the both of us if you want it."

Mac shrugged.

"Aye," he said. "You line them up Barker and I'll switch them off. No bother."

Barker drew on the last of his cigarette and ground it out. Then he turned and looked at me.

"And what about you Vancy Wisdom?"

"She's got nowt to do with this," snapped your father.

"Aye well, there's one other thing you'll need, lad. Patience. Patience and discipline. A fighting man needs to learn himsel the art of waiting before he can learn how to put a man twice his size on his back. And he needs to be ready at all times an all. Fights can come at a day or two's notice and if you're not in shape you're banjaxed. And if you're banjaxed you're dead. And that means no pissing about scrapping in the town on a weekend."

Mac grunted his approval.

"Well you leave it all up to me, bonny lad. We'll get Christmas ower with first and then in the new year I'll put the word out. All the best fights come in the spring time when the travellers are taking to the road."

Mac stubbed out his cigarette. Barker Lovell's cigarette.

"Line them up."

"Remember lad: patience."

"Aye."

"Well then."

"Well then what?"

"Learn it."

"Learn what?"

"Patience you daft knacker," said Barker. "Christ almighty."

*

So what did you do then, Johnny?

We're back on the route now and I'm floating. Properly floating.

I feel like I've lost half my body weight and though I've not yet shagged a lass I've still just done more than I've done before, and it felt bloody great. Top of the world, marrer. And after

92

me dander had done spurting like a bloody burst water pipe, she's gone fucking hell – there's loads of it, and laughed, but not in a bad way. She'd laughed in a good way. Like she was amazed and impressed and mebbes feeling as good as me. *La Vida Loca*. I'd even had a good feel of her tits and rubbed her fanny through her pants, acting like I'm some kind of dab hand at the auld sex game.

And the best thing is, afterwards, when I've cleaned me knob off on this auld duster I keep to wipe dead flies off the windscreen she's gone there's plenty more where that came from. If you want it, like.

If I want it, I'm thinking. *Course I bloody want it.*

Oh aye, I say trying to play it cool like and nearly breaking me neck with a shrug. Oh aye.

And now we're back on the route and the sky has cleared a bit and we're smoking and it's like the past few minutes never happened. She asks us where I'm living and it's like we're back to the formalities of conversation, so I tell her about me flat, then we sit in silence for a bit, and then that's when she goes so what did you do then, Johnny?

I knew she'd ask us this. Of course she'd ask. About what I did. Everyone's the same. They want to know what type of rotter they're dealing with: a pathetic one, a dangerous one or a cool one. They want to know whether you rob auld biddies or rob banks. It makes a big difference to some people, though to me it's all robbing, and it's all what lazy wankers and povvy charvers do. Simple as. She's basically asking us why I lost five years and me whole bloody family, and why I'm weird and stunted and a loner, and living in some povvy flat that even little Coughdrop turns his little wet nose up at.

And why I've ended up here, in charge of this spaff-coated van.

It's not an easy question to answer, even after she's emptied my nadgers and I'm feeling brand new, like a bloody king or summat. Because even though I'm floating there's still a stone in my stomach that's stopping us from totally soaring sky high. I mean, I feel A1, but even now the past is still here in her question, tainting the conversation like a shadow or a ghost or a fever.

I draw on my tab and exhale slowly, then clear my throat, then feel mesel frowning.

I was, I say. Er. Well, I was a bad lad, like.

You and everyone else round here Johnny. But what did you do? Five years is a canny long time to be locked up. Especially for a young lad. It must have been at least some burglaries. Did you rob houses?

Nor. Did I bollards. I've never robbed owt in my life. Twocking is for numpties. I hate thieves, me.

I'm not bothered you know, she says. You can tell us. Personally, I reckon it was summat violent. GBH or summat. Am I on the right track?

I shrug.

Mebbes.

Did you bottle someone when you were leathered?

I look at her: Na. Not even close. Anyways. I've never been leathered.

What you've never been pissed and that? I know you're weird but that's summat else, man. What the hell have you been doing with your life?

I say nowt.

Did you nick a cop car and drive it into the Wear, then do a runner?

Nope. You're not even warm.

Erm... how about drugs. Was you knocking out gear, but then one of the boys found out and came to tax you but you knew he was coming so you were waiting for him and when he stepped up you shanked him in the neck with a rusty screwdriver.

I smile. Na. It wasn't drugs. Or screwdrivers.

Oh aye, I forgot: Mr Clean. So did you do a dump in the font at the cathedral, then use it to write FUCK THE POPE UP THE SHITTER on the wall.

Christ, I laugh. You've got some imagination, you. And anyroad, the cathedral isn't Catholic, so that would be a waste of a shite.

Did you rip some student's ear off and cook it in a frying pan.

Oh aye, I say. That's it. You're bang on there. Ear and chips.

I say nowt for a bit and neither does she so we drive along in silence. I turn the radio on hoping that that *Vida Loca* song will come on again, but I get the news instead, so click it back off again.

Well, she says finally. You don't seem like a psycho to me, John-John. I mean, you're definitely a bit weird like, what with not drinking and them clothes you wear – and you're not exactly the greatest talker either – but you're no psycho. And you're nowt like any of the other lads I know, that's for sure. I mean, you've got a job and a flat and that, you're not on the dole and you divvent chor stuff either. And then there's the travelling thing.

Does that bother you, like?

Bother us? No.

She thinks for a bit.

No, not at all. Why would it? I always wanted to see the world.

I smile at her.

I divvent know about the world, I say, feeling a bit confident and cocky now, but there's neewhere in this county worth knowing about that I've not been. Play your cards right and mebbes one day I'll take you to Sunderland.

She digs us in the ribs with her elbow and I stick the ice cream music back on again.

*

The morning frosts began to melt quicker and tiny shoots started to push their way through the grass that surrounded the van. It had been a harsh winter there in the field miles outside of town, surrounded by nowt but the few other vans and only the hooting of owls cutting through the syrupy darkness that settled across the fields for sixteen hours of every day. Ice, snow and wind. As brittle as the husk of a pond reed.

But spring was on its way and life was returning, unfolding, stretching and yawning. And in the first days of daffodils I discovered I had fallen pregnant again.

My parents had been right. Of course they had. Mac Wisdom was from bad blood. Of course he was. Those Wisdoms. Rough lot. Untamed field beasts, them.

I'd already had plenty of chipped teeth, sore jaws and shiners to show that no-one escaped his fists.

I kept a steak in the ice box especially.

But you didn't talk about these things. Not even with them next door; them that can hear it all. No man nor woman interferes with another man's family business like that. You'd rather pretend it isn't happening.

I soon came to understand that if Mac fighting on the cobbles meant there was less of the rage left in him then it was better he beat a willing man than me.

And there was summat about your Dad that made us believe in him. I reckoned there had to be otherwise there was no hope. And life without hope is death. So I told myself I did see summat in there, deep and dark. Summat ancient and immoveable in Mac, like a rock. Summat that sat there making him indestructible, mysterious.

This was the year that he would make a living for his family on the traveller's circuit. And so it was with the first daffodils now drooping and my belly swelling he hitched up the van and we pulled out.

We left behind us a bleached-out rectangle of yellowed grass and a fire-blackened stone-ringed circle that had scorched the *soil of land once blackened only by the riches of the earth, them dusky diamonds of the north-east fields – coal.*

*

I had a friend once. A proper marrer who wasn't made up, or didn't have four legs, or didn't turn on us and take the piss. A proper human one.

Fingers, he was called.

It was the summer before they sent us away; the last summer I had outside until this one.

I was fourteen, fifteen. Summat like that. It was when I was hanging around the town all the time to dodge me Dad's swinging blows and trying to see if I could slot in somewhere amongst the rest of the world.

Fingers was this little homeless gadgie. He slept in a bush down by the river, on that nice green run that stretches from the weir below the cathedral – the view you see on all them postcards they sell to the touroids – along to Framwellgate Bridge.

I met him down there one damp June day, when the both of us ended up sat on the same bench doing nowt but smoking and watching the wet-backed river rats pop up from their hidey-holes in the bank side.

Fingers had the main two fingers missing on his right hand. He said he was on the run from the law. Then the next day he'd say he was on the run from gangsters in London, or some fella whose wife he'd shagged. When he said this he made like he was shagging some housewife, backskuttle. He was always going I'm a wanted man me you know and I'd be thinking, Aye right you are Fingers. Right you are.

Fingers said a lot of things. Fingers was full of shit.

Fingers was me marrer.

Whatever the weather he always wore this kiddies' ski jacket and git big fat trainers that he'd got from a charity shop or mebbe a hostel or the cop shop, and he had this tongue that he

97

used to poke out to wet his lips. When he did that he looked like a lizard. Always wetting his lips. He had these beady eyes too, Action Man eyes that moved from side to side like they were always looking for an opportunity. A bottle to lift. A dimp to smoke. Someone to tap up for summat. For owt.

I never knew how old Fingers was. He could have been forty-five, he could have been seventy.

We spent that whole summer walking the town together, the gypsy and the tramp, the both of us just glad of the company. We must have walked every inch of the town a hundred times ower, and when we'd done walking and we had some coins in our pockets, we'd go up the hill to the park with some cans and some kets and some tabs and we'd have ourselves a little party as the orange sun sat itsel down behind the cathedral over on the opposite hill. Sometimes Fingers would have a bit of tack with him and he'd roll these really crooked spliffs that he'd suck on, his lizard's tongue wetting the roach til it was sopping, then he'd offer it to me, and I'd say no ta Fingers, I'm alreet, but don't mind me mate, knock yersel out.

And he had stories, mind. Hods of stories. He was always going on about he used to be an ace face down in London and other places besides. About how you could walk into any snooker hall in King's Cross, Tiger Bay or the Gorbals and say his name and you'd get a big drink bought for you, no questions.

"Just say you're a marrer of Auld Fingers."

Me and Fingers were down the river banks every evening, as it turned dark, him working on a bottle and me mebbes drinking a can of pop or summat, the both of us avoiding what it was we were both avoiding.

Other times we'd find ourselves up at Palace Green, standing on the lawn out front amongst the DO NOT WALK ON THE GRASS signs and staring up at the cathedral. When that happened Fingers would fall silent, and he'd lick his lips and say howay kid let's have a gleg inside, and we'd pad across the grass that was clipped so that every blade looked the same length, over to the big wooden door with the gargoyle knocker and we'd push it open and step into the cathedral, both of us feeling like tiny insects.

Then ower to the same place every time: the great stained-glass window down at the bottom end of the cathedral.

Looker, he'd say, and he'd point up, and we'd both stand there for a while, looking at the hundreds – mebbes thousands – of little pieces of coloured glass that had been clipped and shaped and painted and placed to make that window what it was. The most beautiful sight in the whole town. Summat to properly take your breath away.

Look at that, he'd whisper. It's bloody magic that is. Have you ever seen owt so beautiful?

And I'd start to answer, but he'd shush us with a finger to his lips. Remember where you're at son, he'd say. This place is not for talking.

So we'd stand there in silence, and there'd be blue and red and yellow and orange and green and purple light streaming down through the window, shining down on us, shining through the glass, beams of light, dozens of them, and we'd just be stood there, not saying owt, both sort of drifting off into our own little worlds, better worlds. Everything was bathed in colour and the only noise was the faintest echo of footsteps and murmured voices like the sound of long-gone monks or summat, and even the musty smell of stone and ancient dust was like perfume to me nostrils, and there'd be no trouble only colour and silence.

Then we'd walk back down to the river so Fingers could finish his drinks, and he'd just be sat there, licking his lips and staring at the water, like a shadow had crossed his funny little face and I'd become invisible.

Then when the sky was settled and even the moon was yawning and slumping ower the water we'd walk back down into town, and Fingers would nod his goodbyes and then nash along the river to his bush with the cathedral view and I'd set off to walk downstream for an hour, walking through fields and woods, and I'd get back to the site shagged and hoping to avoid the auld man.

I'd get under me blankets and I'd be thinking about Fingers out there in his bush and I'd wonder who had it worse: me stuck up here with this mad, cruel lot for a family, nee money, nee schooling and nowt that you could call prospects, or him down there, with nowt but the foliage and the worms and a tarpaulin to sleep under, his family scattered, his dreams full of regrets and mistakes.

Then one day late in the summer when the grass on the verges was parched and golden, and you could grasp a scent of burning leaves on the breeze, we were sat on a wall near the mental hospital. Out of nowhere this jam sandwich screeches up with its siren light swirling but the sound turned off.

Before I could even blink Fingers had it on his toes. He was fast for a gadgie whose joints had gone rusted from all them damp nights sleeping in bushes, but the polis were faster and they grabbed auld Fingers quick-sharp. They just scooped him up by the collar of his kiddies' ski jacket so that his little legs were still running like a bloody cartoon creature running off a canyon cliff.

Now then Fingers, gans this copper while looking at me sideways. You're a slippery one aren't you?

Been looking all ower the bloody shop for you, says the other musker, the one who'd been driving. And he smiles as he says this. A smile of amusement.

Fingers said nowt though. He just casts us this glance and does this shrug that says, I telt you I was a wanted man. I telt you.

Howay then, says the first musker. Off we go.

You want to watch who you're drinking with, the other says to us.

I divvent drink me, I say, but they're already away, leading Fingers into the back of the car, where he looked so small like a lost bloody child or summat. They pulled away and as they did Fingers gives us a little wave of the hand like he were the bloody Queen or summat, and that was the last time I saw him – the one person I could call a proper marrer.

And it was not long after that that everything turned to shite for us.

*

The lights of the Scotch Corner cafeteria bathed the surrounding flagstones in patches of orange.

In a few hours holidaying gorger families would be pulling up to stretch their legs and picnic with sandwiches and tartan flasks of milky tea on the green grass surrounding the car park, the same people that looked down on us travellers for doing much the same thing the rest of the year round.

It was here where north met south and east argued with west just off a major A1 intersection where your Dad was fighting in a car park.

Off in the far corner of a truck stop where the lorries were parked in such a way as to make an enclosure away from the canteen and the petrol station forecourt, Mac Wisdom did take off his shirt, roll his neck, crack his knuckles and step into a barrage of blows from a sinewy, game young traveller known only as Yarm Kenny.

It was pre-dawn and the lights of the trucks were on low, dipped into the ground to avoid attention.

Shirtless, the two men stood toe-to-toe, grim determination painted on pink faces already swelling with knots and welts. As fist struck skull, the breathing of the two men was matched only by the scraping sound of boot soles on glass and gravel.

A jostling crowd of thirty-odd watched on. All had known about the fight but none had been told the location. That had only been revealed a few hours earlier. Many of them had been up drinking since the previous afternoon in places across the north and midlands. They were grafters, fighters, thieves, gamblers, scrap dealers, truckers and horse men, and there was more money at stake than their appearances suggested. Five hundred per bet was seen as standard.

They fought to find their stride, your Dad and this Kenny one.

"Smash him Mac-lad," encouraged Eddie from somewhere over to his right. "Cave his cunt in."

"Shut it, you little twat," said another voice from the crowd.

They separated and Mac smiled through his fat, bloodied lips.

Barker was stood off to one side, quietly observing with one hand tucked in the breast pocket of his waistcoat.

Mac took the front foot and they came in low together again. He feigned with a left and then as Yarm Kenny ducked, unleashed a hard right that caught him on the cheek. It was enough to provide an opening. Mac went straight down the middle and struck him hard in the solar plexus. It was a bullseye shot. He knew Yarm Kenny would feel that punch into next week. The fight was his.

Yarm Kenny stumbled forward. His hands were still up but his mouth was gasping silently for air. His face read panic.

"Have that, mush," said an excitable Eddie.

A small row broke out between Eddie and one of the men. Your Uncle responded angrily by saying "Or what? Or what?" over and over again.

"Turn it in Eddie," said Mac out the side of his mouth, not daring to take his eye off Yarm Kenny, who was clutching his throat now. "Or I'll put you out mesel. Brother or not."

The men liked this and laughed. Eddie was silenced.

Kenny was desperate now – and as slow as a caterpillar. Your Dad sidestepped and put together a machine gun combination that opened up his opponent's eye and mouth. Yarm Kenny spat blood.

Mac rocked on his heels, savouring the moment for a few more seconds, then he was on him again. Two more punches had him sitting down and spitting more blood.

"Best?"

"Aye. Best."

Mac dropped his fists. He spat, rolled his neck, then spat again.

"Right," he said to nee-one in particular. "Time for some bloody nosebag. I'm starving, me."

*

I'm sitting and smoking and hockling greeners onto the ground and having me morning time with *Robinson Crusoe* in the sunshine, reading about that stranded lad eating coconuts and that, when Arty comes down the depot.

Now then young John-John Wisdom.

Now then Arty.

How goes it – fare thee well?

Eh?

I'm asking if you're alright bonny lad.

Oh aye. Canny.

I put my book down. I shield the sun from my eyes and look up at him.

Takings seem up, he says.

Aye.

Good.

Aye.

Keeping out of trouble and that?

Oh aye. Keeping out of town helps.

Good lad. You've not let us down – you're doing alreet, you.

Thanks Arty, I say. Have you heard from your Tony?

Aye. Had a phone call or two.

How's he keeping?

He's alreet. Surviving. He's going to make it, I think – so long as he doesn't get back on the gear when he's out, daft little get.

Good.

Here – mebbe you can show him the ropes. Get him on the route with you.

Mebbes, I say, though I'm thinking bollards to that, because marrers on the inside don't always translate to marrers on the outside, and anyroad, if Tony joins us in the van I'll not be able to take Maria or Coughdrop out with us any more, and Arty's already telt us we're not allowed anyone with us unless we're getting hassle or summat.

Then as if he's reading my mind he says: Nee bother on the route then?

Nor, I say. Not really.

Not really?

None.

Sure? Nee hassle from the charvers on the estates or them woollyback sheep-shagging clodhoppers out in the villages? Nee-one chorring owt?

Nor.

And what about that other business?

What other business?

The tack and that.

What about it?

Nee-one minds that you're not knocking out at the moment.

Nor. And there's nee 'at the moment' about it Arty. I'm not dealing.

Aye, well. All in good time. How's the flat?

Shite.

Arty smiles.

Aye, I say. But as soon as I've got the cash I'm going to get mesel a van.

What type of van?

A bloody caravan of course.

Arty nods at this.

Well, that's the traveller in you isn't it.

Aye, I say. I'm no good in this pokey little flat they've got us in Arty. It's too much like the cells. Anyways, I'm used to the outdoors, me. It's in me blood whether I like or not.

Oh aye, I don't doubt that. Your lot have been around these parts as long as the castle.

I smile at him.

Your Dad. He had a right name for himself. He was hard to avoid really. He was quite a character round town, was Mac Wisdom. A big man, in all ways.

Hmmph, I'm thinking. Not all ways, like.

Unbeatable, he was.

Not entirely, I'm thinking.

I bet you like hearing the old tales, lad.

Like a punch in the cock, I'm muttering.

Aye we came up together says Arty, all oblivious. We're of a similar age, me and your Dad. When he was younger he had a reputation as a good lad when he was sober – hard as fuck like, but a canny lad all the same. But then when he got the drink in him he was a demon. Oh, he was bad. Temperamental, you know –

I interject to stop his rose-tinted blethering.

So you knew him all the way back to before?

Before what?

Before what happened to him. Before he got his dome stoved in.

Late 70s. Aye. Terrible business that. Terrible. Before you were born. They said he was never right after what happened. But then, that's the gamble with fighting. It's a tough old game.

Arty pauses, lost in thought. Lost in the 70s.

Aye, he says again. Tough game. Ever fought on the cobbles yourself, John-John?

Not by choice.

Right, he says. Right. Because you've not got his build have you? Funny that. How your Dad and your Bobby were so big and broad, and you're just a wean really.

Aye bloody hilarious, I'm thinking.

Like you got handed down the wrong genes or summat. Still, I bet you've had a few scraps though haven't you. Tough little nut, I bet. Aye, he were a character, was Mac Wisdom. Larger than life that one.

You want to try being the son of Mac Wisdom and see what happens, I think. And then I say,

He was a bastard.

Who's that then?

Him, I say. Me Dad.

I stop for a bit, feeling like I'm saying too much as it is – like I'm letting my guard down to another fella for the first time in years.

He treated us like shite, I say. Especially me. And our Charmaine. All of us. He ruined everything but he's not gonna ruin my life no more. I won't allow it.

Aye well says Arty, and I reckon he's mebbe a bit surprised by me outburst. We all remember what happened. It was all over the papers at the time. Beat a dog every day and soon enough he'll bite back, you know what I mean?

I don't even need to answer that. Of course I know what he means. I, more than anyone else, know what he means.

Aye, but things were different then.

How'd you mean?

Well, says Arty, drawing the word out dead long. He might have knocked you about a bit, but they were more innocent times weren't they?

How do you work that one out?

The world has got harsher, that's all I'm saying. Crime is soaring these days.

Aye Arty, I say. Junkies everywhere. They need locking up. I blame the parents.

That's not what I meant, he says. Our Tony's a good kid really.

Oh aye?

Aye. I just meant that everything's shit isn't it. The government doesn't know its scut from its earlobe, you've got bloody foreigners all ower the shop and there's nee jobs for the younger lads so they get bored and they get out of line...

You're talking a lot of fugging bollards you are, Arty. Anyroad, you're bloody Italian.

Aye well, that's different. Italians roam the world – it's what we do. We build empires. Always have done, always will. We're fighters. Gladiators in spirit.

Is that right.

All I'm saying is, mebbe if I had clouted our Tony a bit more when he were younger he'd not be where he is today. You can't bloody raise your hand these days without someone calling the polis. I know you had your reasons for what happened son, and I don't think bad of you –

Aye, the rest of this stinking place does though don't they, I snap. Treat us like a bloody leper. They never had to live with Mac Wisdom did they.

All I'm saying is John-John, try not to hate your father too much. It'll just eat you up. There must be some good memories.

I'm biting my lips as Arty says this. I'm biting my lips red raw because it's taking all my willpower to stop mesel from shouting what the fug do you know you sodding gimlet? Bloody bell-end. Have you ever been kicked across a field of mud like a football or chucked out into the night at eight years old, starving-hungry and nithering your nadgers off, just because your auld man is pissed and hates you so much he can't stand the sight of you sleeping? And then have to gan to school covered in mud to have the shite kicked out of you by ten lads, all of them laughing and hoying stones and sticks and bottles and that. Good memories, my arse.

Arty's full of so much hot air I don't even know where to begin. So I don't.

Instead I do what I always do and that is zip it and keep quiet. Just bury it like we buried me Dad.

So I sit and smoke and hockle and wonder why the world is so messed up, then I say, well, I better get ganning and though

Arty slaps us on the back like we're best marrers after this man to man talk, deep down inside I'm thinking you're just like every other twat out there Arty bloody Vicari – just another selfish knobber going on about hitting kids this and bloody foreigners that, and even though I'll keep grafting for you, I'll never trust you. Because you're as thick as pig shit, you are. And I'm watching you.

And when I've got enough bloody cash together, I'm bloody gone.

Gone, marrer.

*

Then he left us. Your Dad took us back to the site, set down the van, give us a kiss and said where he was gannin was nee place for a pregnant lass. "I'm away grafting on the cobbles with Barker," he telt us. "I'll be back in a bit."

I'd not done fifty miles and I was already back on the same bleached patch up at Edenside, only this time with nowt but the clucking hens for company. A bairn in me belly again.

All I heard for the next six weeks was the odd blank postcard shoved into an envelope with a few tenners, and sent to the post office in the village. There were cards from Kent, Dorset, Norfolk, Sussex. All over the shop. Each postcard was like a kick in the teeth to me sat up on the site with nowt to do but brood and stew, your Uncle Eddie popping in on us now and again while your Dad and Barker were following the travelling vine, that tangled line that sits beneath the English soil, a world of gossip and bloodlines and birth rights, vendettas and knuckle fights.

And that vine did bring them no shortage of scraps that season as they criss-crossed the country in Barker Lovell's transit. It was a summer of knotted knuckles and ice buckets; blood-flecked spittle and red raw grazes. Torn faces, chewed ears and teeth marks.

It was at the horse fairs that the big money was to be made, and there came none bigger than Appleby in June, the most important date in any British traveller's calendar. That's why your Dad let us join him for this one.

You'd see them travelling in from every corner, two, three weeks beforehand. Vans and vardos by the roadside. Little camps in car parks and lay-bys all the way across Yorkshire, Lancashire and Cumbria.

Your Dad picked us up at Edenside in the van on the way and acted like he'd just nipped down the shops for a pint of milk. A peck on the cheek and then we were off again with no mention of his six week adventure.

We'd only been there two minutes when Mac got into an argument with a showman by the name of Lee Lerner while drinking in one of the packed tents. Your Dad took umbrage at the stranger flicking a spent cigarette butt too close for his liking, and that was that. It wouldn't end until blood was shed.

Lerner worked the fairgrounds, collecting coins and spinning waltzers up and down England. The gaping gap in his front teeth suggested he was nee stranger to trouble himself. He was a git big ugly thing an all but, as your Dad was fond of saying, anyone who'd had his teeth knocked out couldn't be that good a fighter.

The tent was too tightly-packed to fight properly. It took half a dozen good men to pull them apart. One of them was Barker.

"You want to fight," he said with one hand on each man's chest, both at least a head taller than him. "Then fight. But not here. You'll do it properly."

"And who be you?" said Lerner.

He had a thick accent. West Country maybe, thought Barker. Some Cornish too. And mebbes a bit of the Irish. A showman's accent.

"He's my marrer, that's who."

Mac lunged forward but more hands pulled him back. Lerner laughed a gummy laugh.

"Your boyfriend, more like."

Lee Lerner's lips curled around the words as they came out and his eyes darkened. "I'll panel the both of youse," he said to the tent, "This big lug first – then the sprat for afters."

"Right you're on," said Mac, interrupting him before he could say any more. "One hour's time. Flashing Lane field."

*

The Nook is humming with tension like a railway track when a train is coming.

There's fresh glass on the road, more cubed confetti to crunch between me warm tyres and the summer-softened asphalt.

The sun is high and business is good. People are out in the streets drinking and nattering, scheming little clusters of them. The season is still a novelty as the sun blazes down on pale bodies that slouch and bask like lazy cats. Even the smackheads have slowed their morning scuttle to a more leisurely clip.

Mind, it won't last of course. It'll all change later, after dark, when the sun's gone down and the birds are roosting and the booze has turned bad.

That's why I never drink, me. I saw what it did to my Dad. Saw what it did to all them knobbers inside, weakened and half-mad and still only in their teens. Above all else though, the grim potential of me with a skin full scares us.

I drive with me elbow sticking out the window and I pull up every couple of hundred yards to sell pop and crisps and cones and Rizlas.

And all the way round I'm keeping my eye out for the lass again. Maria. The girl with the nice dark eyes and the smile and the way with her tongue. I've realised what it is about her that's got us all worked up: she's the only living person I've ever actually talked to. Properly talked to, without stuttering or stammering or grunting or getting into a barney with.

I'm about to leave the estate when I pull ower one last time and sit for a bit with the engine running in case there's any stragglers after owt. I do a rollie and smoke it while I watch people pass by.

On the corner I see Maria's friend Kelly, and the way she's standing there smoking a bine and wiggling her arse looks like she's mebbes a prossie touting for business though I cannot be sure like. I don't see Maria though.

I see kids on mopeds and auld biddies pushing hand carts and gadgies bent double from carrying the weight of the world for too long. I see two women walking and arguing and waving their mobiles at each other, then a pumped-up doorman type with a Staffy tugging at his chain, followed not far behind by a wifey with nee bra on and the biggest tits I've ever seen, massive heavy swinging things down around her waist they are, proper milkers, and she's got names inked onto her arm. I see a kid on a BMX waving what looks like a machete around, and it's gleaming in the sunshine like a lightsabre from that fillum, and I even see a big fat rabbit hopping out across the bloody road in front of us. But I don't see Maria.

I don't see her and I don't see the lads who are suddenly crowding my hatch either. I recognise them though as the charver lads who are always outside the house that plays the shitty music.

There's three of them about my age, late teens or summat, mebbes a bit younger, and they've all got that look about them. They're skinny from too much speed and not enough vitamins and fresh air. Borstal complexions. They all have their tops off and one of them has a baseball cap on that looks like it is fixed to the tightest setting to fit on his cropped pinhead noggin. They look like plucked chickens in a butcher's window. A right shower.

The lad with the cap on's eyes are tiny black mirrors in his sunken face. There's nee hope in them. And they make us nervous. Guarded.

He leans on the counter and looks in the van, squinting.

Who are you?

I'm selling ice creams I say, keeping me voice steady.

He looks at his marrers and laughs at this. Even though I've said nowt funny it's a laugh I recognise. I've heard it a hundred times before from a hundred other fugging sarcastic blowhards inside and out. They're beasts, this lot. Beasts of the field. Clear as day.

Nor, he goes. *You don't say.* What happened to the last one, like?

I dinnar.

He was a puff, you nar.

Was he, I say.

Aye. A right proper bummer. He used to try and touch the young boys round here until we ran him off.

I never knew him.

Aye. Well he'll not be back round here again. We proper mashed him up.

His marrers grunt in approval. I just stare at them.

What the fuck ye looking at man, says one of them.

His shoulders slide away dramatically to these long arms that dangle there like they're seeking a purpose. I notice there's not a hair on his body either. He's like a bald chimp. Misshapen. A proper knuckledragger.

Have a good gleg, why don't you, says the other, their sentences overlapping. Fucken dorty cunt. Here, are you a bummer an all? You better not be.

Knowing there's nee right way to answer his question, I keep quiet.

And why're you wearing them stupid clothes, the lad with the cap says.

I look down at mesel, then shrug.

They're just clothes.

Well you look like a fucking mong.

They laugh again. I say nowt.

He looks like a kid playing soldiers or summat, says the hairless chimp.

Do you want to buy owt I say, me voice still steady.

Aye, says the one with the cap. The ringleader. I'll have a thousand 99s please. And can you put some fucking spunk on top.

They all burst out laughing. But their laughter isn't real. It's forced. Same as them little shits last week: there's nee joy in it, only a feeling of relief that they're the ones in control here. Like I say, I've met a hundred twats like this before.

I pop an elbow up onto the pump, dead casual.

Nee bother. That'll be five hundred quid. And a fiver extra for the spunk.

Baseball cap flinches at this and the smile fades from his greasy face for a second then returns, more forced this time.

I telt you he was a puff. You're a fucking bender, you.

You're the one who wants to eat me spunk.

Who the *fuck* are *ye*? he snaps.

I telt you, I say, making sure me voice stays nice and calm and level, and there's nee violence in it like there is in theirs. Mebbes all that bollards we did inside about anger management and avoiding confron-whatsit has worked after all. Dickhead Derek me probation officer would be proud.

I'm the ice cream man, I go.

Who do you think you're talking to? says the third lad. You look like a fucking pikey, you. Are you a dirty fucking gyppo? Is that what ye are?

I don't say anything.

Cos if you are, he continues, I'll put you in the fucking ovens where you and your lot belong.

Aye you fucking mong, says the ringleader. The one with the cap. Just give us some tack on tick before I smash your fucking face in.

Sorry. I divvent sell tack. Only kets and ice creams and that. I've got some cheap baccy an all, but nee tack.

You fucking mong, the hairless ape says again. Dirty fucking gybsy.

His voice is surprisingly high and squeaky and has a tiny trace of excitement in it.

It's gypsy, I say. *Gypsy.*

Get this radge cunt, says the main lad. Coming here with his fucking ice creams and attitude. Hacky cunt. Get a wash, man. Povvy pikey bastard. We divvent want your fucking heather and we divvent want our drives doing neither. Just give us the tack and then fuck off before we do you.

The others laugh.

Howay lads, I say, raising me hands palms up. It's a lush day and I'm sure you'll be able to pick summat up elsewhere. I'm not after any trouble.

All the while I'm thinking three punches is all it would take to spark these skinny little twats.

If you fight him he'll just try and bum yer Banny, says the squeaky one. Look at him – the spacker. Thinks he's in the army.

Reckon you're hard do you, says the the leader. This Banny one. You want a go? I'll put you down, man. I'll put you in the soil where you dirty pikeys belong. I'll bury you man.

I shrug and keep it zipped, but inside I'm starting to bubble and boil. I want to smash their faces in and stamp on their bollocks and break all their limbs until they have to crawl home using their fingertips. I want to put their teeth on the kerb. I want to do keepy-ups with their eyeballs. Tear them new scut holes. They're wimps the lot of them, just like they always are. Wimps and whatsits. Bigots. Just like them twats at school and just like all them bullying bastard gobshites in prison. For the first time in yonks me temples are proper throbbing and the old red mist is coming in.

Here lads, says Banny. I reckon I should do this cunt.

Look I sigh, trying to flatten the waver that's starting up in me voice. I've got work to do, me. I'm a lover not a fighter.

Aye. A lover of young boys.

Then all three of these charvers are talking at once.

Give us some tack, bender.

Fucking pikey paedo.

He's soft as shite, man.

Oh bollards to this, I finally snap. I've got work to do, me. I snap the window shutter down and scramble to the front seat.

They bang on the glass with their palms and then they start to rock the van back and forth as I fiddle with the keys in the ignition. In my rear view mirror I can see that one of them has run around the other side and is putting more weight behind the tilt. I put the van into gear, take off the hand-brake and drive off down the crescent as they chase us, hoying stones and rocks at my back window and shouting things I can't hear. Some smaller kids on bikes join the chase until I turn back out of the estate and lose them somewhere out on the main road, just past the tatty video shop that sells dodgy animal porn – you know, fillums of women noshing off horses and licking pig dick and that.

*

Flashing Lane was where the traders run their horses up and down for buyers, a busy, narrow lane tight with animals, trotting carts and travellers.

Over to one side of Flashing Lane was the main market area where the beer tent was and across the other side of the lane there was nowt but fields. It was here, behind these tall hedgerows where travellers settled their scores and where your Dad did fight this Lee Lerner one with Barker Lovell giving out odds of 2 to 1 on the showman winning the square go. Barker oversaw it all.

"What's your name son?" he says.

"Lee Lerner."

"You heard it here folks. Lee 'The Gorilla' Lerner" – laughter rang through the tent at this – "will fight Jimmy 'The Anvil' Smith in a sporting boxing match, fought the auld way and the fair way: a bare knuckle boxing match between two evenly matched men of the road."

In the early days Barker and Mac didn't use his real name in fights. Instead Mac always used the most common travelling name of Smith. It not only protected them from any repercussions with the law, but allowed your Dad to fight as an unknown entity. Barker turned to Lerner again.

"Where are you from, son?"

"Fuck off."

"There you have it gentlemen: Lee Lerner from Fuck Off will fight Jimmy Smith out of the north-east."

"He's no traveller," sneered Mac. "He's just a bloody showman. I'll flatten him like a spatchcock."

"What'll you give on the lummox?" said a voice from the crowd as the two men sized each other up.

"Which one?"

There was more laughter from the men at this. The afternoon drinkers were enjoying the spectacle that was unfolding before them. It was what they expected at Appleby. What they came for. Bloodspill was a tradition and they would each take home with them more stories to tell round camp fires and in back room bars.

Barker made to scratch his chin. He weighed Mac up and down and shook his head.

"This man is a game cock, I'll give him that. I've trained him up mesel. But he's not match-fit and he has broken knuckles from his last tussle. So for that reason – and I'm sorry to have to say this in front of these lads, Jim – I'd have to say 4 to 1."

"Bollards to that," said Mac, pre-fight adrenaline coursing through his veins, unaware this was still part of the elaborate set-up. "My knuckles are fine. I'll put this plastic traveller on his back."

"You what?" said Lerner, raising his fist.

Looking round conspiratorially, Barker ignored him and pretended he was addressing Mac and Mac only.

"You can't win if you can't punch properly, Jim," he whispered.

"It's a bluff," said another voice. "They're all in on it. The north-east lad looks pretty fit to me."

"No – I've been here all morning," said someone else. "I saw these boys nearly kick off a minute ago. Proper, like. I don't know about this broken knuckle stuff but they're no marrers."

*

Like I say, I've met this Banny before. Not him, but plenty like him.

There was hods of them inside. Shitehawks. All mouth and nee trousers, and always with an entourage of brown-nosing little cling-ons. Get them on their own though and they whimper like drowning kittens.

Mind, I remember one time not long after I first went in. I was fifteen and frightened to bloody fug what with all them newspapers stories alerting all the lads inside to the tale about the wild gypsy kid.

There I was five foot-nowt-much in my stocking feet, skin the colour of someone from the soil. A carnival curiosity.

The first day in the dorm they laughed at us. They took the piss for hours, talking shite about eating hedgehogs and selling sprigs of heather and that, and they pointed at us.

That is the pikey we read about?

I've shat bigger jobbies than that kid.

Look at the fucking lugs on him!

It only took a couple of days before some git big lump with plenty of bum-lickers backing him up tried to take it further. Tried to show us up and break us down, like.

A big wide lad by the name of Mackem who was thick as pig shit and twice as smelly. His trousers were always hanging round his arse; he was just another Cat A twat getting by on swagger, strength and psychosis.

But I knew he was too big to be quick and too stupid to expect the unexpected.

117

First this Mackem lad done a shite on my mattress and even telt us he done it, the daft knacker.

I just done a shit on your bed, he said, just like that. Like he was remarking on the weather or summat: the sun's out but there's talk of rain later. I just done a shit on your bed.

I telt him I wanted nee trouble and did nowt about it. Just made a glove out of bog roll and scooped it up and hoyed it down the shitter, sprayed the mattress with deodorant and then went down to ask the man for a new sheet.

It was hard to get that type of stink out though. It seeped into me sleep, the bastard.

Then the next morning when I was having a shower he nicked all me clothes – every single stitch. Strides, kecks, shirt – the lot. Me shoes an all. So I had to gan back to the stores in the nud, shivering and freezing and cupping my junk, everyone laughing and trying to grab us down there and jabbing us up the scut with their thumbs, and even the screws just stood there laughing and shaking their heads. And Mackem's stood laughing an all, and everyone's patting him on the back because they're all a bunch of greasy bum-lickers who are just glad it's me whose bed he's shit on and my clothes he's nicked, and not theirs.

Still I did nowt. A day or two later, at breakfast, Mackem comes over and hockles in me corn flakes. He just leant ower and done a git big rubbery greener. Some bad boy you are, he sneers at us. Fucking dirty little pikey.

And still I did nowt. Instead I spooned it off on to the floor and carried on eating those corn flakes it hadn't touched while the other lads looked on, howling in disgust.

Look at him – he's fucking eating it an all!

And I waited.

I waited until we were watching telly one night in the rec room, and everyone was all relaxed and sitting around smoking and joking and scratting their balls, and that was when I made my move.

One minute I was sat there staring at the back of this bullying bastard's over-sized noggin and the ripples of fat where his skull met his neck, the next I pounced on him from behind.

He was sat with his feet up on the chair in front of him and his hands down his kecks when I made me move. It was a dirty suckerpunch move, and I wasn't proud of it, but then so is shitting on a bed or picking on someone who just wants to get their head down. And that's one thing me Dad taught us: there's nee rules in fighting. Why would there be? Games have rules. Fighting's nee game.

So I grabbed the big ugly lump by his lugs and bit into his fat hacky neck, right where the vein pumps bluest. Summat must have come ower us because I went at it like a terrier, shaking me head and tightening my teeth and growling. I was proper riled. I bit in and I didn't let go.

Mackem's neck tasted warm and bitter and metallic, though no worse than the liver an onions they served us every bloody week. I loosened for a second then went at him again, nearly dislocating me bloody jaw. There was a crunching sound and me teeth nearly met in the middle and I must have hit some veins or summat because the blood started pouring out of his neck. Human flesh doesn't tear easily. It's noisy stuff.

And this git big bully boy of the wing who must have had four stone and a good foot in height on us started yelling and screaming like a girl. Proper mewling, like a right mimsie. I'd have laughed if I'd not had me mouth full.

That was when some of his boys got to giving us some kicks and digs to get us off him, but I was blind to the pain, and then some of the other lads who weren't too keen on Mackem and his lot starting punching *them* off to let us have our dirty go in peace.

There was quite a scrap going on around us at this point, it wouldn't be long before the screws turned up but I paid it no mind. I was lost in terrier mode. Everything but this bully's neck was invisible to us.

When I finally unclamped me teeth and stepped back a circle had opened up where the chairs had been and Mackem was in the middle of it, thrashing about on the floor like a right dick, his eyes rolling and his mouth gaping like a big bloody goldfish that had leapt out of its bowl. Gasping like a bloody gimlet he was. Blood everywhere. Then he started retching and gagging and grabbing his flapping neck and I just leaned ower him and said dead quietly, I telt you I wanted nee trouble.

There was blood all round me mouth and chin and a bit of it down the front of me trackie top an all and I must have had a bit of a mad look in me eyes because when I turned round and saw the look on the lads' faces they'd stopped fighting each other and they all sort of breathed in at the same time and said nowt except the odd fucking hell and Jesus Christ he's proper mashed the cunt, and they all gave us a wide berth when I passed them to go to the bogs to get me mesel cleaned up and straightened out.

The whole thing only lasted a few seconds. Five, mebbe. Ten at most. That's all it took. Ten seconds from him laughing and watching telly and turning his eggs, to having his life changed in such a way that he'd think twice about picking on someone next time. Ten seconds to earn us five year's peace from the lot of them.

Mind, Mackem lost some blood that day. He had a load of them butterfly stitches put in his dirty stinking neck and had a good scar to show for it an all, so it wasn't all bad for him.

And that was that.

He never came back at us because he knew he'd have to kill us. I'd shown him what kind of a lad I was. A little bloody terrier, just like our Coughdrop.

Because it's not about size or strength or numbers when it comes to dealing with people like Mackem. It's about having enough about yoursel to say, Na, I'm not having this. No bloody way.

*

Part II
The Green Cathedral

I'm four weeks out.

Four weeks out and it's early in the morning of me first day off in ower a week and I'm sat drinking a brew and thumbing through me tatty copy of *Robinson Crusoe*. I'm up to the bit where's he's just met his man Friday and he's not alone in the world no more, and mebbes it's all going to be alreet, but even then, after everything he's just been through, all the coconuts and worry and that, he still cannot help himself and he starts getting all up his own arse, saying he's going to 'civilise' Friday and this and that. You can see that he's pissing away his own paradise by being a proper numpty just like everyone does in the end, and I'm scratching little Coughdrop's pink hairless belly and thinking if I find paradise I'll not piss it away, when there's a banging on my front door.

I've not had a visitor before; there's been nee-one that's ever wanted to come see us. So I jump a bit in my chair and so does Coughdrop and he starts yapping and I slop a bit of hot milky tea on me crotch and it stings like all hell, and me heart is thumping in my chest like a bloody jackhammer.

I feel like Robinson bloody Crusoe when he sees the ship that first time. All bloody nervy and confused at the thought of another human coming into his waters, like. Coming on to that island of his. Invading his quiet little corner.

I hold Coughdrop to me chest and put me hand ower his mouth and as I do he gives us a little nip with his puppy teeth. Sharp, they are. Like little needles.

I quietly lean back in my chair to get a gleg down the hall corridor. I can see there's a face pressed up against the frosted glass of the front door. Whoever it is has his hands cupped around his eyes and his nose is squashed flat. He looks proper ugly, like one of those old-fashioned bank robbers that used to wear lasses' stockins on their head, and when the face moves away from the glass his sneck leaves a greasy print on the glass, the hacky twat.

John-John-lad, says the voice. You in there?

It's Arty. Bloody Arty Vicari. Banging away.

I gan and answer the door.

Before I can even get a word in, Arty says you need to get yersel a phone lad, and he walks right past us and into the hallway like he owns the place or summat, nee invite or nowt, and that irks us, because everyone knows you don't just walk into someone else's place, whether it's their bloody caravan, their bloody cell or their pokey little bloody probation dive. You ask first. Or better still, you wait to be invited. Any good travelling man knows that.

And you offer to take your bloody shoes off an all.

There's nee socket for a phone I say, not feeling much like blethering to the big man today. It's too early and I'm still on that island with Crusoe and his goats.

And anyroad you barely pay us enough to buy me tins of chilli and me razors and baccy, I feel like adding. Never mind bloody phone bills.

Arty clicks his fingers in front of us.

Well get yersel a mobile then. Howay man, it's the twenty-first century in a couple of months. You've got to get with the times, kidder.

I shrug.

I'm not arsed me, Arty.

But half the world's got a phone these days, John-John man. You need to get upwardly mobile. Join the human race.

Fug that, I think. I tried it and look where it got us.

Half the world's got haemorrhoids Arty, I say, but I'm in nee hurry to join them.

Shaking his head and frowning, Arty walks into the living room. I put Coughdrop down and he runs up to him and starts yapping and scratching at his shins.

Who's this then?

It's Coughdrop.

Is he yours?

Aye.

I love dogs, me. And they love us right back.

Arty bends down to pat the pup and little Coughdrop bites him on the hand.

Ow – yer little bastard.

I start laughing. Good lad Coughdrop, I say. Good lad.

So this is your place then? He looks around the room.

Obviously.

Bit pokey isn't it. Where's all your stuff? It looks like you've been robbed

What stuff?

You know – your bits.

What bloody bits?

Possessions and that. Your things.

I look at me feet, then I say, Well, I divvent have owt else.

Hmm, says Arty. And what about furniture?

I point to me armchair. It's there.

'Kin hell. It's a bit minimalist isn't it?

It's how I like it.

Arty shakes his head then jerks his thumb back behind him. Is my van alreet out there?

How should I know.

Bit rough round here innit.

I shrug. Aye, mebbes. I'm not stopping long though. The probation's got us here so's they can keep tabs on us. I've got nee choice in the matter.

Arty takes out a cigarette and sparks it up. He seems to be in nee hurry to say owt, so I decide to get things rolling. I want to get back to me book and me tea.

So, I say. Um. What's happening? It's me day off.

Well I would have just rung you if you had a bloody phone, Arty says taking a big draw on his Benson. Half an hour it took us to drive ower here. Or I could have just emailed you.

Aye, well. Like I said – nee phone.

You divvent need a phone to get emails you daft knacker. It comes on your computer doesn't it.

Oh aye I forgot, I say, though I reckon Arty's just trying to humiliate us now.

Christ. Do they learn you nowt inside?

I have to give this one some thought. While I do I pass the ashtray to Arty.

What, I say. Like how to speak proper, like you?

Eh, he says oblivious, then: Do they not give you computers and that?

Na. We had a snooker table though. You should ask your Tony about all that.

Bloody hell. A snooker table. Nee wonder you're all straight back at it when they let you out.

Not me.

Aye, well, mebbes, says Arty in a way that pisses me right off. Like he doesn't believe I'm serious, Like he thinks I'm just some robbing junkie like his son.

Then he goes, Well, either way, get yersel a phone or a computer or summat so next time I divvent have to haul me arse out of bed and ride halfway across the county just to come to ask if you can work today.

Work?

Aye.

Today?

Yes. Down at the fair.

Which fair?

The fair down the race course in town. The one that's on *every single year*. The one they've been setting up down there all week.

I shrug.

Bloody hell Wisdom, get with it man.

Arty clicks his fingers in front of me face again and I'm thinking do that one more time and I'll bloody bite it off and feed it to our Coughdrop with his Winalot. Cheeky get. I thought Arty was alreet but now he's just getting on me tits, lording it ower us and that.

Here, he goes. You're not on the gear are you?

Of course I'm bloody not. I telt you, I've never done drugs in all me life.

Oh aye. Not even the tack.

You're the hypocrite who's knocking out, I'm thinking but I don't say that because when all's said and done I still need this bloody job.

Anyways, says Arty. I can't stop here all day so are you free to take the van down there or what? The sun's out and we'll clean up, no doubt. There'll be a nice bit of extra cheddar for you. It's usually Bomber's patch but he got waylaid.

Who's Bomber?

One of the lads. Git big sweaty thing. Used to be a Hell's Angel. Married to that fat boiler. Looks like a ginger Giant Haystacks.

Who – him or his lass?

Arty thinks for a minute.

Both actually. It doesn't matter. Look I need an answer – work today on double time and you can have the morrow afternoon off, how does that sound?

I dunno. I mean, I had plans.

What? Staying in and wanking yersel blind?

I have to crack a smile at this.

Nor, I say defensively. Anyway – that means I'm just swapping a day off for a half day off. I'm not daft, Arty.

Alright, you can have the day after off an all.

Aye, alright, I say. Aye I'll do it.

Good lad. It gets a bit hectic down there but I reckoned you'd like to be back amongst your people.

My people?

Aye. What do you call them – carnies and that? Showpeople. You can speak their language, can't you?

What language is that then?

Gypsy chat and that.

Aye, well. A bit. But I'm not a bread-and-jam boy.

You what?

Bread-and-jammers. It's what travellers used to call showmen. You know – penny pinchers. Hedge-creepers and that.

I never spoke the auld lingo in the first place. Not properly anyway. But me Dad and his marrers and all me uncles used to sometimes, when they were round the fire, pissed up and that. We're passing it on little lad, they'd say. Take note. Our fathers and uncles learned us the auld words and now we're learning you. When I asked why, they'd say because it matters son. Because it's part of you, like it or not. And if we don't pass it down it'll die. And if the language dies, we'll die too. And if the travellers die off so will everything. It'll all be fucked. Because even if people give us grief, a world without travellers is a world without freedom. Do you understand that little lad?

And that scared us right enough. Scared us enough to make us listen and make us listen hard. Aye, I'd say. I think so. Good lad, they'd say, then carry on drinking and belching and spitting in the flames and chatting in that strange coded language that soon enough was a part of me too, like it or not. And even now, even when I've not heard it for years, it's still there. It's still inside us, bubbling up now and again.

Here, the van's outside, says Arty, breaking me train of thought. You've got the pitch from ten so drag a comb through that hair of yours. A bit of deodorant wouldn't go amiss either.

He looks around me living room again and shakes his head.

You can drop us off on the way.

*

He stayed away the whole summer, your Dad. June, July, August and into September too. He didn't return to town once. He just left us there, on the site, in the van, knocked up.

The envelopes of cash kept coming, but it was scant consolation. Betimes he sent them by post and other times he sent them back with people he could trust who were passing through. He'd ask them to stop by the site to look in on us and that's how I knew where he was at or where he'd been. But never where he was going. Because when you're out roving, you just go.

So Mac and Barker did drive across to Scarborough, to fight a traveller on a site near the North Bay, or so I was told. Then the next day he scrapped round the back of a frozen pizza factory on an industrial estate in Middlesbrough. They drove up to Glasgow for a fight in a pub garden, then he fought the same man's brother in Cumbernauld a couple of days later.

They went to London, to Bethnal Green, where your Dad was to fight a bouncer with a face that Barker reckoned could make an onion cry. That was a bare knuckle bill organised by some twins who were meant to be a big deal down there, but the fight fell through so they had a night wandering the West End of London drunk, your Dad filled to bursting with his first ever taste of Chinese food. He sent us a blank postcard of one of them gadgies with the big furry hats that mind the towers.

A day and a night was enough; Mac couldn't wait to leave the city. Barker too. All that noise and people rushing everywhere, hemming them in like bloody moo cows. And the straight lines did their heads in. The fields and lanes, that was where they belonged. The fields and lanes and woods. They needed to feel nature's jumble. Anywhere you couldn't see the sky for the buildings was no good.

They went west for a bit, to Wiltshire, then up through the Cotswolds and onto the Midlands, sleeping in the van, and living

127

on Barker's stews and steamed jam puddings that he made with flour and suet tied tight in a piece of cloth. They drank with auld marrers of Barker's and they'd be taken out in the woods for a bit of exploring and a bit of moon-lit poaching.

They made many new acquaintances that summer, and the odd enemy too.

Then finally as August crept into September and the skies began to turn, they headed north again and your Dad returned one wet morning with a broken nose, chipped teeth, a permanently dislodged knuckle, and a brick-sized pile of bank notes

He never even noticed the new bump beneath me dress.

*

The fair is chocker by lunch time and stays that way all day. There's screaming bairns running riot all ower the shop, getting sick and dizzy from the sugar and the rides and the sun, while their parents get pissed and stoned and turn pink in the heat of the afternoon.

I'm parked up at the top end of the slope that runs down to the river and I've been working the ice machine all morning without a break. I get the cone, pump the handle, swirl the ice, stick a flake in it. I must have done five a minute for the first three hours. That's summat like nine hundred ices before I've even stopped for a piss or a tab or a brew or owt.

Sweat drips off me brow and all day I'm worrying about whether I've got enough change in the float or enough cones or enough hundreds and thousands or monkey blood to see us through the rush.

I cannot complain though: I'm outdoors and the sun's on me face and there's nee screws telling us what to do or daft knackers leaving logs on my mattress.

And then when I'm done, when the summer's ower and I've grafted just enough to get mesel a nice bundle together, and Dickhead Derek and them lot have signed us off and unleashed us proper, I'll be off into the sunset. I'll fetch up and nash off past that horizon to set up somewhere new, away from this town. It's this thought that got us through a five stretch, and gets us through each sweaty day and each lonely sleepless night an all. Mebbes Maria'll come with us for a wander. We'll be like Bonnie and Clyde, only nee-one'll be after us.

There's this look on the faces of the customers today. They've got this sort of wide-eyed looseness about them. It's a look of whatsit – aye, rapture – though that could just be the cider and the pills and the beer and the spliffs and that.

Then as the sun paints the clear August sky first pink and then orange and the lights of the rides flicker and twinkle into life and the cloudless sky means the temperature drops and the sweat on me back turns cold, and the childish chatter of the fair is replaced by the howls and flirty screams of the pissed-up adults, business begins to drop off. Neebody wants an ice cream at night.

I get the glass eye out from me pocket. There's little flakes of baccy stuck on it so I give it a rub.

What do you think, I say.

The eye stares back at us, silent-like.

Aye, mebbes you're right. We should call it a day.

I turn off the ice machine, lock the float box and then gan out onto the back step with a brew and a tab and take in the scene. Even though I'm not from showfolk I can see that there's summat magic about the place, a type of magic you might try and chase.

It's tragic at the same time though, because a funfair is just an illusion, an escape from everyday life for all them who come here, with the lights and the candy floss and the rides that make you think you can fly providing a bit of colour and escape. That's all it is. Temporary escape.

Because when you look at it closely, look past the pink lights and the screams of the rides, you see the litter flapping around ankles, the vats of dirty chip fat and the screws coming loose on the scaffold beneath the Waltzer. You hear the splutter of a generator kicking out nasty fumes and you'll see a pissed-off looking gadgie packing away an empty Hook-a-Duck stall that's seen nee business all day, and he's got armfuls of bagged up goldfish that you know'll be dead by the morrow.

Stuff like that cuts us up. Especially animal stuff. Animals never asked to be dragged into the shite human world. Animals do just fine without us lot interfering.

Still though, it's strange how all the fairground rides can change a space – how they can make an ordinary field seem ten times its actual size when you're in amongst it all. And there's a feel about the fair that has us thinking back to them places our Mam and Dad took us when we were nippers off on our summer travelling. The horse fairs and showgrounds and that. Special places. Places where owt could happen.

And after years of being away, days of grey and beige and stone and lino, of noise and echoes and stale sweat and aggro, all the colours, sounds and smells of the fair drag us back to childhood, back to a life tainted with pain and fear and only the odd hour or two of joy.

When I've finished my brew and sluiced away the grainy dregs I lock up and gan for a walk amongst the lurch and sway of the people with their faces lit by unreal colours, and the circular screams from the rides can be heard ower the grind and rattle of the rusted castors rolling in their well-worn ruts, as they're spun by some tough-looking bread-and-jam lads. *Hold tight*, bellows the auld lad at the controls. *Here we go!*

You can spot the showfolk and the travellers easy enough an all. It's in the way they carry themsels about the place, their bodies built for working by long summer seasons spent as riggers and scaffold men, as operators, mechanics and all-rounders hired for their family name and their ability to break down a show in half a day. It's in their same darkened earthtones as me Mam and especially my Dad. And me an all I suppose. The traveller's tan.

I overhear the odd accent from across the water an all. Because there's Irish showfolk working here too. The Monaghans mebbe. Or the McGintys. Families who've been spending six months of every year travelling the show grounds of England for a century or more.

Mind, it's a decent fair this one. Proper. They've got rifle ranges and one of them old Kentucky Derbys with the little lead men riding the little lead horses. They've even got a tin can booth and all the other auld style stuff that's slipping away these days to be slowly replaced by the big new rides with their airbrushed fronts of Hollywood characters who I don't recognise and blond lasses with huge tits. Spew-sprayers with names like The Destructor and The Superscud-X and stuff like that. It's what the kiddies think they want these days.

Down the far end of the fair there's a fun house called The Crooked Cottage that's got a clattering cake-walk out front, then next to it a Ghost Train that's back-lit in green, and further along one of them giant Tea Cup rides. There's also the swings, a pirate ship that tips up near vertical and a Helter Skelter slide that's shut down since all the bairns have left, a pile of hacky door mats stacked up all wonky by the pay booth. There's a half-deflated bouncy castle too, crumpling and leaning as a couple of lads set to unhitching the giant pegs from the guy ropes and folding it away.

The stars are pin pricks in the tight blue band of darkness that's stretched ower us all. I'm glad I've got me jacket and combat boots on because even though it's been a hot dry day the ground's still clarty from all the feet and there's little muddy puddles here and there.

I'm over by the dodgems when I see Maria. She's in one of the little cars, screaming her sexy head off. Some lass I don't recognise is doing the driving.

I stand and watch from a distance as they crash laughing into the rim round the side, the rubber bumper cushioning them as their bodies flop forward like rag dolls. They're riding the auld cars, the ones powered by them floor-to-ceiling conductors that make sparks on the metal latticed ceiling. The operator is sat in his booth ower the other side. He's a showman who's wearing a thick pair of bottle top bins and taking nips from a hip flask when he reckons nee-one's looking, and there's young lads stood around the side of the track. Their body language is exaggerated. They can't stand still. It's like the floor is electrified as well as the ceiling. Books aren't the only thing I learned mesel to read inside.

I can't lie: hope brought us here. Hope filled me heart as soon as Arty asked us to work today. I wondered, just as I always wonder every time I take a turn around the Nook, if I might see her, Maria, even from a distance.

But now that I have it is not enough. I've spent two decades living life from a distance and now I want that to change. I want to be near to her, to smell her. To touch her face and her shoulders and her tits. I want us to sing that *Vida Loca* song again.

So when the bumper cars slow to a halt and everyone starts unfolding themsels from the cars, I'm straight ower by the other side of the track waiting for her as she climbs out arm-in-arm with the other girl, both giddy, Maria clutching a bottle and still laughing.

Hiya.

She looks up. Her face changes. She seems a bit surprised to see us.

Oh hiya.

What ye doing?

What's it look like I'm doing? Getting monged and gannin on the rides.

She's wearing a hoodie top with the sleeves pulled down ower her hands and her cheeks are flushed red. She sips at her bottle through a straw.

Then – bloody typical – my mind goes blank and I say nowt. There's a moment where we're all just sort of stood there glegging at each other.

I mean, I say. I mean, how are you doing?

I'm mint.

Aye.

What are you doing here, she says, though I reckon it's as much to shatter the awkward silence that's hanging in the air between us as owt else.

I was working, like. Now I'm doing nowt.

Do you work here, says the other lass. At the fair.

Aye.

Not on the rides though, Maria says. John-John sells ice creams.

Oh aye? says the other lass.

Aye.

Aye. He sells them on the estate an all. From a van and that.

Aye, I say. And not just ice creams either. I do kets and crisps and that.

He doesn't sell tack or owt else like though do you Johnny?

Nor, I say.

He's on probation. The way Maria says this, it's like it's a good thing. Like it's summat to be proud of. *He plays for England. He's got the world's biggest dander. He's on probation.*

Probation, says the lass. What for?

I shrug.

Same as everyone else, I suppose. Getting caught.

Here, says the lass. John-John's a funny name though innit.

Aye, mebbes.

Aye, it is like. I've never met nee-one called John-John, me.

I'm just stood there feeling embarrassed.

Here – are you in the TAs or summat?

The what?

The TAs. You know – the army for losers.

Maria laughs.

133

Speccy gimps that roll around in the mud at the weekends and that, says the lass.

Johnny just likes to wear combat clobber, says Maria. Don't you.

She smiles when she says this, then she looks around and takes another sip from her straw. She looks good pissed. She's glowing. It suits her, like a nice hat or summat.

Why's that then?

Because they last a while, I suppose. They're just clothes.

Do you not have to wear an ice-cream man uniform or summat?

I shake me head. Nor. I pause for a moment, then I say what's your name then?

Polite isn't he, says the girl. I'm Olivia.

Aye, says Maria. She's Olivia. Here – show Liv your glass eye.

I reach into me pocket, pull out me fist then unfold it so that the eye is sat there in the palm of me hand glegging right at her. Dead casual, like.

Fucking hell, says Olivia. Did you win that on one of the stalls?

Nor, I say, it's made of glass, that is.

What for?

What for? So someone could wear it.

Wear it?

Aye.

Where like?

Where do you think? In their bloody eye-hole.

Who would want to do that?

I shrug. Just someone.

You're mental you are, says Olivia. You talk funny an all.

I go, do you reckon, a bit defensive like.

Aye, your accent's dead weird. Are you from Newcastle or summat?

Nor.

Ireland? You Irish? Then to Maria: Is he Irish? Me uncle's Irish.

Nor, I say. Not Ireland.

Johnny's from here. From the town.

Are you? You divvent sound it though, do you.

That's because he's a traveller. You don't mind me telling Liv, do you John-John?

I shrug, acting all whatsit. All nonchalant.

What – like a gypsy and that?

Aye, I say.

Do you live in a caravan?

I used to.

He's lived all ower haven't you John-John, says Maria her eyes widening in what I take to be encouragement to keep blethering.

The way Maria's talking is weird. It's like she's putting all the words in me mouth for us, in case I say summat stupid, summat that might embarrass her.

I knew some gyppos at school. They were dead hard.

Were they.

Aye. They never had no glass eyes in their pockets though.

I stand there, then I say what were they called then.

What do you mean like, says this Olivia one.

What was their family name?

I dunno, they were just called the gyppos and nee-one ever messed with them. Are all travellers hard and that?

I wouldn't know, I've not met them all.

What about the ones you have met, she says with this little smirk playing around the corner of her mouth like mebbe she's been taking the piss all along.

Come on – interrupts Maria. We've got to get going Liv, remember?

Oh, aye. We've got to nash.

Where to like? I ask.

We're meeting some of me mates.

Aye?

135

Aye.

There's another awkward pause while I wonder if they're going to invite us and it's like Maria can read me mind again because then she says, I would invite you along for the crack John-John but it's a girly night out and that, you know how it is. Lasses only.

Right, I nod.

You've probably got work stuff to do and that anyway?

Aye, I say, even though I haven't.

Olivia has her phone out and is pressing the buttons on it. As she does this it rings, then she answers it – What? – and sucks on her straw at the same time.

So, I say.

So, says Maria.

I'll buy you a hot dog with the trimmings if you like?

I cannot, John-John. Not now.

Or I can gan and get youse some ice creams and pop from the van if you like. On the house, like.

No, not tonight John-John.

How are you keeping, I say, trying to keep the chat rolling along. I mean, I was hoping I'd see you.

Good. But we've got to get gannin though. Mebbes I'll see you on the round?

What about the morrow?

Aye, mebbe tomorrow.

Cos I was just thinking, like.

What *am* I thinking exactly, I wonder.

I mean, I say. I mean, can I take you out? The morrow?

As the words come out, I surprise even mesel. I've never asked a lass out before.

Olivia is half listening to her phone conversation and half listening to us and still sucking on her straw, but when I look at her, she looks away smirking that smirk.

Where to?

I dinnar. Somewhere dead nice.

136

What – like the Metro Centre?

Nor man. Somewhere in the countryside.

Are you not working, like?

Nor. The boss has given us the day off.

I'm not sure about the countryside though.

Why not? It's mint.

It's muddy and that.

Well, I say. If it is I'll give you a piggy back.

I'm only joking but she doesn't even crack a smile, instead she just sort of looks away again, like her eyes are trying to pick someone out in the swollen crowd of the fair, then she mumbles into her straw, through her teeth, can you pick us up?

Aye, of course.

Not at home though. In town.

Aye, I divvent know where you live anyway.

Oh aye, she says, looking round again. If you can pick us up in the market place mebbes I'll meet you.

What time?

I'll text you.

You've not got me number.

Give us it then.

I've not gorra phone.

Oh aye.

So....

Say twelve-ish then, she says I'll probably be hungover, mind. I'm already pissed and I'm planning on getting mortal.

That's alreet.

Look, I've really got to get gannin, John-John.

So, aye. Well. Enjoy the fair.

I will.

Tomorrow?

Aye. Tomorrow.

*

The money was gone within a fortnight. He put a down-payment on a new van. A second hand nineteen foot long Vickers Lunedale sold at a bargain price by a traveller boy down in Darlington who was stopping his wanderings to settle down into a council house with his old dear.

It were only five years old and in prime condition. Palatial. It was one of them flash stainless steel and chrome ones. Twin axle, double bumpers. The works.

And the inside.

The inside was all two-tone, polished oak and formica. It had camber-fronted storage drawers, glass fronted-cupboards with mother-of-pearl insets in the handles and hand-engraved insignias in the glass. The carpet was patterned Axminster all the way through. Even the light fittings were sunken and chrome-set. The centre piece though was an over-sized wood-burning stove range made by Smith & Welstood of Scotland. It was the very best of the best.

He got us a new china tea-set as well, some clothes for the bairn and the rest him and the lads drank.

*

It might be summer but there's nee cloud cover and being stood around has made us proper cold, so I decide to do one. Little Coughdrop'll need a walk yet an all.

I've just walked away from the dodgems into the shadows round the back of the side shows and am heading away up the bit of hill to where the van is parked when suddenly he's there in my face. That twat from the other day on the Nook. That Banny. Banny and three of his sackless marrers.

They're crowded into a little huddle in the shadows.

Wahey! It's Mr. Whippy.

They look up from their huddle and I see that they're all dipping into a little plastic bag and rubbing shit onto their gums and sniffing it up their snecks. Whizz probably. They've got that look about them. It's there in their eyes; like there's nee reasoning with them. Lads used to get on it all the time inside. They'd take a load of billy then sit twitching in their cells all night. I never saw the point, me.

Lads, I say and make to give them the big body swerve.

I'm in the shadows of this git big artic and there's a generator next to it that's chugging away and pumping out petrol fumes. It's making a right auld noise. Out front is the fair with its lights and bustle but round here there's nee one else about. Behind us the darkness creeps off across the stretch of open grass they call the old racecourse, down to the river. I can just see flashes of torn silver moonlight on its back.

Here Bannon, says one of the boys. He looks like he's in the army or summat. Look at them threads.

He doesn't look like much of a soldier to me.

That's cos he's a woofter. They divvent let cream puffs in the army do they, Bender?

I turn to go back the way I came.

Whoah. Where do you reckon you're gannin, like? What's the hurry?

Bannon's blocking the way. He puts his hand on my chest, dead lightly like. It's the lightness of touch that unnerves us actually. And I can see his eyes are wide and blank and his smile is the same. Whizz face.

I've got to be off.

Howay. It's still early, Bender.

Me name's not Bender.

Well what is it then.

I shrug.

Why, I say.

I'm only asking you your name man, you fucking flid.

It's John-John.

John-John?

Aye.

Fucking John-John what like?

John-John Wisdom.

Fucking John-John Wisdom? That's your name? *John-John Wisdom*?

Aye.

Banny turns to his marrers, who are all facing us now. I recognise one of them from the other day. Mebbe two of them. I recognise the look an all. Pinned eyes and crooked smiles. Trouble, basically. They'll not let up until they've had a taste of it. That much is obvious. I can *smell* it.

Fucking John-John Wisdom, he says again, in a voice that's too loud. Sounds like a cartoon character or summat don't he?

Aye, honks one of the lads. Bloody looks like one an all. Fucking spacker.

I'm sure I know that name me, one of them says. Where ye from, marrer?

I keep me head down and grit me teeth. I try to side-step Bannon again.

Hang on a minute, he says. My mate's talking to you. He asked you a question.

Suddenly the lights and noises of the fair seem a long way away.

I've got to get going.

Aye. You said. But me mate here is talking to you. Or mebbes you're too good to talk to us, are you?

Nor.

Aye he is, says another of the povs as he takes a swig from a can of beer. He's a stuck up little poofter.

I'm not, I say quietly. And I'm nee poof either.

Here, you should see this daft cunt, says Bannon ower his shoulder, his eyes still on us. Drives round the estate all day in his army clothes selling bloody sweets to little kids. That's his job. Selling sweets to kids. What a fucking knobber. Can you imagine deeing that all day?

They laugh.

I push past Banny and head off into the darkness. The generator is still ticking ower and the petrol fumes are stronger

140

than ever. I hear a scream from one of the rides, a snatch of a song from the waltzer; the sound of synthesizers stretched and distorted. A relentless drum beat burrows its way into the soil.

A hand grabs me shoulder and swings us round. We're right in the shadows of the lorry now.

Divvent fucking walk away from me you smelly little twat.

Banny says this.

Look at him – he's shitting himsel. Pikey cunt.

I gan to walk away again.

Reckon you're hard do you?

Bannon spits this at us. There's bits of hockle round his mouth, his hand is scrunched into my chest and his face is all twisted up. He's taller than us and his cheekbones are sharp. He looks like a skinny monkey. There's a crescent-shaped scar above one of his eyes. It looks like a tiny moon. A quarter crescent planted by a sovereign ring.

Nor.

You want to fucking gan do you?

He's fuming now. He's working himself up into a rage ready to fight us. I've seen it before. He's trying his best to summon the red mist, but it's not summat you can just turn on and off. Still. No way I'm sticking around to fight four of them.

Nor, I say.

Have him Banny, says one of the lads.

Aye, knock the cunt out Banny.

Here hold this.

Banny passes his can to one of the povvy gets, lets go of me coat and pulls back. All his movements are geared towards throwing a punch but he's slow and easy to read and in that second I drop to the ground and roll under the artic lorry. It's even darker under there but it's dry. I scramble out the other side.

I'm back in the fair, and on my toes.

I don't get far though. There's too many of them and they're too quick. It's probably the whizz. They can smell blood an all.

Whatever has been started now needs to reach a conclusion that satisfies the group. This is how things go. They snowball.

They come at us from both sides of the lorry shouting, then Bannon is steaming into us. He puts the nut on me but I step back and he only catches me brow, just above me left eye. And his body follows through with him so he's off balance and I've used me hips to keep upright while I backpedal and circle away.

What's all this, like?

A voice comes down from above.

I look up and there's some auld gadgie climbing down from the cab of the lorry that I rolled under. He's got a hat on and has a tab hanging from his mouth. He's a showman. A traveller. An auld timer. Looks about a hundred and four years old.

Nowt, says Banny. Nowt to do with you anyway.

Aye, fuck off, says one of the lads.

Fuck off? says the gadgie. Who ye talking to like?

You, you eggy auld fart.

They laugh. All of them. Like seals at feeding time. All of them except Banny who is smarting from making an arse of himsel trying to chin us like that.

Inside I'm wincing and looking around for my exit route.

The auld gadge slowly climbs down from the lorry and tips his hat back, scratches his pate, then moves his hat down again. His slow, considered movements are enough to distract Banny from putting another one on us.

Having a scrap are youse?

What's it look like? says Banny. And it's nowt to do with you.

Aye, well. That's true. Not really a scrap though is it? Four of you on one, like.

It's not four, says Banny. It's me and him.

Aye, and when you lose the rest of youse'll stomp him is that right?

As he says this, someone else appears from round the other side of the artic. All of a sudden he's just there, a proper big lad in a thick jumper. He's holding a wrench in a greasy hand. The wrench looks like it's part of him. Part of his body. An extension.

Alreet Da?

Aye, I was saying to these lads – four on one. Not much of a square go is it?

Oh aye. Not fair at all that, no matter who's fighting. Two can worry a bull and all that. Mind you, they look like a bunch of jellies to me. Proper softies.

Fuck off are we, says Bannon.

That's twice you've telt us to fuck off now son says the auld gadgie, and I divvent even know your name.

He's Bannon, says one of the lads.

Sherrup Shotter, Banny snaps back. Dickhead.

And what about you?

The auld timer's talking to me now. I say nowt. I just want to get home to little Coughdrop who'll have been sat in his pen with only his turds and some butcher's scraps for company all day.

Not much of a fair fight, he says again. Eh son?

The big lunk, who I reckon to be the gadgie's son, shakes his napper.

It's always the way isn't it, he says. It's always the bully boy lads who need their marrers behind em.

What about you, the gadgie says to us again. I don't suppose you're up for fighting four lads at once are you?

I just sort of look down and shoe the ground and say nowt.

Well here's one more question for you – do you reckon ye deserve the tanning they're about to give you?

No, I say quietly. I've not done owt. I'm just trying to get home.

Well then, says the git big lunk with the wrench. Like I say, that's not a square go is it? Sounds like bullying to me.

His accent is thick with travel. Both of them are. There's all sorts of regional flavours in there. It's an accent bent out of all shape; warm and deep, but with a sharp edge to it, like every question is a statement or a challenge. It sounds like nails being driven into a piece of four-be-two.

What's it to youse says Bannon, but his voice isn't as loud this time. There's confusion in it. He's seen the wrench, sized up the lunk and heard the strange showfolk accents. He's rattled.

Nowt, says the lunk. We just don't like to see bullying, that's all. Can't stand it. Eh Da?

'Sright, son.

And this is our bloody patch and our bloody lorry and we don't want nee blood on our bloody gear neither. Eh Da?

Aye. It's a bloody bugger to scrub off. What's your name son?

He's talking to me again.

Me?

Aye.

It's John-John.

The gadge glances at his son and raises an eyebrow, draws on his tab then back to me.

John-John, is it?

Aye.

Town lad are you?

Roundabouts.

Thought so. And are these lads mates of yours?

I shrug. Nor.

And has he done owt to piss you off the lunk says to the lads, who are quiet now.

Aye, says Bannon. Being born.

They laugh at this, but they're less sure. The odds have changed. They're high. They're confused.

So you're a bunch of cowards then aren't you. Takes four of you and that. Yellow bellies, the lot of you. Little pissants.

Na, snaps Bannon. I could panel this little paedo on me own, nee bother.

He points his finger at us as he says this.

What do you think, son? says the gadgie, to me. Reckon ye could have this charver?

I shrug. I touch the glass eye in me pocket.

Cos I've got a hunnerd snoots here that says you can.

Eh?

If you muller this cocky little bastard – what's your name again, son?

Bannon.

I'm saying if you can muller this Bannon without him being mob-handed, there's a hundred snoots for you.

And what about when I knack him, says Banny. His voice cracks as he says this, like it's breaking for the first time.

Then you take the ton. But if you lose you all empty your pockets into mine. All four of you. Every single penny. And it's a square go, mind. Fists only.

What if that bender loses, says Bannon. What does he have to do?

Nowt, says the lunk. The hiding will be enough.

That's not fair, says one of the lads.

Neither is four on one you little cock-snot.

Watch it Banny, I hear one of the lads whisper. They're fucking pikeys, these two.

They're what, says the auld gadgie.

Nowt.

Funny, cos I might be getting auld but I'm sure you just called us pikeys.

Aye that's what I heard too Da, says the lunk. Remember the last fellas who called us that?

Oh aye, chuckles the gadge. As I say, blood's a bugger to scrub out.

While they're all talking I'm just stood there, thinking how the hell has this happened? One minute I'm on me way home for a shower and a cuppa and a wrestle with little Coughdrop and the next I've been pulled into all this shite. It's like the world'll not just let us be. Bloody hell. The last thing I want to do is to have a scrap. But at least this way I'll not get gang stomped. And this Banny doesn't look like much.

So, the lunk says to Banny, are you on or what.

For a hundred quid, says Banny. Too fucking right.

What about you kidder?

Everyone looks at me.

What if I divvent want to, like?

Nowt. We'll leave you lads to it.

I'm not a fighter.

Aye. You're a fucking chickenshit bender who bums bairns, says Banny.

I take a deep breath.

Alreet, I say. Let's go.

*

He wanted a boy but when the bairn was born at the tail end of winter out comes a girl. A lass with black hair, matching wide coal black eyes and a strong fist that gripped her father's big fingers.

We called her Charmaine.

Your Dad didn't hide his disappointment; girls couldn't do the things he did. Girls couldn't fight – not properly. They couldn't drink like he could drink and they never hauled scrap or poached or did any of them things. They were too dainty. Always crying about something. Always moaning and getting narky.

There was nowt he could do about it, except mebbe make another one, which he set about doing as soon as I was stitched up.

Every night he was at us, pawing and scratching. His beer breath at me ear. He reckoned he liked us best when I was carrying. Reckoned I looked full of life. Said I was wearing nature's make-up.

Barker sent work his way that winter, and I was glad of it. Lifting and loading, mainly. Scrapping and hauling. Physical stuff. Crushing cars. And minding Barker when he was doing a bit of buying and selling with people he didn't know.

Because your Dad looked the part. The fighting and training had shaped him.

He still wore thick wool-knit trousers, a starched white shirt, jacket and boots at all times. It were a style that set him apart from the recent explosion of colour favoured by students around town, who were now wearing floral prints, beads, bellbottoms, dungarees and shoes with platform soles.

He had grown his hair out though, and took to wearing it in a thick dark, unwashed mop.

And there was summat new in his eyes. They were cold eyes darkened by violence. Eyes on guard. Eyes as warning signs. Feral, like.

Within two months of giving birth to Charmaine, I fell pregnant again, twice in one year, and by that Christmas I'd had our Robert. Robert Wisdom. Bobby. A great gurgling bundle with a mop of black hair just like his father.

*

We're well away from the fair, ower in the shadows of the field, and there's the auld-time traveller and his son and there's the three lads and there's Banny and there's me.

And there's the fairground and there's the darkness, then there's us.

The rides and stalls are just smudges of neon in the distance now and the music and the screams seem lost in the night.

And suddenly I'm not even bothered. I don't even care that there's more of them than me because these two fellas being here suddenly makes it into a fight rather than a beating. A square go. And I don't care that I'm on probation either because it's not like Dickhead Derek and that lot are going to find out.

It's just like being a kid again, the way I'm just minding me owns beeswax one minute and suddenly the next I've got all these lads wanting to knack us for nee reason. I don't care though because this time I know the outcome. I'm going to knock the living fug out of him.

I carefully hang me coat from the hedge that we're tucked in behind, then I pull off my top so I'm bare-chested. It's cold but the adrenaline is working its magic.

What's he doing? shrieks one of the Nook knobbers.

The gadgie looks at his son and nods and smiles. Then he says to the lads, he's getting ready for a straightner isn't he? I suggest your man does the same.

Sod that, it's freezing says Banny, then realising how soft that sounds reluctantly takes his top off.

He might be bigger than us by a good few inches or so, but there's nowt on him. His white flesh and flat little rib cage look ridiculous in the moonlight. He looks like a pigeon or summat. And he's pissed and high. And he's a fugging idiot who's full of it. So I'm already winnin.

The lads are around us, pissed mortal and whizzing too. They're hungry for it. They still want to see blood and fear and humiliation and submission, now even more than before. They want to see their man win. They want to see their game played out to the conclusion they expect.

But here in the moonlight he's just another idiot.

And I cannot help but think about me Dad. I hear him too. All that advice he used to give us. Beat into us. *Keep your fists up. Remember your footwork. Always gan forwards. And most of all: a Wisdom never backs down. Never.*

While Banny limbers up and hoys some jabs I roll my neck and just stand there, fists clenched at my hips. I'm already warmed up from the day's grafting and I feel dead relaxed. Almost too relaxed. It's like five minutes have passed since all them days in the fields and lanes with me Dad and Bobby and Uncle Eddie and Big Slice and all their marrers, all them days they spent learning us how to fight lads twice me size. Bloody barbarians that lot, but in the moment I'm almost grateful for the education.

Do him Banny.

Aye, smash the bender, Banny.

Whenever you're ready lads, says the gadgie. Ned here'll be the referee.

Aye, says his son. This is boxing, so there'll be nee dirty business. Fists only. You win by knockout or getting your man to give best. And any biting or gouging and that and I'll put you in the river mesel. Clear?

Aye, I say.

Banny says nowt. He just sort of snorts through his nose, then he says, Come on then cunt, and he comes at us and that's the first mistake he makes, because a good knuckle man never steams in like that. You weigh things up and you ration your energy. You don't know how long you're going to need it for.

So he's opened himsel up right away, daft bastard and I step to him and he walks straight onto a short arm jab, thrown from in tight. I'm rusty so it's nowt to write home about but I get him plum in the eye and the silly little turd yells out. Actually yells. *Aye-az.* He doesn't even have his guard up properly.

Gan on Banny, man.

Hit him.

He swings recklessly and catches us on the cheek, only catches us mind, and then our bodies clash, cold skin on cold skin. It's nowt. It's like being tickled or summat. So long as I move my feet I know he can't hurt us.

We separate and I throw two more quick right jabs to his face because it's softer than his thick head and I don't want to knack my hands, then I smack him hard in the kisser. It flies straight through the middle and properly mashes up his lips. Teeth on bone.

There's nee subtlety to any of it and any decent fighter would have seen that smack coming a mile off. But he's too wound up to concentrate. Me, I'm the most relaxed I've been in yonks.

Gan on Banny, man.

Then he makes his second mistake: he loses it. Proper loses control. Panics, mebbes. He charges at us, half kicking and half punching but not doing much of either and all I have to do is move me feet a couple of inches and mind me balance a bit, and me whole body follows. These are the things that you have to be taught. The short-cuts. How to use your whole body as a weapon; how footwork can win a fight.

He flails and I treat him to a smack in the solar plexus. I've thrown harder but when summat like that hits the target it's still a devastating, dismantling punch; once felt, never forgotten. The breath shoots out of Banny.

Suck it up, mumbles the gadge.

I stand there, casual like. I even drop me guard to give him a chance. I've still not taken a step back.

You want to carry on? says the lunk.

Of course he does, says one of his marrers. Gan on Banny. Tan him. Tan the cunt.

Banny wipes his nose and nods, but he cannot talk and I know his will is cracking, breaking, the fight already as good as ower. He charges us with a flying head butt. It's a dickhead move. Desperate. Dirty an all.

He misses and snarls in my ear as he goes past, and I think, well I've had enough of this bollards, so I push him back to open him up and follow it up while he's still reeling.

All you can hear is the slapping sound of my punches landing and the *thump thump* of the bass line from the music way off in the fairground.

I'm working him ower good and proper when there's a massive cracking noise then a bang above us and Banny's face lights up and I can see blood running from his nose, but in this light it looks blue. It's the fireworks. They're colouring the whole scene.

Another one explodes overhead. Then another. The colours are so beautiful I pause from panelling Banny for a moment, but then he comes at us with a wild, wide circling right and as his body is following through I punch him on the nose. Then again. Two punches in the time it takes for a rocket to explode. His sneck crunches and softens, broken beneath my knuckles.

Summat gives in Banny then. You can see it in him. In his eyes. His whole body slumps forwards and downwards an inch as blue blood runs from his nose. He looks properly deflated, the fight gone from him. Even gravity is kicking his arse. His marrers say nowt.

Then the whole sky proper lights up this time with fizzes and cracks and pops and ower in the fair you can hear people *ooh*-ing and *ahh*-ing, but here in this dark corner there's only heavy breathing. The light changes from blue to red to yellow and the colour of Bannon's blood changes with it.

I reckon it's over, says the lunk.

Aye, says his father.

As expected.

Aye.

It's like they're commentating, these two traveller men. It's like the rest of us aren't here.

Do you give best, son?

Banny just stands there, gulping for air. He touches his hand to his mouth, then looks at his fingers.

He doesn't say owt. He just turns away and pulls his top on.

Fucking hell, says one of the lads quietly.

That'll be a yes then, says the lunk. He steps forward, holds my wrist and raises my arm.

The winner is the young Wisdom lad, he says. Well done.

Ta, but there's nee need for that I say, pulling away.

The lads don't know what to do with themsels so I turn to the hedge and put me top back on. The povvy charvers just sort of stand there sideways on, not knowing where to look. Aside from one hot cheek from the one glancing blow he got in, I feel like I've barely broken sweat.

I'll be off then I say.

Had on a minute lad, says the wiry auld timer putting an arm round me shoulder and guiding us away. Divvent forget your winnins.

I'm not arsed about that me I say, because though I'd like the cash, money like this always comes at a greater price. It's obvious these gadgies aren't running a charity here.

Here, Ned. The lad says he's not bothered about his winnins.

The big lunk smiles and shakes his head.

The wee bugger must be daft in the napper he says, then turns to Banny and his marrers. Right then, he says. Turn them out lads.

The lads just stand there.

Your pockets.

How that's not fair that, says the lad called Shotter.

Turn them out or I'll rip them out, and your bollocks with them. A deal's a deal.

The lads leg it like a bomb's gone off but big Ned is expecting this and grabs Shotter by one of his lugs, nearly pulls it off, and Shotter howls, then still holding him with just one finger and his thumb Ned digs through his pockets as overhead the sky keeps fizzing and popping.

Here, looker, says Ned. This one's got a nice mobile.

Ah howay man, says the lad. I only just got that.

So you'll not be too attached to it then. The lunk takes a close look at the phone, presses a few buttons, then pockets it.

Fucken hell, you thieving –

The lunk grabs him by his shirt and presses his face up against his. He's way bigger than the lad. You could fit two of the lad inside him.

Say it. Gan on – *say it*. I dares you.

The lad shuts up and says nowt. He's not that daft. The lunk shoves him back. Gan on then, piss off.

He legs it to where his mates are waiting and as they disappear, Banny raises a hand and points at me.

Wait till you're by yersel.

I just look at him.

We'll find you, shouts one of the others. We'll find where you live.

You're fucking dead you are Bender, shouts Banny.

Well he doesn't look it to me, says the auld timer, the tab dangling from his lip.

*

With two kids mewling, the new trailer seemed to shrink in size. And Mac did begin to get the itching. It was only last summer that him and Barker had toured the country but all that freedom seemed a long time ago.

Now he was a young father to two and he had that violence burning in his belly. Drink dampened the flames, for a while. But then it came back hotter and sometimes even a good scrap wasn't enough to douse the fire. Even after he and Eddie, or he and Simey Samways and Jim Brazil or any of the local traveller lads, or sometimes even just Mac by himself had clumped some bouncers, or whoever happened to get in their way down the snooker hall or outside a pub or at the taxi rank, the bus station, the market place – even after he had broken chairs and tables and noses and jaws, he would make his way back to the site where he would find a reason, any little reason, to start a fight with me over some daft thing. Summat small, like his tea not being ready, even though it had gone cold hours ago. Or the smell of the shite in the bairns' nappies. Or the weather. Any little thing.

And then.

And then he'd become too big for the van. His eyes would go first. They'd just turn black like clouds had crossed them, and he'd start bellowing and throwing things and smashing things and punching things. Things like plates and pictures and me, his wife.

Fists in me mouth and stomach, the bairns crying. Me on the floor being kicked and stamped into the corner. The van rocking.

But you didn't have to go and make a spleen over it. You took it. It was part and parcel of marriage.

And when that still weren't enough, he'd take off looking for it again to anywhere that there was gobshites and braggarts who he could put on their arses just for looking at him funny.

Soon he was barred from all of the pubs around town so he had to widen his circle. He began to spend time around the villages outside of the city. The funny little places. Pit villages. Backward places, some said. One road in, one road out places.

Places like Wheatley Hill and Wingate.

Nowt more than hamlets, some of them. Clusters of houses and a couple of barns. A pub and a church perhaps, or the foundations of a new housing estate marked out in the fields with chalk like corpse outlines.

Then further afield too, widening the circle further around the city to take in Fishburn and Trimdon.

Places you'd need a magnifying glass to find on the map.

And out towards the coast as well. End of the world places. Places perched over the North Sea. Working places. Dirty places. Rough house places. Places unchanged.

Places he fit right into.

*

The fireworks are ower, and there's just me and the gadgie and his son, who I'm secretly calling Ned the Lunk.

We're sat outside their van on the edge of the showground, drinking strong brews and smoking tabs. It's getting late and the last rides are closing up for the night. The fairground is darkening as the lights are turned off one by one. There's a vague dull throb in me right hand.

So, says the gadge.

Aye, I say.

How's your face?

Me face?

Aye.

That charver caught you, didn't he.

I never felt it.

And your hands?

I turn them over in front of us.

They're fine.

We sip some more tea and I'm wondering what I'm doing here, and looking for an excuse to cut out because I've still got to get the van back to the lock-up and get home to little Coughdrop. The auld gadgie reaches into the inside pocket of his jacket and pulls out a massive wedge. It barely fits in his hand. Tens, twenties and a flash of red from the odd fifty. There must be thousands there. Thousands.

Here you are.

He peels off some notes. There's a hundred there.

Thanks. I'm not bothered though.

You've earned it.

I shrug.

Fair enough, says the gadgie. You've a right to wonder.

Wondering why you're giving us this you mean? I say.

Aye – and it's because you earned it, son.

Aye, but –

It's alreet, there's nee catch. We're men of our word. Isn't that right Ned.

Aye, says his son. That's right. And a good travelling man never stiffs another travelling man.

How do you know I'm –

The gadge takes a slurp of his brew and interrupts us.

I could tell, just like I could tell you'd handle that streak of piss back there.

How?

Because bullies like that are crap at scrapping. They only win fights when they can jump on someone. Mob-handed. And that to me's not fighting.

Aye, I say. But you could have lost a hundred quid there. And you can't have made owt much from rinsing out his charver mate.

Doesn't matter, says Ned.

But what if I lost?

I knew you wouldn't, says the gadge.

Aye, but how? I mean, you've never even met us.

Ned and the gadgie glance at each other.

We've seen many fights, says the auld fella. Many, many fights.

And we knew you'd win, says Ned. Because it's the quiet ones you've got to watch.

And because you're a Wisdom aren't you, says his Dad.

This catches us off guard. I fall silent while I try to work out how they know who I am. Then I realise he said my name before without me telling him it in the first bloody place.

It's alreet, son, says the gadge. You've nowt to worry about.

How do you know me name though?

Because travellers just know don't they? We *know*. And – he pauses – because we remember Mackie.

This surprises us again. Me Dad, I hear mesel saying, me voice a little too high and squeaky for my liking.

Aye.

How come like?

The gadgie drains his mug.

I knew him back in the day, he says. We used to run around together. On the fighting circuit, like. Ned was only a young un' back then – and you weren't even born – but me and your Da were pretty tight for a while.

A fighter were you?

Me? says the gadgie laughing and then coughing, then looking at his tab. No. No. Our Ned here's the fighter in our family.

Aye?

Aye, nods Ned.

I've always been more of a facilitator you know? An organiser, like.

How do you mean?

I used to line up men for your Dad to bray.

Honest?

Me head starts reeling. I draw on me tab to try and stay calm.

Aye. Mind, there was more to it than that. It meant a lot of organising. And it meant putting up the cash, driving him places, taking bets, then getting him out of there if things came on top. We went all over the place, me and your Dad. I suppose you could say I was his...manager.

I nod, feeling weird to be hearing all this stuff about me Dad. Because if this gadgie knew me Dad then he knew what happened to him an all. So I say nowt.

Then like he's reading me mind Ned says, Aye and we heard about what happened. How things turned out, like.

I don't say owt.

There's nee secrets in our world. But mebbes you knew that already.

I still say nowt.

Crying shame all that business, says the auld fella. But he always was a wild one, was Mac. Lost his marbles by all accounts. Proper tapped. All that fighting...well, it messed with his wiring. Turned him funny. Couldn't work out right from wrong, that was his problem. Just a shame you bairns had to bear the brunt of it. But then you know all about that.

Aye.

We sit in silence for a moment.

I'm speechless. There's a thousand things I could say, but nothing will come out. The auld fella breaks the silence.

When did you get out son?

I stare at what's left of me tea and swill it around for a bit.

Not long back.

And you're getting by alright?

Aye. Right enough.

But what about them twats tonight.

I shrug, drain me mug. What about them?

Didn't look too friendly.

They're just a bunch of knobheads them lot, that's all. Local lads.

157

Had many other fights recently? says Ned.

No. That's not my thing.

What about inside?

Sometimes. Here what's with all these questions, like?

We just remember what happened son, that's all. Lots of us do. And we know it weren't your fault. Your Dad had gone bad and there was nowt me or you or any of us could do about it.

I look down at the ground, dig the toe of my boot into the soil.

And your Mam.

What about her?

Keeping well is she?

I keep glegging at the ground, keep digging at the soil. Me eyes have gone misty. I cannot hardly even see the toe of me boot.

How should I know, I mumble. Anyroad, what about youse.

What about us?

What family do youse belong to?

You're dead right son – here we are asking you all these questions and I've not even introduced mesel properly.

The auld gadgie extends a gnarled hand.

I'm blinking away the wetness in me eyes. I'm not going to bloody blub in front of these two. I've not cried in yonks and I'm not about to bloody start now.

I shake his hand.

I'm Barker, he says. And that there's Edward. Ned for short. We're Lovells.

Lovells?

Aye.

In me head I can hear bells ringing. Big bloody bells of whatsit. Familiarity. As loud and clear as the cathedral bells.

Your name sounds familiar to us.

Aye.

The gadgie – Barker – turns away and flicks the dregs of his tea out into the night and nee one says owt for a while. We just sit there in the darkness on plastic chairs. Then summat occurs to us.

So was me Dad as good as they say he was – at fighting, like?

Barker nods.

Aye, I reckon he was. At one time I had him as the best knuckle man of all the gypsies. And everyone knows the best of the gypsies is the best in the land. That right, Ned.

Definitely.

Ned here's on the way up himsel.

Aye?

Aye, says Ned. They say I'm the best man in the North on the cobbles. Fought me way through the counties and not lost yet.

'Sright, nods Barker.

What about the south? I say.

Soon enough. They're all jessies down there anyway.

We sit for a bit then I say, I'm not into fighting me.

Well, that's understandable considering, says auld Barker. But sometimes violence chooses you. Sometimes there's nee choice in the matter. Especially when you're on the outside of life.

Aye well, I say. I'm sick of being chosen. I've seen enough violence to last us a lifetime. Inside and out. I've never started nowt either. It's always others. I'm sick of it.

That's understandable, says the auld timer. Your Mac was a one off. For better and for worse. And anyways, what happened happened. It's in the past now.

I grunt, thinking it's easy for you to say. It's not you that's stuck living round here, with his bloody name and his bloody genes, seeing his face every time you look in the bloody mirror, worrying that you're going to end up half-mad and doing the type of things he did. That's why I could never have kids, me. I couldn't risk it. Couldn't risk putting them in the same position I was.

Here, I say. They say he was never the same after he took a tannin down in Wales or summat, I say. Did you know him then?

There's a tiny glance between Barker Lovell and his son, then he reaches for another tab, sparks it and exhales. He says nowt for a bit. Then he says Aye, as I recall I did. But it's getting late isn't it, and me and him's still got work to do.

I take this as a sign to leave. We all stand up. Barker is small and lean, like me. Ned towers ower the both of us.

I'll tell you this though young John-John, the auld man says. It took courage to take on them numpties tonight, and it took courage to be raised by a man like Mac Wisdom, not knowing whether you're coming or going. Can't have been easy. No. Can't have been easy. You just remember this though – you're stronger than you think you are. We saw you. You never took a step back. You've got this far in life, and you'll go further still.

Aye, nods Ned. Here, how old are you anyway?

I screw me face up.

Twenty or thereabouts,

Barker Lovell whistles.

Or thereabouts? says Ned.

Aye.

You don't sound too sure son.

I shrug.

How come?

I dinnar when me birthday is, do I.

How's that?

Nee-one ever telt us.

Not even on your birthdays and that.

I shrug. Me Dad reckoned it was not an occasion to be celebrating.

Aye, but still, says Lovell. You're young, and that's what counts. Nineteen, twenty, what's a year or two when you're young. I'll tell you summat else, I've seen many fighting lads and though there's nowt on you, you've got what it takes. Of that much I'm certain. You're only little, but that just means you're harder to knock down. Size doesn't matter on the cobbles. What matters is you've got that solid concrete thing inside of you; that thing that can never be destroyed. You've got the true guts of a traveller. You've got courage, man. Your Dad had it before he went cuckoo. Ned here's got it. And you've got it an all. You're tough as pig iron, lad. You could go all the way on the circuit if you wanted to.

Ned grunts in agreement.

I dig the toe of me boot into the ground again and gan, I'm not arsed about that like.

Aye, well. We're just saying like. A hunnerd quid is nowt. That could just be the start of it for a young lad like you. And it's not about the money anyway is it? It's about being the best of the best. It's about pulling yoursel up from nowt and becoming fucking royalty. You've got the fire in your blood and with a bit of work we could get you up there, right up at the top. Who wouldn't want to be King of the Gypsies?

Aye, nods Ned. Me Dad's right.

Ta I say, standing. And ta for helping us out with them lads, like. And nee offence, but I've seen what being King does to you: fug all. I reckon I need to get gannin now.

They both shake me hand.

We're around. Come find us if you need owt. Or let us know when you change your mind.

I won't.

You might.

I won't.

*

They knew him out there in them hamlets. Outsiders were noticed, especially when big, wild-haired travellers like Mac and Eddie Wisdom, or Pete Dimes, or Simey, or any of them lot, would stand up and formally issue friendly challenges to entire pubs. It was your Uncle Eddie that usually did the talking.

"Now, my brother here is not only the best bare knuckle man in the county, but the best in the whole of Britain. Traveller or not, you might have heard of him and if you haven't you soon

will. His name is Jim Smith and I have a hundred quid for any man that will fight him. If you lose, I'll only take twenty-five and one large round of beer off you. Now. Who wants a sporting go with a living legend?"

There was no shortage of takers out in the villages. Hard men. Hopeful men, men that worked the quarries and pits. Men who drove cement mixers or laid tarmac, or lads without work happy to take a battering if it meant getting a week's worth of groceries in. Drunk, fearless men. Men who still spoke in the Pitmatic tongue, that language of the old coal fields.

And when there was a taker they'd do it the old way, like gentlemen, and they'd remove their jackets and they'd step outside, with half the pub following them. Your Dad liked to go easier on these pitmen and farm labourers with big hearts but no technique.

He'd let them get a few punches in; just enough to give them a bit of confidence in front of the villagers that they had spent their entire lives amongst. Just enough to avoid total humiliation when he panelled them good and proper.

And then, when your Dad was warmed up he'd thump them hard enough to put them on the floor. Just enough to rattle them. Put a dent in them. Something to remember him by. Just enough for them to hand over twenty-five quid, which he'd then use to buy them a pint – and one for their missus to keep her quiet too. And another.

And so it went: a round of drinks for everyone. On and on.

And afterwards, after Mac had spent his winnings, and they'd all shaken hands and sung songs, and the locals had laughed along with their new gypsy friends, he'd wake curled up on a bench in a dark pub, or in a static caravan or the back of a strange car. He was always ready for another pint to straighten him out before he made it back to me and Bobby and our Charmaine, and their nappies and their screaming, and the same unchanging view across the barren paddock, the trees in the distance forming a fence against an outside world I rarely got to see for mesel.

She's well late. Double late.

I've been sat in the market place on the steps of the statue of the fella riding the horse, watching the town hall clock on my Jack Jones for bloody ages. It's not even funny.

I've already done me morning round, cleaned out the van, gone home, walked Coughdrop, given him a wrestle and a bit of nosebag, then got mesel changed into my best togs, driven back into town, parked up, and got to the statue by twenty to.

And now it's twenty past and there's no sign of her.

It's busy. Saturday busy, like. People everywhere, making us nervous.

The outdoor market is on and the smell of a hog roast fills the air. Smoke and flesh and that. Animal fat and stuffing. They must have been roasting pigs in this square for a thousand year or so.

And the statue of the fella on the horse. That's been here a fair while an all. The story goes that the man who sculpted it said that it was a perfect representation of a horse like, and if anyone could find fault with it, he'd have to kill himsel from the shame. Of course it was only a matter of time before some clever wee shite found summat. Turns out it was a blind man who gave it the once over with his hands and declared that the horse had nee tongue. So then this sculptor gadgie – an Italian by all accounts – stayed true to his word, and went straight off to kill himsel, which he did quite successfully. Daft bugger.

I look up at the horse above us now, and it's a sort of rain-based coppery green, and I see that it does have a tongue after all, and probably always did, and reckon that mebbe that story is a load of bollards. A whatsit – aye. An urban myth. Shite, basically.

Everyone's out doing their shopping and I'm thinking how when I used to come here as a kid it was a lot different. There was nee McDonalds or Subways to eat at back then, only Bimbi's fish restaurant and Greggs the bakers. The indoor market stayed

163

the same though. It's still selling videos about steam rallies and pick and mix kets, plucked game birds, fishing gear and dried veggie shite from the hippy food stall. Nuts and seeds and that.

But the big change is they've built a whole new street since I went inside, and they've filled it with coffee shops with Italian sounding names, and stationers and clothes shops, and they've tagged on a shopping centre down one end too. It's mental. I gan away and it's a multi storey car park, and when I come back it's "a whole new shopping experience for the new millennium". The first time I saw it when I came in to town for me probation meeting I had to rub me eyes and do a double take. It was like it had landed from outer space or summat.

Because nowt stops still. That's what I'm starting to learn. Nowt stops still. Nee-one'll wait for you.

Some things will never change though. Not the good bits anyroad, like the cathedral and the castle up on the hill and the way the river loops and snakes round them both, built to protect those on the inside from them on the outside.

I'm still daydreaming and thinking about all this shite when someone flops down beside us going soz I'm late I'm proper rough, and it's her, Maria, and though she does look pretty hungover and puffy round the eyes she looks alright to me. Denim jacket, sunnies and her hair down. She's drinking an Irn-Bru and sucking on a tailor made.

It's alright, I say.

You been here long?

Nor, just got here, I lie. I thought mebbe you'd not make it though.

I said I would, didn't I.

I thought mebbe you'd forget.

She seems nervous or distracted. She sort of keeps looking round, her eyes darting all ower the place, everywhere except to me, but mebbe that's just the hangover. Finally she looks my way.

Here – you've not got your usual army clothes on.

Aye.

How come?

I dinnar. I just fancied a change, like.

You look...different. More normal and that.

Ta.

She draws on her tab and sips from her bottle. I reach for my baccy pouch.

I feel dead rough me, she says again.

How come?

I've been up most of the night. Ended up at a house party. Proper fucked.

Where at?

On the estate. Where else?

Whose party was it?

Just some lad.

What lad?

Nee-one you'd know.

I might do.

Why, jealous are you?

She smiles at this. I blush. Turn into a proper plum.

Nor.

So where you taking us?

I thought mebbes we could go to the pitchers, I say.

What's on?

I dinnar.

Maria sighs.

I divvent really fancy the pitchers today John-John, she says. It's too nice a day and I'm too fucked to sit in the dark with a bunch of kids hoying popcorn about.

I'm sort of relieved she's said this because I didn't really fancy the pitchers either. I've seen fillums but I've not been in a cinema before so I wouldn't know what to do when we got there. How it all works and that.

Then Maria goes, I reckon I just need some fresh air. Can you take us somewhere quiet? Away from all these people?

Of course.

Any ideas?

Aye. I know just the place.

Have you got the van?

Aye.

Mint. Where?

It's on a meter just up at Palace Green.

Let's get out of here then John-John, before I gip.

*

Your Dad ran the site with an iron rod.

He decided who came and who went. If anyone was daft enough to come poking round in the night they had to get past him.

And there were rules. There had to be when you lived like we did, out here, away from the estates and the roads and the ways of the house dwellers.

We've always had our own ways son, you know that. The old ways. Tried and tested ways.

They were simple rules, like how only familiar family names were allowed, or if you were a traveller passing through, you had to be vouched for. Fighting with weapons was not allowed either. Weapons only brought wounds and holes and hospital visits, and hospital visits brought the polis calling. And so did the storage of chorred goods. Stolen stuff. Stick it down in them there woods if you have to. Hide it. Bury it if needs be, but keep it away from the vans and the kiddies.

There was the animals to protect too. Our Charmaine's earliest memory was of falling asleep to the sound of the riderless Skewbald cob stallion galloping around the paddock next to the site, its hooves vibrating through the soil and up into the van, the snorting of its nostrils amplified in the stillness of the blue night.

Stealing from another traveller was worst of all. No. Definitely not. Mac wouldn't have it. Because if you couldn't trust your own, you couldn't sleep at night.

166

This only happened the once that I can recall, back in the mid 70s, when a lone visiting traveller from Cumbria who was doing some road-laying work around the town did get himsel caught inside a van belonging to Mac's cousin Jim Brazil. Filling his pockets, he was.

Punishment was instant – your Dad broke both his arms. Just laid him out there on the grass and stamped him. Stamped him hard in front of everyone. He only stopped screaming after he had fainted from the pain. Snapped his arms like bloody kindling, he did.

Then he picked him up, all floppy he was like a rag doll, and a couple of the kiddies were crying, then your Dad and Jim Brazil drove him through town and dumped him on a bench outside the hospital.

His van and all his possessions were sold the next morning and the Cumbrian lad was never seen again.

*

It's funny, I thought about this place I'm taking Maria to so much when I was inside that I'm not sure whether it still exists, or ever even existed at all. Mebbes it's just an image I concocted to keep me mind from flipping out.

I spent so many days sat indoors straining my neck to see the tops of some trees beyond the fences and walls, that I retreated to this rustling wonderland of me imagination's making. The green cathedral.

All them hours spent yawning my way through the compulsory carpentry and car mechanics classes, and listening to bad jokes fall from the mouths of numpties. Entire days sat in Attitude, Thinking & Behaviour classes, doing the compulsory Drug Awareness courses and Money Management workshops with the piss-takers, the knuckle-draggers and the young career cons, all of them smoking and spitting and smirking their lives down the bog. Well – you cannot blame us for letting me mind escape, if not me body.

Because the only thing that got us through all that was the thought of tasting green freedom again; the chance to wander through the fields and hills, away from all of mankind and to have the wind and the rain and the sun and sky for company. I had all these special places I re-visited; the places I fled to in childhood when my dad would turn up pissed and radged and looking for a punchbag; all them times when me mother would be screaming and Bobby and Charmaine would take off to their gorger marrers' houses and leave me to bear the brunt, and the only place to go to would be me real mother's – Mother Nature.

I'm surprised I remember how to get there now, but mebbe it's inside us, in me blood, the traveller in us like, because it's like I've got a compass where me heart is or summat the way I drive me and Maria up to this green cathedral of mine without a map, and without getting us lost once.

It's a fair hitch out of town. We drive and drive, from ring road to dual carriageways to B-roads to this dusty track far away from the bustle of the market place and the Saturday shoppers.

I take us high up to where the rivers get narrower and the valleys deeper and the moorlands bleaker. We're out in the country now and Maria is squinting and smoking behind her shades, the breeze blowing and me whistling and nee bloody ice cream music blaring for once.

Sometimes she points summat out through the window.

But mainly she doesn't really say owt much at all, and I'm fine with that, because they say that silence is golden and I've had enough noise and aggro to last us a lifetime.

After a while Maria turns to us and says, dead casual like, Oh aye I heard about your Dad, and suddenly I'm tensing up because it's like wherever I gan at the moment people want to mention me fatha.

Dickhead Derek, Arty, the Lovells and now Maria; there's nee escaping him. It's like he's following us round like a shadow. Like a bloody ghost.

And I'm also thinking: heard what exactly? There's that many stories surrounding that bastard she could be talking about owt.

I swallow a grimace and keep me eye on the track because it's narrow and bumpy and there's pot-holes and dark patches where the thickness of the canopy overhead is blocking out the sunlight.

Oh aye, I say.

Aye.

There's a long pause, then she says. Sounds like a right madman.

Hmm, I say.

Was he really the bare-knuckle king of Britain?

I shrug.

I dinnar about that. Him and me uncles and their marrers reckoned he was King of the Gypsies. But so do fifty other travelling fellas at any given time. It's not like it's official or owt. It's not like he wore a crown.

Still. He must have been canny hard though.

Aye, mebbe. But he was soft as shite an all.

How's that?

Anyone who beats up women and kids must be.

She nods. She doesn't need to ask which woman, which kids.

Couldn't handle his drink either.

Oh aye? she says. Lightweight was he?

Nor. He could drink twenty pints, but it would just make him even more radged than he already was. By the time I were born he was already mental from all the kickings. They reckoned they loosened the wiring in his head or summat. Sent him loopy. Here, how did you hear about him?

Word gets around dunnit. The town's not that big a place.

I suppose.

It can't have been too easy for you.

I don't know what I'm supposed to say to this so I just keep quiet.

It must have been weird though, she says again. Living in a van with him.

Aye, I say. If it wasn't him knocking the crap out of us, or making me fight our Bobby to "learn us the ways" it were the lads at school, or in the village or in town who wanted to knack us an all.

Why?

I don't even know. For being a traveller I suppose. For being the son of the local hard man nutter. I'm still trying to work out why mesel.

But you're alright now aren't you. I mean – you can look after yoursel.

Aye mebbe. Why?

Cos like if anyone else started on you or if anyone was after you you'd be able to handle it and that?

I wipe me nose cos it's feeling runny and say, why would anyone be after us?

I'm just saying like if they were, it wouldn't be a problem, because you've had far worse when you were growing up, everyone bothering you and stuff, or mebbe when you were inside and that?

Aye mebbe, but I'm not planning on getting into any of that though. I've had enough of all that shite, me.

Good. Like how it's best just to keep your head down and that?

Aye.

We fall silent again.

*

When he was auld enough to walk and talk our Bobby was auld enough to own a gun. You'll not remember, but your dad would take him across the fields, over the dual carriageway, down the back lane and into the woods that flanked the river by Godric's Abbey.

They'd spend a day shooting and setting snares. Snaring rabbits and shooting squirrels. Mac would learn Bobby how to get the truest aim. How to merge and meld with the scenery; how to become invisible. And he would always have a line and a hook with them in case there were any nice trout lurking. He knew all the spots. He knew them woods like the back of his hand. Your Dad did know every tree root and hidden ravine. He could navigate them woods in the pitch dark.

I never went down there though. There were summat about that place. Too many shadows, too many secrets buried in the soil.

But all the while a violent desire burned in Mac's belly. Oh, it burned.

He began to treat me differently. I was a mother now. A mother who had endured one miscarriage and two births. I was a body that fetched the water and gathered the wood and kept the fires going and cleaned the clothes and the van and scolded the kids and kissed them better and worried about her husband when he disappeared for nights and days.

He turned on us.

"You've always got that face on you," he'd say. "Like a slapped arse. Never giving owt away, you. Martyring yoursel like that."

"You've lost your figure," he'd say. "Nee-one but me would have you – you know that don't you?"

And then he'd beat us and he'd kick us and twist me fingers and pull me hair and nip me tits and rub me face in me tea and all sorts, and me biting the cloth to stop me screams.

*

I drive down this track about as far as I can go then pull in at a passing place. A whatsit. A lay-by.

And I'm thinking, it's a bloody good job we're here because the holes are proper screwing the suspension and we're wobbling all ower the shop. The towers of cones in the back are toppling ower and the float box is rattling and sliding in its locked cupboard.

Arty'll kill us if I knack his van, I say.

Where've you brought us John-John?

I cut the engine and open the door.

Howay. You'll see.

We step out the van and are in the middle of the woods. We're right in the heart of all the trees, and it couldn't be a more beautiful day. I look around us to check we're at the right place. The place I visited in my waking dreams.

We are.

I look for the familiar right-angled tree, a sign post, and there it is after all these years, this one odd alder that has a massive branch growing out perfectly sideways from it, about fifteen feet up. The branch is as horizontal as the sky line and nearly as big as the trunk to which it is attached. It looks almost too precise to be natural. It's off doing its own thing, away from the main growth. It's a freak of nature, that tree. A bit like me.

Howay, I say again and start to walk off into the trees.

Where we going?

I don't reply. Instead I take off down the track deeper into the wood.

She stands by the van for a moment, smoking, her hip cocked and her nearly empty bottle of Irn-Bru in her hand.

Come on I say, waving me arm. You said you wanted somewhere peaceful and that, so that's what you're going to get.

She chucks her tab on the ground, and I wince because I once read that dimps take summat like six hundred years to whatsit. Bio-de-whatsit.

Here, look at that tree, I say and point to the tree. That's how I know where to get where we're gannin. If you park up and look for the alder tree with the right-angled branch, it'll always show you the way. Even in the dark, so long as you can find the right-angled alder, you'll be alreet.

Aye, she says, in a voice that's not quite as enthusiastic as mine. That's canny clever, that.

Aye well, that's what comes from growing up outdoors. Hanging out in the green cathedral and that.

What's the green cathedral?

This place, I say. Everything that's around us. There's loads of things I could learn you. It's just about reading the signs. You're never bored when you're surrounded by nature because there's so much to see and hear and smell, and all of it is changing all the time. It's like life and death are wrestling each other all the time, and it's better than owt on the telly, or better than any conversation you could have with someone. Better than booze and drugs, better than owt.

I pause for a moment as we pick our way along a path that is actually just a flattened strip in the long grass and more used to animals than humans passing through.

It's a path that you'd mebbe not even notice unless you've got your eyes trained to the ground. Ground that's not seen humans for a long time. Then I continue yacking.

The words come out in a rush.

Like, it could be dead quiet and still and there's not a soul around, I say, and all of a sudden one leaf on a tree will start fluttering and vibrating. Or one blade of grass out of a hundred thousand will start dancing. Just the one. And you're looking around wondering why the hell it's moving and it's mebbes because the breeze has caught this one blade, or mebbe there's a tiny insect walking along that one fluttering leaf, and it's so small you cannot see it, but you can just make out that summat is happening. Summat that you cannot really fathom or explain. A little drama. All you know is that it's Mother Nature doing her thing. I mean, it's like ganning to the ballet or summat, that is. Not that I've ever been like. But I mean, I divvent need to go when there's all this entertainment for free out here. And that's exciting to us, that is. Always has been. It's me upbringing, I suppose. Nature was me schooling.

Maria looks at us and nods so I keep talking. I'm surprised at how easy it feels to be telling her all this shite that's been on me mind for years. But now I'm offloading it, it feels canny good.

Like, the woods to me are as beautiful as the cathedral. It's silent here an all, and you can sit and think and be yersel. And you've got your own stained-glass window when you've got the sun shining down through the tangle of branches like that.

I point to an illuminated clearing over to our right where shafts of lights are beaming down through the latticed tangle of branches above and picking out squares and rectangles on the forest floor. I cannot help but think the sun's timing is bang-on, appearing as it does through the trees like that as if I'd pre-planned it or summat.

See?

Wow, she goes and the way she says it I think she genuinely means it. That's proper mint.

Aye, and like it doesn't cost owt to come into the green cathedral and you've not got some vicar droning on about being a sinner even though he probably wants to feel you up and that, like the gadgie who ran the church when I was inside. He were a right weirdo that one. Proper nonce and that. *And* the church he ran was just some povvy room with a crucifix in it and nowt much else. The green cathedral's different though. There's nee rules other than the rules of nature, and even then there's hardly any other than mebbes summat about respecting nature and not leaving a mess behind.

I turn to Maria.

You alright back there?

Aye.

Good, I say, then continue. And the other thing is Maria, you divvent even need to believe in God and all that bollards if you don't want to. It's not about that. It's not about that at all. Cos like everyone is welcome in this cathedral, so long as they're not up to nee good.

Realising that I've mebbe gone off on one a bit, I shut up and say well, that's what I reckon anyway.

A minute passes then she goes so are you religious then John-John?

Nor, I say. Nor, it was just summat to kill the time inside, going and sitting in that church. But when I come here, or when I'm out in the fields at dusk, and the sun is setting ower a freshly-cut field and the hares are out dancing and boxing and that, or the sun is coming up over a still pond and the fish are rising, or when you're up on the moors and there's a proper storm brewing and the air starts to crackle and the light turns this weird brown colour and all your hairs are standing up on end – well, that's when I know what it must feel like to be religious, or believe in this God they're always ganning on about. The idea of summat bigger, I mean. Summat you can't explain. The thing I like about this green cathedral – about nature, like – is it's real and it's all around you and really it's nowt to do with God or vicars or bibles or shite like that. It's just there, and it's proper class.

I'm sweating now, so I wipe my brow on the back of me arm and say what do you think?

Aye, it's dead nice here, Maria says after a long pause. Dead calm, like.

Aye.

And it's nowt like at home. It's nowt like the estate.

You're right there.

We fall silent for a bit, then Maria speaks, unsure of herself at first.

What you said about the woods being like a green cathedral, I totally know what you mean John-John, about feeling calm and that, only I'd never have been able to put it like you just did. I mean you just described the way I *want* to feel, but cannot.

There's loads more I could show you, I say. There's a whole world around us and it's just past your front door step. It starts where the concrete ends.

We walk on and then after a couple of hundred yards I turn off to an even smaller path that leads up and away from the track.

The path is overgrown with ragwort and other weeds. Some call them parasitic plants, but I think they're as beautiful as any wild flower, me. As we brush past the Himalayan Balsam that hangs heavy from both sides, the swollen seed pods pop noisily, scattering their contents in all directions. And the way the pods curl backwards like springs recoiling never fails to amaze us. Maria lets out a little squeal. We're both showered.

That smells lovely, she says.

Aye, I say. It's Balsam. Originally from the Himalayas.

The what?

The Himalayas. It's some country.

It smells dead sweet, she says. I always think of the outdoors smelling of dog shit and dead things and that. Here, you've got seeds in your hair.

Maria flicks some seeds off us, then I go aye it's not like that at all is it, nature? Things do die all the time, but they're re-born an all.

Do you reckon?

Pretty much, I reckon animals are far less cruel than people. Humans are always attacking and killin for nee reason, but animals only really do it to survive.

Aye, says Maria, warming to the subject now. Cos like when I was young me Nan had this budgie in a cage that just used to bash its head against its mirror all the time and I used to get dead upset watching it. It used to break me heart, that did. So one day I opened the cage and took it out into the back garden and threw it in the air. But because it wasn't used to being outside it just sort of flopped to the ground. It wasn't used to flying and it couldn't use its wings. They'd wasted away or summat. And even though I felt bad, it was necessary cruelty wasn't it – to at least try and set it free like that? To at least give it a chance.

Aye mebbes I say, careful not to make Maria feel bad. Aye, I reckon.

Aye, and that was the fault of humans wasn't it? Like, nee animal would ever lock summat up in a cage for fun would it? It's just us being selfish and that.

I think you're right there. Most animals only kill for one of two reasons. Either because they're hungry, or because they're under threat. Mainly anyway. Everyone and everything deserves a fair chance, I reckon.

She nods.

That makes sense. But we've not been given fair chances have we John-John?

Nor. It doesn't always work out that way does it, I say.

She shakes her head. Na.

Then after a moment she says, I've never really met any lads who know owt about all that stuff. They all sit on their arses smoking tack and sniffing whizz and watching telly and that. Or fighting and twocking stuff, and trying to shag us.

And do you let them?

She shrugs. Says nowt.

By my reckoning we're nearly at the place we're headed. The place I pictured in my head. That place I used to come.

So what happened to the budgie in the end, I say, changing the subject.

The cat ate it.

Oh.

*

They said I had a fine singing voice though. It was summat I got from me mam, your Granma Pearl, who your Dad wouldn't let us see any more.

But he couldn't stop us singing. Even when I was bruised and sore and crying inside, I could turn out a fine tune from between fat lips and chipped teeth.

177

They reckoned I had the finest singing voice of all the traveller women around – and I knew more songs than anyone else. Everyone said so. They said if a record company man happened upon us or if I ever went on that New Faces *programme I could be a pop star, me; not that Mackie would ever allow it, of course. But just saying. They reckoned I was good enough.*

Me favourite back then, before you were born, was a song about the changing ways, written by a country fella. 'Thirty Foot Trailer', it was called. When I sang that song, they all listened. They said I could bring a tear to the eye of any traveller with a heart beating in their chest. Even your Dad. The song reminded him of distant memories, or maybe even memories based on them few photographs he had seen of his ancestors in their plush trailers; made up memories, or memories passed down the Wisdom line.

He had this catalogue that got passed round the sites too, that had trailers like the Palladin or the Eccles in it. Or the gleaming Westmorland Star. Great beautiful beasts with stainless steel Morecambe strips and git big bold headlamps. And there was the insides, with their formica lining and hand-stitched coverings made by Cobdale or Avro or Carlight or any of them companies.

And so I sang that song.

And it would be around about then the women would be blubbing into their hankies and the travelling men would be clearing their throats and rubbing their eyes free of the dust that they pretended they had in them.

They never knew though. They never knew how singing kept us going. Kept me alive through the darkest time. It was all I had besides the kids because even your Dad, even Mac Wisdom knew that to silence us would be to go against the travelling ways.

*

The path narrows to nearly nothing then leads to a small blind bank that hides whatever lies beyond it. Weeds and grasses tug and scratch at us as we push our way through the density of the woodland.

I help pull Maria up the bank by one clammy hand, our feet slipping on the dirt that is dried and compacted from the hot season. The light is changing as the branches stir overhead, redirecting the beams of sunshine so that they probe the ground like searchlights.

As she gets close I can see there are burrs stuck to her top and there's a small twig in her hair that looks like it was placed there deliberately, as an accessory.

And I'm sweating cobs. Proper minging.

Here I say, wait a minute, and pull off the round sticky burrs from her, their bristles clinging to her denim.

It's like velcro innit, she says.

Aye. Actually, that's where they got the idea from. For Velcro, I mean.

Really?

Aye, I reckon. I think I read that somewhere. Nature beat us to most things.

It's hot an all, isn't it.

Without thinking I say, I'm taking me top off, then I peel off my T-shirt. I catch Maria stealing a glance at me torso and I'm embarrassed to be half naked near a girl. But it's too late. I can hardly put it back on straight away. Anyway, it's nice to let me pits breathe again. I'm just glad I remembered to use plenty of roll-on this morning before I set off. If I hadn't I'd be proper humming by now.

Is it far?

What?

Where you're taking us.

No. We're here.

I lead Maria ower the crest of the bank and there it is, the best of the best. A special place. My mental escape. My fortress of solitude.

I'm double-chuffed to see that it is still here, and, better than that, it is almost exactly as it has been in my head for them five long years that I was locked up, only more so. More vivid. Sharper. And more overgrown, because it's August and the weeds and wild grasses are running riot.

Seeing it before us like this somehow amplifies everything about it, even the silence. It makes it more magical. A sensory overload.

The green cathedral is a clearing that looks how I reckon a theatre stage must look, all plush and silent and about half a football pitch in size, with a big cliff face backdrop behind it. And on the stage there are bumps and mounds of grass and a thick carpet of ferns, five or six foot deep in places, and all the mounds are linked by the well-worn tracks and trails of badgers, foxes and snot-dragging snails, and over to one side there's a damp marshy patch with reeds round it. Nooks and cracks and tiny caves go into the rock at different angles and different heights and there's a trickling of water running down the rock, a tiny tinkling waterfall from the sky that I remember used to become a torrent during the wetter months. It's reduced to one long thin wire of water now though.

There's boulders too, scattered about. A couple of them are the size of cars and there's moss on them and the grass is licking up their sides.

And there's more Balsam, more perfume, all the plants and grass and mosses locked together in this one secret corner of the woods, closed off at one side by the rock face and at the other by the little bank of earth that drops downhill back into the woods, towards where we parked up. There's only the sky above and the earth below, and me and Maria stood here on it now catching our breaths, the pollen sitting on our lungs like summat wonderful.

The peppery smell of wild garlic hangs thick and heavy too. The air tastes good enough to chop up and eat.

Wow, says Maria so quietly that the word is just the faintest of mumbles falling from her bottom lip. I look at her and see there are tiny beads of perspiration on her like little diamonds.

Innit, I say.

I've brought a bag with us that's got some kets and some apples in it and some fancy bottled water that I took from the van's fridge and twenty Benson and all, and I say howay follow me, and head over to a raised bit of ground that's squeezed in close up against the rock face, just where it dips in a bit, to form a sort of dead-end corridor right where the sunshine meets the shadows.

It's amazing this place, she says. Proper magical. How did you find it?

I used to come here all the time when I was younger. Before everything. I've slept here.

Honest?

Oh aye. Loads.

Camping?

Aye, kind of. Not with a tent or owt like that though.

With what then.

I'd just bivvy down.

How do you mean like.

I shrug.

You know – just make a little shelter. Or crawl into one of these little spaces in the rocks.

She nods.

Aren't you bothered about spiders and that?

Spiders? I crack a smile. Nor. They're the least of me worries, spiders. Mind, there's deer about here and an all. They're dead timid, deer. You can't get anywhere near them – not unless you're silent as a mouse and you stay down wind from them. This was years ago, but I bet they're still about. Them or their kids. Or their kids' kids. Fawns, they call them. Baby deer. See them narrow little paths?

I point to the tracks that criss-cross the clearing.

Aye.

Some of them are badger runs. And others'll be deer tracks. I bet if you go and look at some of them lower branches you'll find the odd brown hair hanging off them.

How do you know?

I saw some other branches on the way in where all the lower leaves had been chewed at. Nibbled away. That'll have been deer an all, that.

Maria nods at us. It's like she's actually interested in what I'm saying. Because it's all new to her. For a moment she looks like a little bairn being told a bed-time story. It's like no-one has ever told her owt like this before.

So who did you used to come here with?

I shrug.

By mesel.

Did you not have any marrers with you though John-John?

I shake me head.

So you stopped here yoursel?

Yeah, loads.

How come?

Because it was better than being on the site.

You didn't get scared then?

Of what?

Of owt. The dark. Or ghosts and that.

I smile.

Na. Nee ghosts ever bothered me. And even if they did I doubt they'd be as scary as me Dad when he were pissed up and on the rampage.

I shift the bag from one hand to the other. Then Maria says, my Dad's a pisshead an all.

Is he?

So I've been told. On the gear an all.

What, a smackhead, like?

Maria shrugs.

Aye, mebbe. I dinnar. He got clean, then became a pisshead, then he got back on the gear. Last I heard he was inside.

I don't say owt.

Aren't you going to ask us what for, she says.

What's he in for?

She shrugs again, but it's just the one shoulder this time.

Same as you: getting caught.

She doesn't smile as she says this. She looks down and frowns, then snatches at a blade of grass and busies herself splitting it lengthways with her fingernail.

We sit down side by side at the top of the incline, just in the entrance to the man-sized crack that leads into the rock. From up here we can survey all of the clearing and still get the sun, or if it's too hot we can just lean back into the stone for a bit of shade if we want. Best of both worlds.

I point this out to Maria, then I get out the water, the apples and the bag of kets. I've got Rolos and Haribos and mini Coke bottles. Cherry laces an all. Loads of kets.

Do you want one?

I reckon I'll have an apple.

I pass Maria an apple and take one for mesel. I polish mine on me kecks and we bite into them and sit for a minute, chewing and crunching. They're proper juicy. Sweet an all. Just right. We've both got juice dripping down our chins. We chat for a bit about nowt. Where I live, how little Coughdrop is getting on. All that.

Then I hear this noise, a rapid, woody tapping sound. Maria flinches.

What's that? I think someone's coming.

Nor, I say. You can relax. That's just a woodpecker, that.

What do you mean?

I mean it's a woodpecker. You know, one of them birds that pecks the wood.

She looks at us blankly.

How do you know though?

I'd recognise a woodpecker a mile off, me, I say.

We sit in silence again, chewing our apples.

I didn't think places like this existed, she finally says. It's like paradise or summat.

Aye, I agree.

Cos like wherever I gan there's people and bairns and buses and concrete and music and pissheads and smackheads and people dealing and people chorring and people fighting. And they're all bloody hassling us all the time. But there's none of that here.

I could probably find some dog shite for you, if you like.

She nudges her shoulder against mine and pushes her sunglasses on top of her head.

You know what I mean though.

Aye. Aye, I do.

It's like when you took us up that hill the other day and showed us the county from a whole new angle. Everything looked smaller and simpler from up there. But when you're actually down there on the estate, it's like it's all you know, and mebbes all you're ever gonna know, and there's nee escape from it or the people you hang round with or live next to or find yoursel related to.

Aye, I say. Tell us about it.

Because like they always want summat from you, or they always drag you into summat or they always fuck you ower. So you might as well just lower your expectations and go along with it. Because if you don't sometimes it all just gets too messed up and too complicated.

Complicated how like?

Maria sighs and looks away. Squints across the clearing with snake eyes.

I dunno. People and that. They complicate things. Everything. You.

Me? I say, thinking what the bloody bollards have I got to do with it?

184

Aye, in a way.

How do I complicate things?

You just do. In ways you wouldn't even know.

Tell us.

No.

Why not?

I like you John-John and I like being with you. But at the moment I feel like shite. Just ignore us.

That's the hangover, that.

It's not just the hangover. It's everything. It's my life that's shite. My life and everything in it, so I think I just want to sit with you here in the sunshine and mebbe not think about owt for a bit, because if I do, I'll just end up spoiling our day out. Is that alright?

I nod.

Aye, I say. Here – do you want a tab?

Aye. Gan on then.

I pass her the packet, she pulls one out and sparks up. I do the same.

The thing is John-John – and divvent take this the wrong way – you're proper weird.

How's that, like?

You're just different to the lads I'd normally knock about with but I mean that as a compliment.

The lads up at the Nook, I say as I touch my cheek and remember last night.

Aye, Maria says. Like, because even though you've been inside and all that, right away I could tell you weren't like them. You're not a wanker for starters. And you see things different too. Like, nee-one has ever brought us to the countryside before. And if they did they'd have to chor a car or summat to do it because they wouldn't even have the money for the bus fare. And nee-one knows all this stuff about plants and birds and bloody Velcro and all that shite either. Because even though you hardly say owt, when you do, you put it different to everyone else. Not just because you talk a bit funny either, but the way you see things as well.

I smile at her, feel her shoulder against mine again, tap ash into the dirt.

But like I say, she goes, life is complicated.

True.

You make mistakes and that. Or you're born into a mess. Or you fall for the wrong people.

Aye.

And there's always someone trying to fuck with your shit.

Aye.

Aye well. *You* know.

I'm not quite sure what Maria's getting at. I don't know whether she's on about me being a traveller and that, or if she's on about someone else, so I keep quiet and smoke me tab and sip some water and hoy the apple core across the clearing and into the gently swaying ferns, then clear my throat.

I suppose what I'm saying is Johnny, my life is a mess and I don't want to make it any more complicated than it already is. I don't need to create any more trouble.

What trouble?

Any trouble. It just seems to follow us around. There's always summat going wrong.

Aye, I say. Well me an all. Trouble follows us like flies round shite.

So you understand?

No, I think. Not really. But I don't say that. Instead I say: Aye, well, mebbes like.

Good she says. Because I just don't want any more aggro in my life, you know what I mean? I feel bloody knackered and I'm only young.

Aye, I say, wondering exactly what type of bother it is that she's been having. Me an all, I say. I've had enough trouble to last us ten lifetimes.

Me mates think I'm mad for meeting up with you, you know.

I shrug and smile.

Mebbes you are.

She laughs.

But, I say, I'm glad you did.

Good, I'm glad that's out of the way, she says, then she leans into us and starts kissing us, and as she does she slips her tongue in and the way she lets it wander around in me mouth has me cock hard in an instant. Instant hard-on. I feel all hot and gozzy.

Do you reckon there's anyone about, she says.

Nor. Nee-one ever comes up here. It's too far out the way.

Good she says then stands up and peels off her trackie bottoms and knickers in one go.

All I can see is her fanny. It's the first one I've ever seen up close and I'm blinded by it. I can't look anywhere but right at her clopper. It's like a magnet for me eyes or summat.

It's not as hairy as some of the ones I saw in those auld porn mags that used to get passed around inside. Instead she's got this little line of hair that goes down to between her legs, all neat and trimmed and that.

Her arse is round and white and beautiful like the moon. It looks bigger now it's not hidden under clothes. Bigger and rounder. It looks so smooth and new and alien that it makes us dizzy to look at it. Dizzy and scared and hot and gozzy. I've not done owt like this before.

She sits down, then lies back in the grass, in the shade of the rock. I turn and lean over her, and as I do me face casts a shadow across hers. We start kissing again, our tongues wandering, then wrestling, then she properly pulls us on top of her and without thinking about it me hand works its way to between her legs. The flesh feels soft and smooth down there. Different. Then my fingers are finding their way inside her and I'm surprised how easy they slip in.

The way it feels makes us think of animals for some reason. Dead animals that I've just caught. Rabbits and that, and the way they used to feel when you'd skin them, when they were still warm and steaming. When the flesh was so full of life it was a thousand different colours, and your fingers would find their way between the pelt and sinew. It's not that different to this. Flesh and warmth. Hot meat.

I kiss Maria's lovely smooth neck and I gan down to the top of her tits which are wobbling a bit and look dead nice the way they're sat there sort of spread out on her, rather than all pushed up and trapped in a bra, but she pushes me head down even further so that I'm moving past her belly. Then my mouth is on her fanny and it's warm and wet. She tastes hot and salty and better than any dead bloody rabbit, I'll tell you that much for nowt, and I divvent know what I'm doing, but I do it anyway.

I get me hands around the top of her thighs and I lick as she adjusts herself on my tongue. She's not complaining and it feels double cush so I carry on like this for a while. Maria is lying there dead still and me hard-on is digging into the ground and starting to ache but then she starts moaning. At first she's so quiet I can hardly hear her, but suddenly she sparks into life like a house that's just been turned on after a power cut and she lets out this much bigger moan – massive it is – as her legs close around me head until I'm wearing her like a nosebag. It's hard to tell because it goes proper dark and quiet. Then there's a tightening in her, and her fingers are in my hair and pulling at it, and me nose is more or less up her clopper an all, then she does this big shudder and lets out a long moan that comes from somewhere deep inside, a place that I reckon only sex can unlock.

Then she gans all loose. Disintegrates. She collapses like one of them tower blocks being detonated; neatly and from the inside.

When I raise ma head and wipe me mouth she has her phone out.

Here – who are you callin?

Nee one, silly. I'm taking a picture of you.

A picture?

188

Aye.

On your phone?

Aye.

How, like?

On the camera.

Your phone has a camera on it?

Aye. Have you never seen one before?

I shake me head.

But why are you taking a photo of us?

Because you're the first lad who's properly made us cum and I wanted to capture the moment.

By taking a picture of us with me face down here? I say.

Aye. Why – are you shy or summat? Here – don't move.

I divvent like having me picture taken.

Why?

The only people who I let take me picture are the polis.

You're funny. I'll not show it to nee-one, John-John.

You should get rid of it.

You've nowt to worry about. Anyroad – I'm not finished with you yet. Come here.

She puts her hand behind me neck as I crawl up beside her. She kisses us again, tasting herself on me, then she slips her hot hands down my trousers and I get ready to do everything that I've thought about doing a thousand times over, and all the ways I've imagined doing it, and I'm ready to let everything go dark and quiet again. I'm ready for owt me, so long as Maria is doing it with us.

*

Sides from the Appleby jaunt I'd not gone further than the three, mebbes four miles into town since I married your Dad. But that summer I saw there was life beyond the high tensile fence, the chicken coops and the horses snorting in the paddock; past the vans covered in rust spots and the crackle of the fire and the long wet grass. A life beyond the skyline I'd been staring at for months.

The clothes, the haircuts, the cars, the food, the shops. Everything was different. It was a gorger's world. It was leaving mumpers like me behind.

It was as if the mottled concrete greys of the sky and the flat, muted greens of the site's surroundings fields had been pulled back to reveal another world, one I'd all but forgotten about: a world of noise and electricity and laughter and traffic.

Life. Real life.

Colour was everywhere, as if someone had taken a paintbrush and a palette the size of England and coloured in all the gaps.

For months we travelled the country. Up the roads and down the lanes stopping with them that knew your Dad. His name was known down in East Anglia, Kent, Cambridgeshire and Essex, places that seemed like a million miles from our world up north.

Oftentimes we'd fetch up in darkened corners of fields and copses in the dead of night. Each morning the view was different. Sometimes it were a working farm but oftentimes it was the arse-end of an industrial estate or builder's merchant or summat like that. One morning we were in pissing distance of the sewage works.

Your Dad took a few days work here and there, just enough for food and petrol. Or he would buy a ferret from a market and he and our Bobby would spend a day and a night emptying a warren. They could bag a dozen or so rabbits that way. Maybe more. Empty it right out. They'd seal off all the exits with netting which they'd peg into the ground with sharpened staves they whittled themselves and then they'd slip the ferret in and sit back. When the rabbits came running out in a panic your Dad and our Bobby would be there waiting, with their cudgels.

Betimes Mac would have to fight another man, just out of courtesy. It was sport. They wanted to see what all this fuss over big Mac Wisdom was about. Such scraps were the grapevine manifest. Teeth were lost and noses broken, but this was fighting for fun, fighting in lieu of rent. They got family names about.

"You can stay if you fight our best man," they said.

"Tell your lot about the Ducketts of Cray's Hill," they said in Essex.

"The Smiths of Lytchett Matravers fear no man," we were told in Dorset.

And your Dad's jumper would already be halfway over his head.

And they always shook hands at the end.

It was the non-travellers we had to watch. It was in some of the towns that whispers did follow us like shadows. Parked on some land outside of St Albans we came back one day to find the van's tyres slashed to ribbons. On the beach at Scarborough, Bobby and Charm were spat at and called "dirty gyppos."

But even then they knew better than to tell their father, who would give them a good hiding "for not standing up for yoursels".

Right enough the money ran out like water down the drain and your Dad decided he needed to earn something proper; none of this chump change for hops picking or what-have-you.

He had to fight again. Properly fight. He had to be tested. Face death and taste a bit of blood.

He had to muller someone. The fire was burning.

He called Barker Lovell.

*

Afterwards, when we're done, I walk right across to the other side of the clearing and piss into a thick patch of ferns. They must be seven, eight foot high. I've still got a semi-on and there's a glow on my cheeks. The piss sprays everywhere. I feel good.

And then I hear me Dad's voice: *So you're finally a man then. About bloody time. We all thought you were a woofter.*

I shake off then pick a long blade of grass, clasp it between my thumbs and blow on it. It vibrates and makes a reedy, screeching sound. Maria looks up and I wave at her but she doesn't wave back. She just looks down at the ground.

I walk over to the water that's trickling down the rock. It falls the last twenty feet or so from an overhang. I catch a handful to rinse me face and wash me hands. I cup some more and swish it around me mouth, then spit it out. Then I drink a bit of it and it tastes proper dopper, ancient and earthy, so I pour some ower me head and upper body, then give me pits a quick rinse. I feel fresh as a daisy. Alive.

When I get back over to where we were sat Maria is dressed and her knees are tucked up to her chest and she's smoking a tab. She's taking short quick puffs from it. I take one from the packet, light it and then stand there smoking.

She doesn't say owt for a couple of minutes so when I've finished me tab I sit down beside her and offer her a ket. She shakes her head. She's not said a word.

What's wrong, like? I ask her.

Nowt.

You seem quiet. Sad, like.

I just feel like shite.

Did you not enjoy it?

Oh aye, it was dead nice. I've not cum like that before. Not with a lad anyway.

I smile, wondering if she means she's cum like that with a lass or with her own hand, or never at all. I decide not to ask her though because I'm feeling good and don't want to spoil the moment. I'm feeling fifty bloody feet tall. As high and broad as the cliff face whose shade we're sat in.

We're having a nice day aren't we, I say.

Aye.

And the hangover?

She smiles. A tiny smile at one corner of her mouth. You must have shagged it out of us, she says.

Inside I'm smiling but I'm a bit worried an all, because it's like someone's flicked a switch and changed her mood.

What then, I say.

It's nowt.

Are you sure?

Her eyes study the ground. Flick from side to side.

Aye. I mean... I just feel like I've done summat I shouldn't.

With me?

She shrugs.

Did you not enjoy it like, I ask again?

It was dead good John-John, she whispers.

We both go quiet and sit there for a minute and me mind's working overtime because I know she's pissed off about summat, and I'm wondering if mebbes it's summat I did or didn't do.

It's nowt, she finally says through that same tiny smile that I can tell she's forcing her face to crack. It's probably just PMT.

I cannot bloody work lasses out me, I'm thinking. Not that I've ever met many mind, but one minute they're noshing on your dander and taking photos of you licking them out and that, the next they're being all moody and serious like someone's just died or summat. I can't help but wonder if it's always like this after sex. Mebbes it is. There's so much I've still got to learn. And then a thought occurs to us. One that makes us feel bloody stupid for not having had it earlier.

Here, I say. Can I ask you summat?

Aye.

Do you have a boyfriend like?

She looks away, out across the clearing. She inhales on her tab. She doesn't say owt.

This is what I'm on about John-John. Complications and that. Things getting spoiled.

I'm not bothered you know.

You're not?

No. Well, mebbe a bit. I just like being with you, that's all.

Things are never simple though, are they.

Mebbes not, I say. But they could be. It shouldn't always be complicated.

Aye but it always is, she says quietly. Good things never just happen. Or if they do, it's only for a bit, until summat comes along and fucks it all up.

Mebbes we should just stop here forever and never leave, I say nodding out across the clearing, but then immediately feel daft. I try to turn it into a joke.

I mean, there's kets and water and tabs and that, I say. We'll not starve. And I'll protect you from the wild bears an all.

She's not laughing this time though.

Aye, she mumbles. She's still looking away.

So do you, I say.

Do I what?

Have a boyfriend like.

She sighs. Exhales smoke. Looks at us.

Aye. Aye, I have been seeing someone.

As soon as she says this, I know it's him. That lad. That twat Banny. I don't know why or how but I just know, like I know the sky is up above, the dirt is down below and chickens cannot fly proper.

Up on the estate?

Mebbe.

It's Bannon isn't it.

She looks properly surprised when I say this. She finally looks at us and when she does her eyes are open wide. Wide and black. Only for a split second though. Like, half a second. She's about to say summat but she checks herself. Hesitates. Then pretends it's no big thing.

Do you know him, like?

Aye.

How?

I shrug.

From the round, I say. I've seen him about.

Pause.

I want to say nowt but the next thing I know me mouth is flapping and I'm talking in a voice that sounds a little too cold. Suddenly I'm going, so have you shagged him then?

She looks at us sharply. Shoots us daggers.

Of course I've shagged him. I'm not a bleeding nun you know. Not that it's your business.

I think of where I've just put my face, then I say are you in love with him?

She snorts.

Love? What ye on about John-John, man? Of course I'm bloody not. I mean what the fuck is love meant to be anyway.

She sounds proper annoyed now.

It's just summat they sing about in crap songs and that. All I know is Kyle's a knobhead – wait, I go, who's Kyle? – and Maria says Banny, his name's Kyle Bannon, then carries on going yeah he's violent and he's either going to end up in prison like me Dad and half his bloody family – and half the lads on the Nook come to think of it – or he's going to wind up dead, but the one other thing I will say is he's not always as big a knobhead as people think he is.

Oh aye? And that's the reason you're with him, is it. Because he's not a total knobhead all of the time?

I'm not 'with him'.

Sounds like you are.

She sighs.

It's compli-

I know, I interrupt. It's complicated.

We sit for a bit.

I'm not even that arsed I say, but I bet you any money he's knocked you about. *Any money.* Twats like that always do. Bullies and that.

I don't expect an answer to this but Maria replies.

So? she says.

I knew it.

I mean, so what though, she says before I can say owt. Everybody hits everybody don't they? That's nowt new.

They shouldn't though. Lads shouldn't be hitting lasses.

But they do, John-John. Lads hit lasses, lasses hit lads. Brothers hits sisters, fathers hit their bairns, the bullies smack

195

the bullied. Even little kiddies smack each other. On and on. That's they way it is. You know that. It's life, isn't it.

Aye, I go. But sometimes it has to stop. Sometimes you have to say bollards to all this and walk away. Or mebbes you have to hit back. But either way you don't just sit there and let it happen. Otherwise it'll just carry on and on, down the generations, right round the world. People hitting people.

He's not had it easy.

Maria says this quietly and for some reason I feel me hackles rising.

Aye, well. None of us have.

His Dad used to beat him up.

So did mine, I fire back.

He's in the BNP, is his Dad.

Big wow, I say.

Well, they're Nazis aren't they.

Maria pronounces it *Narz-eyes*. Then she goes, his dad does their security or summat. You should see him – he's a nutter. He used to be a proper skinhead when he was younger. He showed us pictures of him with the boots and braces and that. Proper scary looking. Swastikas and that.

I wouldn't know about all that me, I say. There were lads that went on about that stuff inside – about England for the English and that shite – but they were thick as pig shit so I paid them no mind.

Well you should because if they had their way they'd have you lot rounded up and shot. That's what Kyle reckons.

What do you mean 'you lot'?

Gypsies and that. Travellers.

Why?

Because that's what they believe isn't it, the *narzeyes*. Like you said, England for the English and that.

But I am English. And even if I wasn't they could go piss up a rope before they start telling me where I can and cannot live. Daft twats. Honestly.

Aye, well. All I know is they just want everyone to be white.

Well what's the point of that? That's like saying everyone's got to wear the same clothes as each other or summat. It's bloody stupid and pointless.

I'm thinking Christ I've never heard so much rubbish.

I dunno, John-John, says Maria. It's about protecting England or something. White power and that.

But England's shite. And only an idiot would want to protect shite so that it stays the same. And, anyways, I *am* white.

But you're a gyppo.

Aye, so?

So they want to kick out all travellers. And the blacks and the Asians and that. Anyone who's not from England, basically.

I shake me head.

But then there'll be nee-one left but thick gets like Banny and his lazy-arse marrers probably sat around eating, I don't know, bloody boiled potatoes or summat because there'll be nee good food left for anyone. Nee pizzas and kebabs and curries and that. That's just bloody stupid, that is. Anyway, it's a bit bloody late for all that, isn't it. I can't see some of the big black lads I've met inside taking too kindly to that idea.

Maria shrugs. Divvent ask me. I'm only repeating what I've heard them say when I've been round there. Here, his Dad has a tattoo of a dotted line across his neck that says 'CUT HERE' you know. And he's got this massive eagle on his arm. Only it's a *narzeye* eagle or summat. One of Kyle's brothers has the same and Kyle reckons he's going to get one an all. Or maybe Hitler's face on his leg.

I start to laugh and shake me head.

Hitler's leg on his face? Why?

No, his face.

Hitler's face tattooed on his face I grin, taking the piss. How does that work like?

Maria doesn't notice, and I'm thinking God man you need to lighten up. All this white power bollocks.

No – he wants to get a picture of Hitler's *face* put on his *leg*. The radge gadge with the 'tache and that?

Aye.

I grin.

On his leg?

Aye.

I start laughing. I cannot help mesel.

What a twat!

Then I say: Here, mebbes I'll get Kermit the Frog on me knob.

She's not laughing though. She never actually laughs that much, Maria.

Look John-John, all I'm saying is, Kyle's alright if you get to know him, but the rest of them Bannons are proper *narzeyes* and you'd do good to stay away from them. They've got swords and war medals and shit hanging on their living room wall and they go round smashing up corner shops and that. They go on marches and they knock about with other bloody idiots; fat twats with bald heeds that'd sooner stomp a traveller like you as look at you. Do you remember that Indian lad from the Nook that died a few year back?

Na.

Howay, you must do. It were all ower the papers.

No, I don't. I wasn't around, was I.

Aye, well, this lad got proper mashed up, then they set him on fire. Not on the Nook like, but that's where he came from. He was only a young un. Sixteen or summat. He'd not lived there long and he'd done nowt wrong to nee-one. They found his body bloody miles away in the woods, burnt to fuck. Flame grilled like a bloody whopper. Ninety per cent burns they reckoned. They never caught no-one, but everyone knew it was Kyle's Dad and his marrers and mebbes his brother, Ken. His big brother – the oldest one. Racialist attack the papers said. Mebbes even Kyle an all.

I don't know what to say to that. The whole conversation is depressing me now.

But Maria continues.

Here's another question for you: how many non-white people do you see on the Nook?

I think about it for a moment. She has a point but I feel in nee hurry to answer.

Who cares, I say. I don't see what this has got to do with me boffing you just now.

How many, John-John.

I shrug.

Exactly. Because they've all been chased out of there. That's Kyle's family. They run things and they've got rid of anyone they divvent want round there. They let the junkies stay cos the junkies buy their gear off them, or swap it for owt that they've chorred – cars, tellies, owt they can get their hands on – because they're not just into the BNP stuff, they deal an all. Tack, whizz pills, bugle. Wobbly eggs. Brown. Everything. No-one buys or sells owt on the Nook without them knowing about it. They sell to half the county, man. And you don't get away with that by being a nice person do you? They're into owt, that lot. Not just the dealing. Protection. Chorring. They run dog fights and they pimp lasses out. They make porn. Underage lasses. Owt going. Anything bad that's happening, you can bet there's a Bannon behind it. They'll come for you next John-John, trust me. And Kyle's the least psycho of the lot of them.

I shrug.

And this is the lad you go round with is it?

Maria goes quiet.

Hard is he, I say.

Aye, I reckon.

Aye well. He didn't look that hard last night, like. His *Nazi* brothers weren't around then, were they?

There's a moment's silence and I can hear her brain ticking over then she says, Why, what happened last night? Has he been hassling you?

I don't feel like telling her what went down at the fairground with the fight and Barker Lovell and that because I know nee good will come of me telling her about it all, and all that stuff about *Nazis* and swords and burnt Asian lads has got us proper down, and now I'm thinking too hard about bloody nutter fathers and messed up families and me own past, so instead I just shrug and concentrate on smoking me tab down to the dimp.

Has he though, she says.

What?

Been hassling you.

No, I mumble. It's nowt I can't handle.

Cos he's already mentioned you.

Mentioned me? How like?

Aye. He won't shut up about you.

What did he say?

Nowt.

Howay man, he must have said summat.

He was just being a knobhead, that's all. He was just going on about the bloody ice cream gyppo this and gyppo that. Twisting on about you being on the estate and that. Reckoned him and his brothers would sort you out.

What's it got to do with him, the bloody nebby nose *Nazi* get, I say. He needs to mind his own beeswax, that one.

I don't know, John-John. Everyone thinks the Bannons are dead hard and psycho and that, so he just feels like he has to act it all the time. You would if you'd been through what he had. He feels he has a name to live up to.

I look at her and raise an eyebrow and say he's not the only one for fuck's sake.

You swore she says. And sorry.

You don't know the half of it, I say.

So what happened last night?

It's nowt. It's not even worth mentioning.

Was it at the fair?

Aye.

After I saw you.

It was nowt, Maria.

I knew it.

Knew what?

That summat had happened.

You were with him last night weren't you, I say. That's why you were acting all weird with us.

I wasn't acting weird.

Aye, you were. That's who you were gannin off to meet wasn't it. On your girl's night out?

Aye, she says in a low voice. Mebbe. But that bastard never turned up.

Did he not?

Na.

That's because he was off with his marrers, looking for trouble.

I fucking knew it, spits Maria. I knew he'd get into bother at the fairground. Did you see him scrapping, like?

Aye.

Where?

On the ground after I'd put him down.

How do you mean?

It was me he was fighting.

You?

Aye.

Oh, fucking hell John-John. What happened?

Suddenly Maria's all interested in what I have to say. But now that the story is unravelling I divvent much feel like being a part of it.

Nowt really.

Gan on, tell us.

He just started on us, that's all. That's how I know he's a proper dick – cos he'd rather chase after me than spend the night with you. Him and his sackless povvy bastard mates.

Which mates?

I don't know.

I do. I bet it was Boz and Shotter and them lot she says, as much to herself as to me. Were his brothers there?

How would I know? They were all about the same age and all on the gear and looking for trouble.

And they started on you?

Aye. Or they were going to until this showground gadgie stepped in and called a square go.

A what?

A fair fight.

Between you and Kyle?

Aye. Between me and him.

And what happened John-John, for fuck's sake?

Well, I say taking a git big pause. Nowt much. Here – do you want to see me glass eye again?

John-John.

Nowt much I shrug, enjoying Maria's frustration. I brayed him good and proper – put him on his arse like.

Shit. Was he hurt?

Banny?

Aye.

Who cares? He was practically blubbing though. Proper pissed off, he was.

I care, she says in an urgent voice that I don't recognise, and suddenly I see her in a whole new light. Maria's not the lass I met on the round that day, the girl whose just shagged us and shown us a part of her I thought nee-one else would get to see. Suddenly she's someone else; just another lovesick ninny who's fallen for the first feckless bad lad that's come along. The bad lad from the bad family. The family with the reputation. The big fish in the little stagnant pond that's got nee stream running in or out of it. "Oh, but he treats us nice". Shite. Fug this for a game of whatsit, I think. Aye – bloody soldiers.

He didn't look too happy about it, I say. But he'll live. He said he was coming after us, but stuff him. What's he going to do?

Oh shit.

I said he's alreet Maria. He'll live. He just got taught a lesson, that's all.

I stand up again. The sun has gone behind a cloud and it's not so warm just sitting here with sweat drying on me back, so I pull me top over me head.

It was nowt anyway, I say. Just some bollards. But it's over now.

No John-John. You don't understand. If he says he's coming after you, he'll come after you. Especially if you panelled him in front of his mates. It won't be over. He'll keep coming for you. Him and his brothers.

So, I say.

He's stabbed people. He's been inside. They all have.

I shrug. Sounds like you've got a thing for cons to me.

No, she says.

Nazis then.

No.

I thought you said he wasn't as bad as people think he is.

Aye well. He's not when he's with me. He can be proper nice sometimes. But with you...I told you, he's already got it in for you.

He started it, the daft knacker. Let him come.

There's his brothers an all.

I'm not arsed me, I say, though me head's working overtime thinking about what Maria said about them lot dealing and running everything, and how if Arty Vicari was knocking out weed on the Nook, then he was either doing it with the Bannons' permission, or he was selling it for them. An if he was selling it for them, then he's in their pocket. He's working for them. Them bloody *Nazis*. And anyone with half a brain knows that nowt good ever comes out of business like that. It's nee wonder that this Banny lad has got it in for us, me not only battering the twat but also refusing to knock out gear an all.

Bloody typical though isn't it, I'm thinking. Four weeks out and I'm working for the man who knocks out for the biggest rough-arsed plastic gangster charvers around, and on top of that I'm shagging the lass of one of them an all. The one I put on his arse last night. And all I bloody want is a quiet life, just to be left alone in a green cathedral like this place. Christ.

Let him come, I say again. I've taken on worse than him. Much worse.

That's a bad idea John-John.

I notice that when she's serious Maria starts calling us John-John instead of Johnny and although John-John is me name it somehow sounds colder the way it falls off her tongue like that. More formal and less friendly.

A thought occurs to us.

And where do you fit into all this anyway? All the dealing and shagging and that?

You should just leave, she says.

I've only just got here.

Town I mean. You should get away for a bit.

I snort.

I doubt it. There's me job and me flat and the parole officer. And little Coughdrop an all. I can't just drop everything. Any road, I don't want to. I've been running away from bullying bastards like him and his lot all me life. So sod him.

That's a bad way to talk John-John. Kyle's done stuff. They all have.

Yeah well. I've done stuff too, remember?

*

Mac had not seen Barker for many months, but it took only one call from a service station telephone box for the grapevine to deliver him to our doorstep.

We were stopping at a site near Luton run by a traveller called Jimmy Buckle. It was a real midden-heap of a site.

It was an abandoned small-holding that he and his vast family had assumed ownership of. In its centre stood a shell of a derelict house and beside it a dilapidated barn had junk spilling from its mouth: old blue gas bottles, a toppled fridge-freezer, a small tower of rolled up carpets, piles of tyres. There was a caravan too, slumped and rusting on its bare axles. Surrounding all this rubbish was a crescent of haphazardly parked trailers facing inwards, as if to protect these worthless, rotting treasures from the outer world.

Down in the town, the site had a reputation. Few people ever went up there. It was just the type of place your Dad felt most comfortable in.

Buckle was regarded as a traveller who welcomed fellow men of the road; his was a good stopping site before you hit the suburban sprawl that bled into London. He was also known as a knuckle man who, at just over five feet but built like a bullet, earned the nickname Big Slice. Buckle was regarded as a pit-bull fighter. They said it once took six men to pull him off one opponent, and he was impossible to knock over so long as he was conscious.

It was just after dawn one morning when there was a knock at our door. Mac answered it and there stood Barker Lovell in the half-light. I watched from the bed.

Barker nodded and said, "Now then."

Bare-chested, Mac yawned and stretched. Barker noticed the early signs of a slight paunch around your Dad's white waist. He's been on the ale, he thought. No doubt about that.

"You best come in then."

I roused myself to get the tea and toast on. It was as if minutes rather than months had passed as their conversation re-ignited. There was no small talk; like with most true travelling men. Oftentimes if a traveller says he's going for a bit of a wander, he might be gone an hour or he might be gone a month. That's just the way it is.

"Hello Vancy," he said.

"Barker."

I got our Charm and Bobby dressed and sent them out to play with the Buckle lot. Then I made myself look busy tidying up.

Barker parted the curtain with one yellowing finger and looked out. He was dressed the way he was always dressed – wool suit, trilby, silk scarf. The auld way. He kissed his teeth.

"Well, this is a shit hole."

"Do you want to tell Big Slice that?"

Barker shrugged.

"He's like a bloody skip rat, that one," *Barker did say through a slurp of tea.* "Gives us more refined travellers a right bad name with all that shite lying about."

"What do you care?"

Barker reached for his baccy pouch, rolled a cigarette, licked it, sealed it and lit it. Mac reached for an ashtray.

"I don't. I'm just saying, like. Burnt mattresses and broken fridges and that – well. He should make more of an effort. If you look like rubbish, people will treat you like rubbish."

Mac grinned a wolfish grin.

"So how come you always dress like you're selling bloody pegs or summat?"

"You cheeky get."

They paused. Barker drank more tea, sniffed, then sat back on the recliner.

Mac drained his mug and carefully placed it on the side.

"I want to fight," *he said finally.*

"Good," *said Barker.* "Been keeping in shape have you?"

"Aye. Can't you tell, like?"

"Not from where I'm sitting, no. Been training have you?

"Aye," *said your Dad.* "You and I both know that Mac Wisdom on a bad day can still tan any numpty that you care to send his way."

Barker laughed. He was pointing at Mac's new bellbottom trousers, bought from Big Slice at the knockdown price of two pairs for a quid. They were chocolate brown polyester and skin tight around the thigh but fanning out to a twenty-two inch flare at the hem.

"I hope you're not planning on fighting in them."

"What's wrong with them?"

"You look like a bloody woolly woofter."

Mac stiffened and his brow dropped. His hands curled into fists.

"You look like that bloody whatshisname," *continued Barker.*

"Who?"

"You know."

"I divvent, like."

"You do, man. That mincer off the telly."

"Danny La Rue?"

Barker roared with laughter and slapped his thigh, dropping tight little shreds of burning tobacco onto the table.

"No, you daft bastard. I meant Rod Stewart – but, aye, Danny Le Rue'll do an' all."

Mac's eyes darkened.

"Christ man, I'm only joshing you," *sighed Barker.* "Lord God almighty. I hope you're not going to fight Cliff Pike in them."

"Who's Cliff Pike?"

"One of the meanest, dirtiest fucking apes on this bloody island, that's who."

Mac snorted.

"Well, how come I've never heard of him then?"

"Mebbe because you've got your heed up your arse half the time and the rest of the time it's in a pint pot?"

"That's bollocks, that."

"Well," *sniffed Barker.* "We'll find out tonight, won't we."

Your Dad's eyes widened.

"Tonight?"

"Aye," said Barker, drawing on the last of his tab. "You said you wanted a fight, so I got you one. We'll leave this afternoon, after you've cooked us up some scran."

He ground out his cigarette and started whistling a song.

It was some pop song they kept playing on the radio. I recognised it.

'Maggie May', they called it. By that poof Rod Stewart.

*

When I've dropped Maria off a long way from her house and then taken the van back to the lock-up and walked home, it's double late.

As I head through the estate to my flat I'm sweaty, hungry and knackered. It's only half-dark though, like someone has left a light on a million miles behind the sky. I'm feeling dead weird. Weird, because on the one hand I've finally got me oats and on the other Maria's mashed me head and it feels like it's all turning to shite already, like I'm being pulled in four directions by wild horses or summat.

And I'm pissed off because I'm trying me best to keep me head down and just crack on with things. Really trying. And now there's this darkness coming ower us. It's a different kind of darkness. A sense of impending whatsit. Aye. Doom.

It's there as I turn into my close. I can feel it.

The front door is open. Wide open. The way it's hanging on its hinges tells us it has been forced. I can see nowt but varying shades of darkness in there. My radar was right.

I stop on the landing and wait, me senses heightened. I listen but I cannot hear owt.

I walk closer, to the doorway, and stand there. Summat smells funny. It's in the air. A vague tanginess. Like stale piss or summat. A spoilt dinner mebbe. Then I walk in.

I go quickly down the hall on silent heels, into the bedroom and turn on the light. Everything looks just as I left it: mattress, rack of clothes, pile of books. Glass of water. Ashtray. Nowt that's worth taking anyway. I call our Coughdrop.

Aware of every breath I take and every swish me clothes make, I walk into the kitchen – the same. Hacky plate and cup. Bin. Dog bowl. Tins of food. *Robinson Crusoe* half read on the side. Same as ever. But, everything feels wrong. The atmosphere feels different, like there's a charge running through the air and into me. A warning charge. A current of fear.

I go down the hallway again and into the darkness of the living room. I fumble for the light switch and turn it on, and when I do I see summat I can't comprehend, summat alien. Summat that's beyond me understanding and experience so far.

It's long, about five or six feet, and it's flat and it's stretched out on the carpet and it's red and blue and brown and black and purple, but mainly it's black and red. It makes us think of art galleries and butchers' windows, and it stinks. It's like a tear in this dimension. A glimpse into another world.

Me mind races to process what me eyes are taking in.

In amongst it all there are shapes, a suggestion of a greater structure. The over-stretched oval of an eye. A grimace of teeth. A peeled back cheek, ripped from its moorings. The parts comprise a face, or what was once a face, now re-ordered and re-distributed. It's like a broken mask or a spilled dressing up box.

Me body buzzes and surges and lurches as me senses battle it out and that charge of horror that is emanating from this room, down the corridor and out onto the stairwell, runs right through us stronger than ever. I gag then I retch and my hand goes to my mouth in case I gip. Nothing comes. Nothing liquid anyway. It's more of a long moan.

It's the dog turned half inside out.

The mess is little Coughdrop.

Coughdrop with his fur and skin torn and peeled back, and his blue intestines pulled out across the carpet.

There's bloody brown smears on the skirting board and there's a sort of gluey shit-smelling substance dotted around too that's starting to harden on the carpet and is mebbe fat and sinew and snot and everything else that creates life.

His rib cage is open and his guts are stretched out like a discarded flag or the tail of a kite or a pair of trousers that have been kicked off in the dark. I can see other things too. Organs. They look strange and new and too beautiful to be anything manufactured: only Mother Nature could have created these things.

His torso and face are demolished but other parts of him – his legs and paws – are intact so that little Coughdrop now resembles something weird and elongated and exaggerated, but his framework is still in place as if in defiance of his tormentors; as if to let me know he fought them til the end, the little scamp. Splayed there his body says to us: I tried to stop them, Dad. I did me best.

A turd hangs from what remains of his little black arsehole and his tongue hangs distended from the mess as if he's catching his breath, as if he's trapped between two worlds. Forever suspended in sleep.

But he's not. He is definitely not sleeping.

*

They left Luton and headed west.

"Where you taking us, auld man?" asked Mac.

"I told you: to fight Cliff Pike."

"Aye, but where?"

"To Wales."

"Bloody Wales," said Mac. "That's miles away."

A moment passed.

"Had on a minute," said Mac. "I've not got a passport."

Barker glanced at him and then thinking he was being serious, slapped the steering wheel of his BMW and roared with laughter.

*It was the kind of laughter that Mac despised. Patronising,
contemptuous and usually enough for him to knock any other
man spark out. Because the warmth he once felt for Barker was
gone; he didn't like the way this gadgie spoke to him – him the
king of the gypsies. Always using long words and gannin on about
how to dress and the good old days and all that. Well. It took
the piss.*

*"You divvent need a passport to get into Wales, you bloody
div."*

*They crossed Oxfordshire and the Cotswolds and the
landscape rose and fell around them like great green waves.
They went through villages and hamlets of wattle and daub
cottages. They passed lush meadows where the cattle grazed with
the sun settling on their backs. They saw tiny churches nestled
in hollows, drove over chalk streams and past duck ponds and
tightly-planted copses that Mac knew would be brimming with
fat lazy pheasants just ripe for lifting. They drove on through the
evening, chasing the sun.*

*Soon they were headed to that part of the land where England
and Wales rub up against one another and only the widening
expanse of the River Severn holds them apart like a referee.*

"So tell us about this Pike lad, then," said your Dad.

"He's game and he's nails. What else do you need to know?"

"How does he fight?"

"Dirtier than you."

"I doubt that. Square go is it?"

"It's a dirty-as-it-gets-go, lad. Does that bother you?"

"Does it hell. How much am I getting?"

*"Half of the grand his lot have put up, plus I'll cut you in on
the side bets. They've not heard of you so the odds'll be good."*

"I'll muller him."

"Don't be so confident about that, Mackie Wisdom."

Your Dad looked at him sideways.

*"You know Barker, if I didn't know you better I'd say you didn't
have any faith in us. I've not seen you for months and here you*

are appearing on me step at dawn with a scrap lined up for us at a few hours notice and you're talking like I'm some turkey that's ripe for fucking plucking. It just doesn't sit right."

"It's not too late to back out you know." Barker paused. "If you're not up to it."

"Fuck you take us for?" Mac snapped. "I never back away from fights, you know that. I'll panel this Pike cunt and maybe if you're lucky I'll not panel you an all. You just make sure I get paid. How far to Wales?"

"We're in bloody Wales."

"It looks like bloody England."

They were somewhere on the edge of the Brecon Beacons before Barker spoke again.

"So listen. When we get to the pub you just let us do the talking. You just sit tight until we're up at the quarry."

"Hold on a sec – quarry?"

"Aye."

"You never said nowt about a quarry. Here – how well do you know these gadgies?"

"Well enough."

*

It's as dark as it gets at the close of August when I scrape up what's left of Coughdrop into two carrier bags and leave the flat. He feels heavier in bits than he did alive. Not for the first time I know what the phrase a dead weight means.

I'm in a bit of a trance. Numb, like. I'm gasping for a tab but I was shaking too much to do a rollie in the flat and now me hands are full with the carriers in one and a kiddie's plastic spade that was lying in the airing cupboard of the flat in the other.

I walk out through the estate and across the bridge over the dual carriageway. It's late so there's not many cars passing under us.

There's tears on me cheeks and I'm cold. Motorways at night always make us feel sad and lonely at the best of times. And now we're back in the worst of times.

Over the other side I gan past the Kingdom Hall where the Jehovah's worship and around the side of the building and to the edge of the woods at the top end of the valley that drops down into town. The river's hiding down there somewhere; these are the banks me Dad stalked as a young man. Upstream a couple of miles is where the old site is. Was. I've not been back there since that day. That final day.

It's dark, but I've got a torch.

I don't walk far into the woods. Just a couple of hundred yards. Once I've gone deep enough and stood for a minute making sure there's nee-one about, and I'm not on any footpath that's likely to be disturbed come the morning, I get to digging a shallow hole with the plastic spade. The ground is hard and dry but once I've cracked the surface it starts to come away in clumps and after about twenty minutes there's just enough space to put the parts of the puppy in. My puppy. Little Coughdrop.

And I'm thinking, it's my fault. My fault this happened. He was my responsibility and now look at him. All broken up in a bag. It's not right, this. It's not right at all.

Them cunts are going to pay for this, I think. Ten-fold, like.

I put Coughdrop in the hole and then I scrape the dirt back over with the spade but it seems to take ages, and it feels stupid, so I start to use my feet, and I kick the dirt back into place more and more vigorously and then I flatten it down a bit. There's more tears silently streaming down me face. I feel like mebbes I should say summat but there's nowt to say, and nee-one to say it to. Little Coughdrop. Me Man Friday. He cannot hear us now.

So I just stand there for a minute, then I roll a tab and sit there smoking it in the dark, tears and clart streaks on me cheeks and I know it'll soon be light and though I know I'm going to have to do summat, I don't want the morrow to come.

*

It was a hazy summer's evening when they finally reached a pub called The Swan With Two Necks that sat in a clearing in a wood in deepest Wales.

Barker turned into a tight lane that led alongside it to a space that was neither car park nor scrubland.

A couple of transit vans were already there. Beside them men milled around drinking cans of beer and smoking.

"Look at these fucking woolly-backs," said Mac, whistling through his teeth.

"Stay here and don't get out of the car."

Barker got out and went and spoke to them. The men turned and glanced at your Dad hunched in the front seat, nervously smoking a cigarette. A halo of flies circled in the air outside his open window. Then the men all laughed.

Barker walked back to the car and re-started the engine. The men climbed into the two Transits and pulled out. Mac and Barker followed close behind.

"What were youse all laughing at?"

"Just some joke. Nowt for you to worry about."

It was a balmy evening. The sky was pink with the last traces of light, the sun's residue smeared thinly across clouds that were scudding along at a fair clip, like the last sheep being corralled into a stone fold for the night.

From a side lane a small car pulled out and joined the convoy behind them. Mac looked in the mirror and saw three bearded men in it. It felt presidential. Or mebbe funereal.

Your Dad was nervous. He wasn't used to fighting this late. Most of his organised bouts took place just after dawn, as was the gypsy way. But, as he always said, a true warrior should be ready to fight at any time of the day.

"Which one is Pike?" he asked.

"None of them. Pike's up at the quarry already."

"Have you got owt to drink?"

"No."

They drove for twenty minutes down a winding track barely wider than the car, riding rough through puddles and pot-holes. The trees formed a tunnel. A darkening green tunnel that closed in around them.

"Are you sure you've got nowt to drink?"

Then the trees ended and they were in a clearing, where there were more cars and more men. The headlights of the cars were turned on low to cast beams of light into a large, man-made hollow in the centre of the quarry, long since abandoned. Saplings had been planted around it that had now grown to three or four storeys in height, obscuring the quarry from the outside world. Hewn rock lined its sides. Only the sky offered an exit.

Barker turned off the engine.

"Right listen up, lad. This Pike one'll try and rattle you early on but if you stay on your feet you can take this fucking Mammoth. Mind, he's a git big lummock so you'll need to put him down so that he stays down."

"Where is he?" said your Dad. He was distracted. The adrenaline that usually fuelled him before a fight wasn't there. He felt uptight and unnerved.

"In a minute. Let us do your hands first."

They got out the car and stayed in the shadows. Mac pulled off his sweater then bent and stretched and threw a few jabs. His joints clicked and cracked. After hours cramped in the car he was nowhere near warm enough. He swung his arms wide to loosen his shoulders then shook the tension out of his hands. He rolled his neck and threw more jabs. The men glanced over.

"Alright?"

"I don't feel radged enough, Barker."

"Well pretend then. Pretend he's fucked your mother or diddled one of the kiddies. Owt like that. Pretend you've walked in on him with his cock up your mother's arse, and he's grinning at you."

"I don't even know which one I'm fighting though. I need to know the face I'm going to tear open."

215

Barker pulled out a roll of tape which he carefully bound around Mac's clenched fists.

"You'll see him in a minute. How's that?"

Mac just grunted.

"You might want to lose your T-shirt an all. Less to grab on to."

He peeled it off and tossed it through the open window of the car.

"Ready?"

"Have I got time for a tab?"

"No. Ready?"

"No."

"Let's go."

*

I've had a bit of sleep – not much but enough to get us thinking a bit clearer – and I've tried to clean up the stain on the carpet and get rid of the smell that's in the living room: a mixture of shit and blood or summat. Runny shit and puppy blood. Its the smell of the inside of a little dog that's never done owt to anyone except be unlucky enough to end up in the care of the cursed John-John Wisdom.

There's flies in the room. They're manically tracing invisible shapes in the air above the stain that's all that remains of Coughdrop.

Them bastards. Them povvy fugging *bastards.*

They're dead meat, I'm thinking. All of them. I swear down.

Because despite everything I've said – despite the years away and the anger management and the psychologists and the probation meetings and all that cack – despite all that, I still want to do them cunts. Because in a moment like this I cannot help but revert to being a Wisdom; that auld bad blood is pumping and coursing and I want them to fear me. It seems like a taste for vengeance is my only inheritance. It's funny how years of learning can just slip away in a second. Not funny ha ha. Just funny mental. It's like reason can never beat violence.

216

Violence always pushes through, like a weed through concrete. You only have to watch the daily news to see that.

I have to take it slowly though. Not rush into owt. Keep me head.

I'm up and about dead early mulling things over and two things are obvious. One: they know where I live and they'll not leave us alone. That's guaranteed. For not knocking out gear. For the fight. For being a gypsy. And mebbes for fucking Maria an all. Two: summat has to be done. A pre-emptive strike.

So I'm in town for just after the shops open, and I gan straight to the Army & Navy to buy a green kit bag and some other bits and pieces. I get mesel a knife. Then I pick up a pencil thin Maglite, a length of rope and fold-up tarpaulin. I sort a new lock for the door and pick up some scran from the supermarket on Silver Street, some bread and tinned stuff and that, and some fresh baccy, then leave town before it gets busy.

The flat still stinks so I scrub the carpet some more. I give the kitchen, bedroom and living room the once over and I bunch up a load of stuff into bin bags ready to be hoyed out. Parole papers, empty pop tins, jam jars used for ash trays, some auld clothes that I'll not be needing. Just hods of crap. I cannot be leaving the place like a tip when I'm gone. Tidying up like this makes us think of me Ma. How she always kept the van spick and span, and then me Dad would come along and mess it up out of spite and boredom.

After I've put the mop and bucket away I sit down in my armchair and scarf down a sandwich and a brew, then have a tab while looking out the window across the top of the flats opposite over to where the dual carriageway is, and past that to the woods, where me dog's still warm in the ground. I feel sick just thinking about him.

He never stood a chance.

As I'm smoking, one thought runs through me mind: how did they know? How did they know where I'm living when I've barely told nee fucker?

It's pretty quiet for a bit, and then I can hear kiddies playing. Screams and laughter. I gan into my bedroom and fold away my mattress. Take the rubbish out. I pause down in the street and look around at this shite hole they've put us in. I'll not miss it.

I drift off for a bit thinking about how that Robinson Crusoe gadgie didn't have it so bad. Me, I'd bloody love to be stuck on a desert island with nowt but crabs and coconuts for company. Man Friday for a bit of a blether when you want it, but mainly it's just you and your sunburn. No hassles. No parole officers on your back, no boss gannin on about the bloody route, no loose lasses messing with your head, no *Nazis* after you. Bloody lovely. Being stuck out there in a floating green cathedral can't have been so bad. It sounds like heaven to me.

I get me bag, give the flat one final look over then lock up. I stick the keys through the letterbox. Good bloody riddance if you ask me.

I head through the estate and over the bridge. The sun's proper blazing now and it's going to be a rare old English day; one to remember I reckon.

I go down to the Jehovah's church. It's a funny looking place. New, like. Too new to be a church really, but they've got to be built sometime I suppose.

I go round the side and over the fence into the thicket at the edge of the wood. I'm only a couple of hundred yards away from Coughdrop but I can't think about him now, mind. Instead I stick me bag down, cover it up with foliage, then hop back ower the fence and gan back the way I came. In me pocket I've got me baccy, knife, lighter and some money.

There's this bank alongside the dual carriageway. A grass verge with bushes at the top. I walk along it, behind the bushes so that the cars that are whizzing by at seventy mile an hour divvent see us. If I walk along here for a mile, then cut in past the top end of my estate and walk for another mile or so across the industrial estate and the playing fields and past the new

Tesco, it's the best way up to the Nook without having to get on a bus or pass too many people. Hardly anyone'll see us this way.

I walk quickly, a tab jammed between me lips, puffing away and thinking about what them povvy bastards did and how that Bannon couldn't accept a sporting defeat, and how stupid I am for even thinking such a thing exists.

I'm thinking about his lips on Maria's lips, and how she looked when she spoke about him; thinking about how they couldn't just leave it. About how nee-one can ever just leave it.

And I'm thinking about how there's only one person who could have telt Banny and his mates where I live. One lass.

And that's the hardest part to think about.

*

There were two dozen men or more down in the quarry.

They were wild men with thick forearms and scowls, mossy hair and brown teeth. Men with sunken eyes and flattened faces. They were creatures who carried the dark secrets of their valley; they were judge, jury and executioners of their domain. The true rulers of this dark, dank kingdom.

Mac and Barker climbed down a precarious set of makeshift steps, blasted into the side of the rock decades earlier. Hand over foot into a hole in the ground in the wood in the mountains.

A large bare-chested figure stepped out the darkness into the light of the car beams.

A mountainous-looking man. Cliff Pike. He was as tall as Mac, but squarer and with an upper body that seemed out of proportion with his legs. He had a shaggy mop of red hair and a thick untrimmed beard that covered his neck and chin and gave him a wild appearance. Animalistic. Elemental. He smiled.

Beneath the beard and hair, your Dad could see that this Pike one had a flattened face, as if he'd been smacked squarely with a spade. His cheekbones ran down to petulant lips and his eyes were set deep and protected by the scar tissue that had hardened and knotted across his brow.

Mac broke the silence. His nerves compelled him to go on the attack. That was his way.

"You reckon you're the best do you?" he shouted, rolling his neck and walking towards Pike.

A chuckle of disbelief rippled through the gathered men.

"You've got some balls coming here gyppo," said Pike in an accent as thick and bitter as valleys' poteen.

"Speak up you Welsh cunt."

"Watch yoursel," hissed Barker, "Don't forget where you are."

"I hope you've got life insurance," said Pike.

"Fuck off, I'm Mac Wisdom, the best of the travellers and therefore the best in Britain. And I've never even heard of you, you dirty fucking sheep shagging prick."

The air within the quarry changed at this. It tightened. The light was fading but the beams from the cars gave the chiselled-out hole a strange atmosphere. It felt to Mac as if he were standing in a mass open grave. His vision went blurred for a second. The whole wood was humming in his ears like a lone pylon on a hill-side. He wanted this over. He wanted it ended. Cliff Pike said nothing. The men said nothing.

Barker stepped between them.

"Now listen lads," he said, but as he did Mac swung a punch which missed Pike's chin by the stub of a whisker.

Barker ducked out the way and the fight was on, as Pike returned with a punch that did scuff the side of Mac's head. It was enough to wrong-foot him. His centre shifted and his weight was distributed all wrong.

When they came together in a clinch there was no grace or artistry, just desperation and brutality. They grabbed for one another. Two desperate men entangled. Mac could smell Pike. Summat stale. Stale and sweet, like rotten maggoty meat or cream gone sour at the bottom of the churn. Pike could smell Mac. Cigarettes and fear. A fear for his life.

The volume amongst the men grew as they hurriedly placed bets with one another and with Barker, most of them favouring the local man.

"Give us a ton on auld Cliffy-boy."

"This Geordie gyppo needs learning."

"There'll be blood."

"There'll be a bloody murder."

They pulled apart and traded punches for a minute or two then Pike smashed his fist dead on to the bridge of your Dad's nose and followed through with a head butt that connected just above his left eye. Pike's skull felt as hard and cold as the half-quarried seam of stone that held them. Mac's ears screamed and rang and he swung wildly, but Pike punched him deftly in the solar plexus. Mac doubled over as the wind was sucked out of the vacuum that had opened up below his rib cage. He had never known pain like it before. A ball of it sat inside of him, stopped his breathing. Compared to this every fight until now had felt like a walk in the park. And he might as well have been out sniffing daisies for the past six months, the shape he was in. Desperate panic seized him. He was on the back foot.

Pike went to knee him in the face but Mac saw it coming. He felt pain like a hot poker being shoved down his tightened throat, took a side-step and grabbed for Pike's cock and balls.

He found them held firm in Pike's tight jeans and they felt full in his hand. He squeezed hard. He grabbed at whatever his fingers found and squeezed again, pretended it was mutton for his pot, and squeezed a third time, harder, until Pike made a noise like a wounded animal. Mac pulled and twisted until he felt something give, then pop. Pike howled. It was a noise to shatter glass.

"The dirty cunt's got his bleeding knackers," said a voice close by.

Only fear pushed Mac forward now. This had gone beyond a stand-up scrap and had crossed over into summat else. It was gladiatorial. It had to be ended quick. He knew that.

You don't shake hands after a fight like this. Only one walks away.

The blood drained from Pike's face as Mac let go of his crushed ball sac and straightened up. Everything was reverberating and he was breathing in strangulated, syncopated gulps. He managed to throw two head-shots then grabbed his opponent by the beard and pulled him forward to knee him. Pike was hyperventilating. He groaned and fell forward, jamming a thumb in Mac's right eye as he did so. Pain seared through his skull. There was a yanking, ripping sound. He felt fingers being forced into his mouth and his cheek being peeled back from his face. He heard something tear, the sound of trousers ripping, only it was flesh. In desperation Mac did grab for Pike's junk again. Grabbed for anything. To pull and twist and mangle.

But Mac's legs had gone. The earth-line tilted and everything slowed down to a series of fragmented images. He saw the men round him and the quarry stones beneath him and Cliff Pike retching and heaving with pain. He saw it as if he were looking through water. He fell like a brick through treacle, feeling nothing.

As he slumped to the ground his sound and vision in his good eye became crisp and clear, and then the whistling and wailing in his ears became even louder. His head was a bell and his brain was the clapper. Your Dad's head was that twenty-eight hundred weight brass bell up in the rafters of the top tower of the cathedral, and now it was being rung by the feet of strangers.

His head was wet and so was his cheek. There was summat on it that shouldn't be there. A pendulous mess.

Some of the men saw. Between the blows they saw Mac's eyeball dangling on pink tendrils, then summat cold and hard and blunt hit him from behind and boots and fists rained down upon him.

A muffle of breathless voices came through the ringing and roaring in his ears. Hillbilly voices from the throats of mountain men. Excitable grunts. Sexual grunts. Gurgles of pleasure. The music of the pack feeding. They were wild hungry beasts setting upon their prey. They fought each other to get at him.

"Get the English cunt."

Blood slipped down the back of Mac's throat. It was viscous and thick, the taste of copper. His breath was still trapped in his windpipe and his cheek was hanging from his face like comedy glasses.

Then he was on his front and the pain was unfathomable, too real to make sense of as blunt instruments hit him on his elbows, knees, chest. Bolts and jolts. Boots stamped on his fingers. Cracks and spasms. Where was Barker? Fingers found their way into his mouth again, his eyes. His cheek was wrenched back again. A flap hanging in the dirt now. A belt buckle whipped the back of his head. Yet still more punches came as one thought echoed.

Where was Barker?

His trousers did come loose and they were being pulled down around his knees. He lost a shoe. The eyeball dangled and the quarry echoed to the sound of something primal and awful there deep in the woods. There was no shouting now, just the sound of men expending energy.

His body became a limp thing made of string and feathers and egg shells.

Mac was buried at the bottom of a landslide now. An avalanche of pain. All colour drained from the world and he felt himself slipping away. He was certain now that he was going to die. He was reduced to a tiny speck of light far, far away from everything and everyone and the loneliness he felt was even worse than the physical punishment being meted out to him.

Then he stopped feeling anything.

Then things were never the same for any of us again.

*

Part III
In The Topsoil

I'm up on the Nook and the light is changing. Pink fingers are starting to creep across the sky in the far distance. I reckon there'll be a sunset like you see in the fillums in a bit. It's all beautiful; too beautiful for a night like this.

I've skirted right round the perimeter of the Nook. I've gone the long way round through the woods and the places they call the Scrubs, the no man's land of brambles and hidden corners and motorbike tracks. I've been peering over fences into back gardens with Rottweilers and broken motorbikes in them, and checking out all the alleyways and ginnels that lead back out here and seeing which roads are dead ends and what links up to where. Memorising the entrances and exits. Doing a reccy. Making a memory map.

After I've laid low in the bushes deep in the Scrubs for a while it's evening and the sky is still changing. Them pink fingers have turned orange, like someone's set fire to a cloud. Sky arson and that.

I smoke some tabs, scrat me balls and think about what I'm going to do.

I decide to leave the Scrubs and go round the back of the estate again where I count the houses until I find the one I'm looking for. The one where they hang out smoking their tack, dealing their powders and banging young lasses. It's not hard to find – I just have to follow the crappy rave music. The bleeps and beats and squeaky voices of the Toytown rubbish. *Doof doof doof.* Christ. What a din. Nee wonder they're all on the gear. You'd need summat.

I go to the back fence and take a peek. There's nee curtains on any of the winders. Upstairs some of the glass has been put through and is covered with cardboard. It's not that late but there's people all over the shop and they're all getting mortal. There's a big black burnt patch where a back lawn used to be.

I crouch down in the grass and sit for a while, watching the house through a knot hole in the fence. After a while someone comes out into the back garden with nee top on and a bottle of orange 20/20 in his hand. It's one of the povvy bastards. I don't know his name. He walks towards us. He's got a crappy Union Jack flag tatt on his arm. Proper sketchy. He walks down to the end of the garden. He stops and gets his cock out his trackie bottoms and has a long piss on the other side of the fence. He waves it about and sprays piss everywhere. I'm so close I can smell it. It's a bit like Sugar Puffs. He has another slug from the 20/20 and slowly walks back to the house, stopping to hoof a flat football up against the back door. Then he gans back in.

The sun is proper going down now, and it's getting darker and colder and I want to have a tab but I don't. I just sit there in the grass, watching the house through the hole.

The doorbell keeps ringing and people keep coming and going.

I see Bannon at the kitchen window and he's laughing and talking to someone I can't see. Then he disappears. Then I see Maria and she's not laughing. She's stood at the kitchen sink looking out into garden. She's looking right at us. Dead-eyed. Right at the piss-drenched fence. She doesn't see us though. She can't.

Then Bannon is back and he's stood behind her with his arms round her waist and he's either kissing her neck or whispering summat into her ear, but she squirms and pushes him away. Then he grabs her arse from behind, and they both disappear, and I'm wishing I'd properly brayed this twat instead of just giving him a bloody nose.

And I can hear me Dad going: *Aye you should have put him in hospital while you had a chance you soft little shite.*

It gets darker and the party carries on. My legs start to cramp and though it's getting nippy I'm as warm as toast in my combat jacket and even though it's August I put a beanie on because everybody knows that's where you lose most of your body heat.

All of Banny's lot are in there and other people I don't recognise. They're downstairs, all properly hammered, shouting and hoying stuff about. They've got some povvy disco lights in there that are flashing on and off and Maria was right about them being *Nazis* because there's a tatty whatsit on the wall. Aye. A swastika.

A light goes on upstairs in one of the bedrooms. There's two lads and a lass.

The lads are in their late teens but the lass looks proper young. Thirteen or summat. Mebbes less. It's hard to tell. The house is too povvy for curtains so I can see the scene like I'm watching it on a big telly.

The young lass looks like she's half asleep or has mistaken the pills for smarties when one of the lads says summat and gives her a gentle shove from behind. She stumbles forward.

She's wearing a boob tube that's not really got any boobs in it. Too young to be in bedrooms with bigger boys.

I'm thinking about Charmaine at her age.

The lads are sort of facing each other when one of them raises his voice at the lass, then she disappears out of sight, on her knees. The lads are talking to each other, then one of them drops his crackers, tilts his head back and gets a hand around the top of what must be the young lass's head, then starts shoving it back and forward.

And I'm thinking about Charmaine.

He's stood there with his chest out, all proud, his other hand clenched into a curled fist by his hip. I want to smack the pride right off his face. Turn his nose sideways.

Then he grabs her with both hands and goes at her harder.

226

She's too young, I'm thinking. She's too young, you cunts. She should be at home playing Barbie. Or she should be in bed asleep.

The other lad just sort of stands there for a couple of minutes, watching and grinning like a gormless dickhead. Then he gets his cock out and begins to have a wank right where he's stood. He's tugging at his skinny bit of string and he's glegging at the other lad, and they exchange the odd word and laugh, but mainly their faces are serious, as they concentrate on what I cannot – and don't want to – see.

The lad getting the nosh starts jerking about. He hunches over some more and is slamming her face like a demon, and I'm feeling proper sick, and have to force meself not to stand and throw the nearest rock at his paedo head.

And I'm still thinking about Charmaine.

After a bit the lad steps back and the girl stands up. She's wobbly on her legs as she wipes her mouth. I reckon she's mebbes been spiked or summat. She's all floppy, like a puppet that's had its strings cut.

She just stands for a minute then one of the lads says summat to her and backhands her hard. I don't hear it, but I feel it.

She stands with her hand to her cheek. He pushes her forward so that she's bent double and starts fucking her.

Christ, I'm thinking. What happened to holding hands?

The first lad, the one who's been grinning and wanking, says summat threatening to the lass and then she starts sucking him off while she's getting done from behind.

Fucksake I'm thinking. Fucksake.

I look away.

When I turn back the young lass is still spitroasted on their grubby charver cocks. The one doing the banging starts slapping her arse then pulls her hair.

The one getting the noshing responds by slapping her face. I turn away again and look deep into the darkness of the Scrubs, the bile rising, me throat tightening and everything flooding back as the girl's face is replaced by Charmaine's and tears well up then wet me cheeks, and all the while downstairs people are partying and the music is still playing in search of a melody that seems forever just out of reach.

*

Everything was different. It was as if your Dad had been broken down and then put back together but there were parts missing. Vital parts. Summat had broken deep, deep inside.

They kept him in for five months. Them mountain men had broken his fingers and one of his legs. They'd fractured his skull and knocked out ten teeth. They'd broke his nose and his jaw and tore his cheek half off, and it took wiring, thirty-odd stitches and sucking melted ice cream through a straw for weeks to set it right again.

They had cracked his ribs and smashed his elbows. They'd bitten off an ear lobe and broken an ankle. They'd near destroyed one of his kidneys and ruptured his testicles so that he pissed blood for weeks. He dropped from fourteen stone to ten.

And they'd near gouged out one of his eyes. In time they'd make him a false one to fill the gap it left, but for now it were a black hole with a bandage over it. Then he took to wearing a patch.

But he had lost a lot more than blood and an eye – he had lost his heart. It was still beating, inside him, but it was a hollow thing. It was empty. His spirit was smashed and it was like his blood had been replaced with pond water and no matter how many plaster casts or poultices they applied, or drips and needles they inserted, that old Mac was broken.

That Mac was gone now.

*

Them charvers treating that young lass like that have got us too riled to sit still any longer.

228

There's not much I can do sat with me eye to the knot-hole and me legs seizing up with cramp anyway, so I stand up and skirt back round the edge of the estate, down an alley and into the street where the party house is. It's proper dark now but I'm still making sure I skulk in the long shadows cast by the hedges and fences.

There's another alleyway a few houses along from the party and at the other side of the alley there's one of them little power sub-stations where they store the electricity and that, so I bunk up the fence, slide onto the roof of it then press mesel down flat.

The sub-station is quietly humming.

Though the roof is gravelly and bits of it dig into me legs and chest, the sound of the electricity is soothing. From up here I can see the front of the house an all. I lie flat for a bit and suddenly feel tired. The humming from below us and the roof that's still warm from the day's sun makes us drowsy.

It's about one in the morning when there's shouting and a door slamming and I'm looking up at the house. I think mebbes I've nodded off for a bit.

A couple of the lads I don't recognise come out of the house and head off in the opposite direction from us.

I get me knife out and fold the blade out. Then I think, no. Put it away you daft knacker. Nee knives.

Knives make us as bad as them. Knives are what done our Coughdrop.

I close it and put it back in me pocket.

A couple of minutes later the numpty I saw taking a piss earlier on comes out all wobbly on his jelly legs. I recognise him as the lad who was egging Bannon on to bray us at the fairground the other night. Shotter, I think he was called.

He walks down the garden and turns along the road towards us. I ready mesel. Then he turns right into the alleyway where I'm at. When he's as close as he'll get, I push mesel up like I'm doing a press-up or summat and as I do he hears me feet on the gravel and he looks up, but all he sees is a shape against the sky, and suddenly I'm jumping down like bloody Batman or summat, and I'm on him like a nightmare and he's proper shitting himsel, the soft twat. He doesn't know what the bally-hoo is happening.

I don't smack him though. Na. Instead I just get him up against the wall, my forearm across his throat and a fist pressed into that soft bit below his rib, knuckle-first. It's a power point move some lad showed us inside. He's bigger than us like they always are, but I've got the element of surprise on me side, and anger an all. Proper brooding, boiling, quiet anger. And Wisdom blood.

Then he sees it's me, he recognises us, and he's not sure whether he should be scared or relieved because to him I'm just some wee loner streak of piss ice cream lad, but on the other hand I'm the same wee loner streak of piss ice cream lad who just panelled his supposed hard lad of a marrer, the cock of the midden, and now I've got him pinned to the bricks like a bloody lab rat.

It wasn't me he blurts, straight out, the silly twat. He practically shouts it before I've even said owt to him.

What wasn't you?

Eh, he says, confused. Eh? Nowt.

Yes it was, I say anyway. It was you.

It wasn't. Swear down.

Aye it was.

I shove me forearm tighter across his throat.

It wasn't, man.

You killed me dog. You killed our Coughdrop and now I'm going to kill you the same way.

Howay, leave us man. It wasn't me. I've never touched that dog.

I move my hand from his solar plexus and put a pinch on him, right at the bottom of his neck.

Aye-az, he howls, but quietly like because even to make a noise hurts too. That's why the crab is so effective.

You were there though, I spit. You touched the door handle of me flat. You touched me carpet. You were in my room. You breathed my air without my permission. Didn't you?

His eyes widen. They're blood shot. He reeks of spliff so I reckon he's probably getting proper para now.

Divvent lie because I saw you, I say. *I saw you.*

I'm lying of course, but he's as good as admitted it already.

He forced us, he says, the little grass.

Who?

Eh? Nee-one, man.

He's squirming but not very well. I tighten the crab claw and his red eyes start watering. I've got him with two fingers. Two fingers and a forearm are all it takes.

I'm going to have to do what ye did to that little puppy.

Nor. Aw, howay man. Howay, he gurgles.

I'm afraid I have to, I say all friendly. I'd feel bad if I didn't yer nar?

Nor man. Howay man.

Tell us who did it then, I say. *Tell us,* I gan, even though I know exactly who did it. I just want to hear his name. Tell us and I'll not spill your guts on this pavement.

He says nowt.

I tighten the neck claw and go, You've got three seconds before I gouge your eyeball out with me house keys, you cunt.

Banny done it, he says straight away.

I feel like laughing it's so easy. But I don't laugh. I keep a straight face and I keep it close up to his. All me body weight is pushed up against his as I lean in.

Was it long?

Eh?

Did it take a long time?

How do you mean?

Killing our Coughdrop. The dog. Was it quick?

Oh aye. He was out of it.

What do you mean?

231

He says nowt to this so I bite his cheek hard. He cries out from the pain and the shock.

Nor man. *Nor.* It was dead quick like.

He's lying. I know he his. Turning a dog inside out cannot be done quickly.

How did you find us?

What?

How did you find where I live?

I dinnar man. Honest. Looker, I've got nee problem with you. You know what he's like, man. He's a fucking headcase.

And you're one of them *Nazis* an all aren't you, I go. Want to see me and my lot dead and that do you?

Eh? he goes, and the way he says it I reckon he genuinely doesn't know what I'm gannin on about now.

You know, I say. The swastika bollocks and that. Fucking loser.

He just blinks his red eyes.

How did you find us, I say again.

I dinnar.

Was it the lass?

What lass?

You know which lass.

I divvent.

Yeah you do. Maria.

He hesitates and shrinks in his clothes, but I tighten the pinch and he straightens up in pain again.

Aye, mebbes. I dinnar. Banny's shagging her so I reckon it was her. Aye. Aye mebbes.

Why's he after us?

I dinnar, he says in a voice that sounds like he's trying to get pally with us or summat. Like he thinks the worst is over.

You know what he's like, he says.

No, I say. No, I don't.

His face is pissing us off now so as I say this I let go of this fool, pull back and lamp him in the mouth. It's a quick fast jab

that splits his bottom lip right down the middle. There's blood.
He looks shocked. Then I put another pinch on him. Tighter.

Aw – fucking hell, man.

Reet. One more time, why's he after us?

Cos he doesn't like you, does he.

Why?

Just cos, man.

Why?

Cos you're a –

A what?

Howay man, he pleads.

Say it.

You're a pikey.

So?

He hates pikeys.

Why?

Just cos.

Why? Cos you're all a bunch of *Nazis*.

I dinnar. You know what him and his brothers and his fatha
and that are like. Cos.

Cos what.

Cos he reckons you're a bunch of thieves that live like
animals. Reckons you're not properly English and that.

What else?

Eh?

Why else is he after us.

I dinnar man. You'd have to ask him. Summat about dealing
gear and that. I dinnar, man.

I get in this lad's face and it feels weird because though my
eyes are only up to his chin and there's blood on it from his
bottom lip which is torn in two parts, and I say if he knew
owt about us he'd know why I spent years inside. He'd know
about the Wisdoms. He'd know about me Dad. He'd know
about everything I done and he'd think his upbringing was like
a Butlins bloody holiday compared to mine. He'd know I had

233

me cock in his lass yesterday. And he'd know that he's not going to get away with this.

How man, he says. She's up the duff yer nar.

What?

Maria.

This gives us a jolt like when you jump in an ice cold stream or summat. A proper shudder.

What about her?

She's carrying his bairn.

How do you know?

Everyone knows man, he says.

I release the pressure point and put together a quick combination. One, two, three punches. I belt him round the bonce down here in this dark alley. This pissdribbling dog killer. He doesn't even fight back, the soft get. He just sort of stands there all floppy, taking it like a punchbag and looking like he's going to blub or summat. The povvy bloody brimson. I kick his legs away and he's down on the floor, a stoned sack of shite that helped kill my little Coughdrop. I give him a final boot and go, Here, this is for what ye done to me dog.

As he lies there stunned and groaning I take my cock out and piss all ower him. I've been needing to gan for ages so there's loads of it. He starts thrashing about and shouting – Ah, howay man – and he tries to get up but I boot him in the ribs as the piss keeps coming. Hods of hot stinking salty piss. There's so much of it I surprise mesel and I should be laughing but I'm not, because pissing on someone's just never been an ambition of mine. What I mean is I don't feel particularly good about it, but like the gadgie says, I've started so I'll finish.

I make sure he's properly doused then I shake off and zip up.

And this is for what ye done to me cat.

What fucking cat? he says, genuinely surprised.

I gob on him and boot him again.

Tell him I'm coming, I say and then I'm gone.

Down the alley, round the back, off into the darkness of the Scrubs.

*

Jimmy Buckle picked your Dad up and drove him back to his land up past Luton, while me and the bairns stopped on a site near the hospital. Buckle's eighteen year old nephew Little Tater stayed there to watch over us. According to Jim, Barker Lovell emerged unscathed from the woods. Not even the scratch of a pine needle. Now how do you fathom that?

Big Slice also said the word on the vine was that Barker had bet against Mac that night. He'd arranged the fight and set the odds then he had dropped a bundle on Pike, who he already knew to have killed men in death fights.

And if he believed that he would lose to Cliff Pike, then there were things he knew that Barker had not told him about. Like how Pike and his lot hated travellers and hated the English and especially hated English travellers, and how in setting things up his old friend and trainer had handed him a death sentence and it was only by sheer luck or the grace of God that your Dad did emerge from that quarry alive.

That was all Mac needed to know: Barker had bet against him. He knew that if he ever saw Lovell again he'd have to kill him. But he also knew that he didn't have that in him any more. That thing – that burning violence – was gone. The flames had been put out and his blood had cooled. Mac had been tamed.

*

Obviously they'll all be after us. There's nee doubt about that.

Because I know how this works. They'll come after us like pack animals. Half the bloody Nook lot. They'll come after us and they'll keep coming until they've done what they need to do to prove whatever it is they need to prove. It's the same bloody thing that sent me Dad to madness: senseless bloody violence. I've seen it a hundred times ower. And it leads neewhere.

At least I know some people who'll help us out of this spot. People who understand; who never gan on the back foot neither. People who'll put us up for the night, nee questions. Those showfolk. Barker and Ned. Me new marrers.

So let them come.

It's only a mile or so round the back way, across the scrublands, through the trees and over the hill where Nook lads ride their nicked motorbikes down to the river. It's not long before I'm crossing the water by the bridge down near the old swimming baths and heading straight along the path, past the kiddies play area and the bogs where the willy watchers used to hang out, and up to the race course. I walk the tow-path quickly, smoking a tab and feeling a bit jittery.

They'll know by now. He'll have gone back to the party – Shotter – and he'll have telt them what just happened, only he'll edit out some of it out. Of course he will. He'll not mention he took a beating, he'll just say summat about getting attacked from behind and how he got in some good punches before I took off crying and screaming like a jessie. They'll be wondering why he stinks of piss of course, but he'll have some story. He'll say I hoyed a can of it over him as I ran off or summat; owt to make it a little less humiliating for him. And he'll be saying things I never said an all. Things about them, and their mothers too. Dirty things. Nasty, vile things.

It was that gyppo cunt, he'll say.

And if he's not thinking straight or if he reckons he's not getting enough sympathy or the party is too swinging for anyone to get their charver arses in gear, mebbes he'll blurt out summat like: *here, he reckons he shagged Maria an all.*

And they'll all be getting radged now. Proper radged. They'll turn the shitty music off and they'll all be stood up and getting vexed, puffing their chests out and draining their cans, trying to out-man each other with their threats, making out like I'm summat I'm not, summat that needs to be crushed. And there'll be that young lass upstairs sore and sobbing, and gods knows what else going on.

And they'll get Maria. They'll grab her and mebbes she'll say nowt or mebbes she will, but then they'll get her phone. Aye, they'll get her phone and they'll go through the photos and they'll see me with a sloppy grin on me face, all blissed out in the green cathedral.

So now they'll all be getting tooled up. Knives and coshes and that, even though there's only me. And even though they started this.

They started this.

So let them come.

The party'll be turning into something else now. The mood will have turned. Banny will go and get his brothers, the mini-Hitlers. Mebbes he'll tell them that the stinking little gyppo get that works for Arty Vicari, the one that won't knock out gear on the Nook for them and doesn't send any tax their way, the one that's been shagging his Maria, his pregnant Maria, that gimp with the git big ears that dresses like a bloody soldier, the one that's done time, the lad that thinks he can come up on the estate and do what he bloody well wants, is proper asking for it now and is definitely in need of a lesson or two from the lads.

Mebbes the older Bannons, the ones that burnt that Indian lad, the ones with swords and flags on their wall, mebbes they'll be going, aye, that sounds like a laugh, lets go and batter the little scrote.

Aye. It'll be snowballing. They'll all be united in this shared goal. They'll feel good. They'll bond over this.

Let them come. Let them all come.

The field is empty.

There's the odd bit of litter and there are patches where the grass is lighter and more bleached-out looking, but other than that you'd not even know the funfair had been there.

You'd not know that it was only the night before last that the field had been full of screams and noise and laughter.

The rides have been broken down and packed up and carted off to the next site. There's nee-one about now, not a soul; especially not that Barker Lovell gadgie and his son Ned. Them that know about pride, and what it means to be born into a situation that's bigger than you and your life, summat deep-rooted and far-reaching.

Growing up all that gypsy pride shite seemed like a load of nonsense that me Dad spouted when he was pissed. It's only now that I'm beginning to see why this stuff might matter; why travellers feel the need to stand up tall.

Because a world without travellers is a world without freedom.

They were a bit of good luck just when I needed it, them two. Allies. But now it's like they never even existed. Like they were ghosts from another time or summat.

And right now I'm back to looking out for mesel.

I'm not sure what to do so I turn back and head into town. It must be late because the only people about are the odd student and swaying pisshead, and all the clubs are up the other end anyway.

There's a mini-cab circling. I wave it down and when he pulls ower I lean into his passenger side window.

Can you drop us off at The Kingdom Hall please marrer?

The Jehovah place?

Aye.

Hop in.

It only takes us five minutes to get up there – a three quid fare – but I give the gadge a fiver and say can you had on for a minute?

He looks at us funny.

I hope you're not up to owt dodgy, he says. I'll not be an accessory to owt, me. Just so you know.

Nor, it's nowt like that. But me Mam'll kill us if she knows I've been out drinking. I've just got to pick me stuff up from here. I'm meant to be stopping at me mates'. Had on a minute.

He just shakes his head and raises an eyebrow as if to say, aye right, hadaway and shite you lying little get you're probably out on the rob or summat, but he takes the money from us anyway and offers nee change.

I gan round the back of the hall and hop over the fence and into the darkness where I've stashed me gear, then am back to the car within a minute. Then I ask the taxi fella to take us up to the industrial estate.

He raises another eyebrow as if to ask why I'm wanting to gan up there at this time of night and what surprise is going to be waiting for him when we get there, but he has the sense to say nowt. Cabbies are good like that. They just want to make a bit of money and keep out of whatever is happening.

I can understand that.

After he's dropped us on the corner under a street light that's silently flickering on and off in a way that makes us feel totally empty and lonely inside for a few intense seconds, I wait until he's pulled away before I turn off into the industrial estate and walk down through the future world of steel and tarmac and silence until I come to Arty's lock-up.

If it were quiet in town it's graveyard dead here. Proper silent. Proper eerie. I'm not scared mind, because there's nowt to fear but your own company down here. It's when there's people about that you should be worried.

Aye. But I stick to the shadows anyway, just in case there happens to be any prying eyes about like, and then when I get to Arty's lock-up I crouch down and quietly open the shutters with the key he gave us. They rattle a bit, but not much, then I go straight to the van which is just where I left it. I start it up, let the engine tick over for a moment then reverse it out. As I do I hear a crunching sound. It sounds like when you stand on a snail. I put the handbrake on and get out.

There's a red Christmas bauble under me tyre, shattered and glinting. There's tiny shards of silver and red scattered about and it looks stunning in the moonlight, like a stash of uncut diamonds and rubies. It's funny how if you've got the right head on you it can be the cheapest things that look the most beautiful.

A girl's hair clip. A coke can. Broken glass.

The bauble must have rolled off one of the delivery trucks that drives the decorations out from the estate all year round. Standing there I'm a bit whatsit. Transfixed.

I close the lock-up and climb back into the van.

I'm knackered so I crack open a can of coke and scarf down half a Mars bar in a couple of bites then light up a tab and pull out into the darkest part of the night, that bit when everything goes into slow motion and sounds are amplified and all the little creatures come out from their hiding places.

*

They'd left him with a stutter and a limp and other things you couldn't see.

He needed help with everything. Tying his shoes.

Rolling a bine. Wiping his scut.

The rest of the time he just had to lie there on his bed in the van up at the Buckle site, staring out the window at the empty farm house and the piles of junk, too tired to seethe or swear vengeance. His bones and gums and limbs ached as his body tried to restore itself. And though they took his teeth and an eye, they couldn't take the blood that was roiling in his veins now. He was still alive – just.

Your Uncle Eddie visited in November and stopped for a week. He brought Pete Dimes with him and the pair swore vengeance on Mac's behalf. Your Dad was too dismantled to think about it. He tried to summon up the details they would need but all he knew was the quarry and the name Cliff Pike. Everything was mist in his memory, an agonising void.

And then winter was on the breeze and we needed to get back up north.

Finally when the frost had come and the trees were stripped of leaves, and the summer's bounty had been flattened by wind and rain and ice and Mac was well enough to walk unaided, we left.

Big Slice had Little Tater hitch up the trailer and drive us north.

Your Dad said nothing the whole way, his head leaning against the cool glass of the window as he watched the telegraph poles and the fields fly by, his one eye seeing England anew.

*

I don't feel bad about twocking Arty's van. Well, mebbes a bit bad because he did give us a job, but then again he has stitched us up over all this drug-selling stuff, so bollards to him. He knows I'm on probation and still he fed us to the Bannons and that lot. He must have known they'd be after us when I telt them I wasn't interested in getting involved in any of that shite. Silly twat.

I'm just thinking about getting away from here once and for all, and doing what needs to be done so that little Coughdrop can rest in pieces.

The roads are quiet and the van hums on the tarmac. The hedgerows slip by. I keep the radio turned off.

It's still the middle of night but over to the east, off towards the coast, the sky is already starting to crack with light. It's like a curtain is being drawn back an inch and the first chink of light is breaking through to offer the faintest suggestion of a new day dawning. It is the colour of hope. I've never lost hope, me. Hope and the glass eye are the only two things I've held on to these past few years.

Even at the worse of times like when the polis came and took us away that time when I were fifteen or when that judge sent us down or all them nights all alone, no marrers, no family and the odds stacked against us, I kept hope going. Because where there's a heartbeat, there's a hope.

I want to drive towards that strip of light, to chase it, but I'm headed in the other direction, inland towards the darkness but decide to give the town the body swerve in case I get a pull.

So I turn off and take the back roads. The B-roads. The hedgerow highways me Dad used to roam before the limp and madness limited his wanderings.

I tighten my hands on the wheel and light another tab and between drags I try a tune to keep mesel awake and my morale up, just like they do in the army – *Cha-cha-cha, livin' la vida loca* – but it's not the same with just the one of us singing it, and at this time of the day and in these circumstances it sounds like the saddest song ever sung.

So I shut it.

It feels good just to go where the road goes though. Just to let the white line lead us.

I pass through villages and hamlets I don't recognise. I'm in the land of the pit yackers now, driving past shitty little nowhere holes and big country estates. I see broken barns and lonely copses sat in the middle of vast empty fields; turf-topped slag heaps and quarry holes gaping like ugly mouths.

Road signs flash by in my beam and I see I'm heading east towards the sea after all, towards the rising sun and that little orange ray of hope.

There's fallow fields and flattened hills that once held all the carbonised riches of the county and the way it all levels out makes it easier to see the sky above because there's less to block it, less to crowd you in. It's more whatsit out this way. Aye – expansive. And between the spaces, more villages. Places that once offered new houses and jobs and pensions and that. They all had their own way of talking in these places too; a language you'd not even recognise ten miles down the road.

Not now though.

)

I cannot help but wonder where Maria is at and what she's up to this very second. I wonder if she knows about Coughdrop, and about what I done to that Shotter. I wonder if she's really going to have a bairn. I wonder if she's going to let this mess seep into another generation.

And I wonder if she telt them where I've been living.

I cannot allow mesel to believe that. Not yet.

Because even if she did, she's still the nicest, sweetest person I've ever met and the stupid thing is, even if she did set us up, the few times we've had together this summer still cancel out any shite I'm facing now.

*

He became another kind of animal.

He moved differently now. He spoke differently. Everything about him had changed. The rages became more intense.

A winter passed in convalescence eased into a spring of slow mobility. Your Dad stopped washing and eating and the weight fell off him even more. The stream of visitors who had passed through the van that Christmas soon tailed off. They couldn't handle seeing big Mac Wisdom sat in the dark, chewing his lips, spilling his tea, a stammering mess.

Only Eddie kept coming, squeezing a roll of fivers into me hand when he left. He got us a second van for the bairns' safety.

Spring became summer and one morning Mac left the van, blinking into the sunlight like the creature of hibernation that he had become. Nature brought him back, pulled him out into the fields and woods.

His movements did become slower. But he was volatile too. He could only be approached head-on. There was no sneaking up on Mac Wisdom. No surprises. Not after what had happened. No.

Because even after everything the violent burning had stayed alive in his blood, and it sat there in his veins, and when the time was right that blood would start pumping again, and it would spread to his limbs and his eyes and his mouth and flashes of the auld Mac would return. Then he'd be lashing out and punching and biting and kicking and smashing anything within reach – me and Charmaine and Bobby too. He'd grab them and yank them and punch them and shake them. He was a mad auld dog that had survived a kicking to bite anyone that came within an inch of him.

And that's what life became. Rage and rain and animals and mud and the sky and the paddock and the trees. Frosted winter mornings and hazy summer evenings. Hushed silences. Bubbling anger. The violence of Mac Wisdom.

*

Villages flash by through the gaps in the hedges as I carry on chasing the light towards the coast. More road signs tell of places I've heard of but never been, places where the Wisdom name is still known. Places I've avoided for that very reason.

South Hetton and Haswell.

Shotton and Thornley.

Wheatley Hill and Wingate.

Trimdon Foundry.

And then I've crossed the A19 and am passing round the outskirts of Peterlee where I see a milk cart clinking in the dark blue light; the first human signs of a new day approaching.

The sea is close enough to smell the briny seaweed and the salt-sharpness of air that always reminds us of childhood and then suddenly it's there before us like a slice of sky that's slipped below the line of the horizon and turned darker; a shadow of the sky in liquid form.

The North Sea.

I pass through Horden and it's in a sleepy stupor. There's nowt here but houses and offies and a power station. It's the last outpost of the land; a place to fester and rot and die. They can't even be arsed to name the streets here. There's just Sixth Street,

Seventh Street, Eighth Street and so on. It's living reduced to numbers.

Some bloke who looks like he's been on the beer all night tries to flag us down but I fly past because I'm stopping for nee-one today. Then Thorpe Road leads to the Sunderland Road which leads to the Coast Road. I hit it going southbound, the sea to my left and nowt but a strip of cliff-top allotments and the water below between me and Denmark.

The Coast Road takes us to Blackhall Rocks which would be ugly as fug any day except at this time of the morning, just as the August sun is sticking its hot head ower the wall of the brown North Sea and sending shards of light across the water towards us, changing it from shit-brown to golden in the blink of an eye. I swear down it's bloody beautiful. More beautiful than owt I've seen.

The rocks are on fire.

There's a village perched above them. It teeters near the edge where the land starts to fall away to nowt, and it's somewhere just past there that I turn the van down a little track and pull ower.

I get out and walk across a bit of scrubland, towards the edge of England. It's a wild empty place with nowt but the cracking sky and the shimmering water and silent miles of nothingness.

*

Charmaine was becoming a young woman. Turning early. Sprouting, as your Dad called it.

He always said she was a queer one an all. He couldn't read his daughter's mind, and that bothered him.

Bobby he understood. Bobby was a boy. Bobby was strong and surly and tough. He liked simple things, lads things, like the fighting and the poaching and wreaking havoc in the village. Stuff his Dad understood.

But Charmaine, she was different. Always brooding and scowling. Off doing her own thing. And when she was twelve, thirteen, she took to reading The Bible. Carried it with her everywhere for a while. This little leather-bound Bible she picked up some place.

And then one day Charmaine – little quiet coal-eyed Charm – fetched up with a seed in her belly. Thirteen years old and already showing. Pregnant and refusing to tell a soul who it was that did this to her.

He blamed me. Of course he did. And he went on the rampage again, smashing more plates and kicking bigger holes in the walls than ever before. He said some terrible things to her. Unforgiveable things. Things that would turn me mouth sour to say to you now son.

Then he took to the woods for two days and two nights.

Because deep down he understood perfectly. He knew. He knew who the father was. He knew what had been done and what was next for the Wisdom line, and all about how the blood had got mixed up all funny.

*

Seen close the North Sea is still shite-coloured and well choppy, but there's a thousand million flickering flames of orange dancing across it through the darkness as the sun peeps it's head ower the brow of the horizon.

The flashes of gold make it look like there's a shoal of herring sat just beneath the surface. A proper good catch of sun fish.

I'm looking down on it all and smoking another tab and even though everything is crumbling I'm starting to accept that I must have been sold down the river by the lass to the povs on the estate. There's nee way I can return to me flat, me job or Dickhead Derek without getting grief one way or another – and even though what's left of me family rejected us long ago, and everyone else thinks I'm a weirdo, the way the sun is illuminating the stack of rocks like the cathedral at night and the thousand million dancing flames are setting the North Sea ablaze, reminds me that hope is still there. Just. The fires still burn.

I sit like this for a while, smoking tabs down to the dimp and watching the flashes of gold disappear as the day gets lighter and the sea loses its magic and mystery and returns to just being the choppy, sloshy, brown angry thing I always remembered it to be.

Far down below us on the pebble beach I can see some wifey walking a dog that's chasing the tide in and out and yelping like a maniac. The dog is black and right away I'm thinking about little Coughdrop and how he's now just a stain on the carpet and a bag buried in the woods, and I'm wondering why violence poisons everything that's good, and if it's this way for everyone, or if mebbes I really was just born under a queer moon or summat.

*

He had tried to hide it, of course. He tried to nip it in the bud early on, your Dad.

He had heard all the horror stories and the jokes and he knew things could get twisted; that the bairn could come out backward or weird or inside out, like. That it could be born with tiny eyes or extra teeth. Too many fingers. Or mebbes not enough.

It had happened before. He'd heard all about it. Of course he had. All those stories passed down the vine.

Blood stories. Family myths. Wisdom accounts.

And he'd seen it plenty too and not just amongst us travellers neither. It went on in some of them places he used to hang about. Them little one-track hamlets and farm settlements up in the dales where people would nod and nudge and wink and say see that couple over there, with the bairn? Brother and sister, they are. Why else do you think their kiddie wears them callipers?

And hadn't he known plenty of cousins that had married?

Anyway, this was different. This was any father's right.

Better me than some young hooligan coming in, he reckoned.

And that's exactly what he'd telt her that first time he took her down the woods.

"It's only natural," he'd whispered. "The love between a father and his first born is the most naturalest thing in the world. It's a bond, see. And you can bet your last red penny that none of the lads round the town would be as caring and as loving as I am."

He said it wasn't his fault. Said it didn't matter. Said they were already bonded in Wisdom blood.

That's what he said. That's what he whispered.

And he said he couldn't be blamed. Said his head wasn't right. Not since Pike and the quarry.

She'd thank him for it later, he said.

Soon she'd be out dating lads, he said.

Soon she'd be engaged to be married. Now she'd be broken in. Ready for them. Less mess this way, he said.

So he broke the girl, my daughter, and he kept going back and breaking her some more.

And there was no loving tenderness. The gentle instruction about what goes where was forgotten when Mac Wisdom got his knotted hands on my daughter down there in the trees. That had just been talk. Words to coax her down with. Down into the wood. Down onto the ground.

And he kept at it. Taking her away. Our Charmaine. Piece by piece. Just chipping away. Taking bits of her. Holding her and breaking her, his gnarled fist on her face, his thick legs spreading hers.

"Don't you dare tell your mother."

I'd seen it all myself. Experienced it. That grimace of his. That twisted look.

Spittle on his lips. The hair in his nostrils. His dirty fingernails.

Her Dad's arse bobbing up and down above her. Cloying. "Don't you tell nee fucker."

He'd been at it for months until he'd filled her mould with a new version. His own daughter. Like a devil.

*

It's still the best part of the day when I get to the woods. Early.

Clean slate o'clock.

It's so hazy it's like the air is wobbling. Everything is perfectly still but distorted by distance. An orchestra of unseen birds argues in song. The natural perfumes of the country lanes chill us out a bit.

I've been driving around for a while weighing up me options, thinking about the implications and the whatsits – the repercussions. Even though me brain is working double-time it's like I still want to believe there's some goodness in her. Maria. Because she's what I'm really thinking about. All I'm thinking about.

So I've headed to the place that makes us happy. The place that made us both happy, the green cathedral of Mother Nature's making.

I'm parked up in the woods with nowt but me bag with me bits in, a van containing a quarter of a tank of petrol and about four hundred cones, wafers, flakes, a miscellaneous assortment of confectionery and a massive fugging chip on me shoulder.

I'm feeling proper shagged, like I can't be arsed to run any more, like I just want to roll over and curl up and pull the soil over us like a blanket and sleep forever in silence.

But I cannot do that here, in the front seat of Arty Vicari's van, so I jam a few chocolate bars, packets of crisps and bottles of water into my army bag, lock up and head into the woods.

As I walk through the trees there's that same smell of Balsam again that I'll always associate with Maria. And there's the lingering smell of perfumed sap being squeezed through timber and bark an all. And the wild garlic. And a hundred other smells besides, all of them proper lush.

The trees are like auld friends. The dry, impacted dirt is a carpet and the birdsong symphonic.

It's still a place of worship this. This green cathedral of mine. A last refuge.

As I walk I'm thinking about how if only that sackless Banny twat could have took his defeat like a man, like men used to, all of this could have been avoided. But things have changed from them auld days. Twats like him would rather slit your throat than show weakness in front of their marrers. There's nee courage or conviction left. It's all just knives and gang-bangs and that.

I mean, we're only weeks from the end of a millennium and it's like nowt's changed since the end of the last one. It's still the ruthless heartless animals that reign in this living hell. We're all just savages. Beasts.

And I'm sick of it, me. Properly.

*

He couldn't let it enter the world. No way, he said. Not a bairn. No way. Not a bairn by his own daughter. No chance. People might know. And people might be able to tell. They might tell just by looking. No chance. Not a babby; a new-born by his first born. No. Not a bloody half-breed. That's bad blood, that is. Bad news for everyone. You have to think of the family. The Wisdoms. The future.

And he never even telt us, the bastard. He let it all come out in the wash, over time. That poor wee girl. My girl. My Charm.

Instead he fetched his tools.

Aye. He fetched his tools and he took her down into the woods again. We'll get you fettled, he said. Fix you up.

He drove down in there to a different spot this time. Somewhere far away from the site. Miles, it was.

They drove for a long time until the track didn't look like a track any more. Then he parked up and they went on foot down there. He took her by the elbow and when she flinched he took her by the back of the neck, down to a place he knew, a dingy dark wet spot on his poaching rounds, where the tips of the trees joined hands to form a dark dome of branches that clicked and clacked and split the sky and rationed the light, divided it into cubes and oblongs and rhombuses and trapezoids. That's what she concentrated on. The shapes. The shapes in a lifeless place. That damp, musty rotting place.

My girl. My poor daughter.

They left the path and he took her in there, into the trees, off the path, and this time she knew that summat else was happening. Summat even worse than the usual. Much, much worse.

The bag of clinking tools told her so, and her father not saying anything, just walking and grunting and dragging his bad leg, his breath heavy, twigs snapping as they went in deeper and darker into a place, his hand still clamped on the back of her neck.

She'd have been able to feel his calluses.

His tools. A git big clanking bag of rusty things by his side. Swinging by his leg. His bad leg. A bag of saw blades and screwdrivers. Drill bits and blades and tubes. Lengths of coathanger and coils of wires. Washers and spanners and cutters. Attachments. Appendages. His bits from the site.

All hard things though. Nowt soft. Nowt soft about your Dad, ever. His bag was full of angles and edges, twists and turns. Crude shapes. Man-made things. Functional things.

The tools he once used for levering tyres off flat-bed trucks and driving in posts and dismantling washers and tellies and fitting new tow-bars and fixing up trailers and making pens and kennels and snares and shelves and traps; tools for fixing and building and tools for dismantling too.

The bag swinging by his side, his other hand on her. Gripping and pushing. The calluses. What did they always say? 'Too big for his own body, that one'. No room could contain him. Belongs outside, that one.

Their feet slipping on the carpet of leaves and the mud beneath.

Then the bag was open, the tools were in the mulch and Charmaine was on her back on an old blanket he'd thought to bring. Flung down on the topsoil. A nice touch. Thoughtful, like. Considerate.

The two of them deep in the woods. No soul for a mile or two. Father and daughter, her sobbing and silently shaking and him saying "Shhh girl," and making her drink whisky and saying "Keep still or you'll make us slip", and him selecting something else from the bag, something unseen, something out of her view because all she can see is the primitive look on a dirty face framed by her shaking thighs, his tongue protruding with concentration as he leaned in, squinting.

My girl. My poor girl.

And then things did get torn and they did get ripped and she must have bled a hell of a lot. Blood on the leaves and blood on her legs and later, when she went to the bog, it'll have felt like fire, and she'd have vowed never to go into those woods again.

Mac fluffed it. Got the shakes. Nerves shot.

He scraped and scratched but he didn't destroy that thing inside.

It was dark in there, in the woods – it was dark in her – and he'd not thought to bring a torch. He knew nowt of the female anatomy, knew nowt about what went where and how things joined up. He didn't realise bairns grew that far up. He thought he could just pull it out and stick it in the ground and that'd be it.

And Charmaine was tougher than he ever knew. A right tough girl. He'd underestimated her. And you never underestimate a Wisdom. He should have known that.

Then that night and the next night too she did ball up her clotted knickers and rheumy sheets faster than I could boil them, and that's when I knew summat about this was rum. Summat was off. That's what I mean when I say it started to come out in the wash.

Three days later Charmaine was still showing so the bairn was still in her and everyone did know about it now, and there's Mac Wisdom pretending to be enraged that some wee shite had got his little girl knocked up, while Charmaine chose dignified silence.

Only then did I see it: it was all show. Show for me, his wife. Blind to it all along.

This time your Dad had gone deeper and darker than I ever could have imagined.

*

The green cathedral is calm and quiet but I'm all churned up so I spend a good while just wandering the woods, following the flattened grass of the animal trails and losing my way, then finding it again. Walking is the only way I'm able to control the hateful images and ideas that are flickering through me head; images too nasty to dwell on for long. Stuff from the past – memory photographs of smashed skulls and skinned animal faces. Stamped bollocks and strings of sloppy intestines being pulled still twitching from ragged wounds. Teeth chewing through cheeks and noses and thumbs twisting into empty eye sockets. Things that go pop and thud and crunch. Me Dad whipping off his belt and looming over us.

That look in his eye.

Being down in the woods.

Deep in the density of the trees, away from paths and clearings, I sit down against a tree and light a tab and decide to have a good old think about things. Rationalise, like. Ditch these grim visions rising in us and instead try and do what one of the shrinks inside called a personal inventory.

On the positive side this is all I can come up with: I still have me freedom. Freedom to go wherever I want, though it does mean having to break all the parole rules and going on the run so there'll be a warrant on us.

Oh aye, and I have lots of kets and crisps and that, so I'll not go hungry.

And that's about it.

The negatives we know about.

I rest me head against the rough ridges of the bark and close me eyes as I draw on the dimp but even though I'm proper shagged and I've been running on adrenaline all day I cannot switch off because there's this voice in me lugs. It's been muttering all day but now it's getting louder. It's the voice of me Dad, Mac Wisdom: *What ye waiting for?* he's going. *Do them cunts you soft little shite. Let them come to you – and they will come – then do them. Do them quick. Do them for travelling men everywhere. Do them for your Ma and for Charmaine and Bobby. And if you can't do them for your family then do it for yoursel. Do them in their beds if ye have to, but just make sure you end this because if you nash now, you'll be running away forever.*

I flick the yellowy dimp out in the trees and exhale.

Sherrup, I'm thinking and me heart's pumping just thinking about it. You just sherrup. It's you that caused all this, I'm thinking. It's your fault, you twat. You bloody bullying bastard. Fugging headcase. You bloody predator. Beast. You caused all this. You made us come out small and runty. Destroyed our family. Tore us apart. Made us a freak.

You soft little shite.

Sherrup. You're the reason. You're the bloody reason. You're the bloody reason I'm in this mess. You're the reason everyone hates us and laughs at us. You're the reason I've been running for twenty year. Cursed from day bloody one.

I hear mesel saying this in a cracked voice I barely recognise and I can feel me eyes getting puffy and sore as hot tears rise and well and spill out down me hacky cheeks and there's salt in me mouth as a big fugging sob shakes my chest. I sound like a git big bloody bear with its paw stuck in a trap, and as I start proper blubbing alone here in the woods I realise it's the first time I've allowed mesel to cry in years and years.

And now that I'm blaring I cannot stop and there's snot coming out me nose and there's so many tears that the green cathedral turns into a watery blur that's swimming away from us like I'm sinking to the bottom of a very deep lake, and the saddest thing is there's no-one about to witness us drowning alive.

And it's the story of me short stinking life.

*

And so the bairn was born in blood and membrane on rough blankets on the floor of the van with me and a couple or three of our travelling neighbours too, with hot water and strong arms to hold her down, and all the while Charmaine saying nowt the entire time, barely even a scream. Only a moan and a whimper then the mewling of the newborn, under-sized and barely alive.

That night the moon had crossed the sun and the light turned queer in the moments that it slid out.

Born under a bad moon, said the women between muttering their muted prayers. A bad moon.

And it was you, my son. It was you.

And Charmaine did bear you. She was your mother. Not me. Her.

Her and him.

And you. You were a tiny thing. A funny looking thing. Not big and strong and roaring like the Wisdom bairns, but a slight creature, brittle, with nowt on you but a wisp of dark down on a conical head.

It's the moon they said. It's a bad un. The moon knows this one's a bastard, they said, but I shushed them and told them to keep their curses.

"I'm calling him Kane," said the mother. "Kane Wisdom."

"Funny bloody name," said the women.

"It's from the Bible," she said. "Like Cain and Abel. But I'm spelling it wi' a K."

And your Dad did speak up just the once on the subject: "You'll call him John-John after my Uncle John-John Wisdom, as good a man as there ever was."

"But I'm calling him – "

"John-John's a family name. A good Wisdom name. We'll hear nee more about it."

"I want to – "

255

"Well you can't. The little cabbage is John-John."

And there you were, my son, and I did raise you, as if I'd birthed you meself. Raised you as my own.

And that's the bare truth of it.

*

I pull mesel together and blot the voice of the ghost out. Have to.

I stand and trace my steps back through the woods to the passing place where the van is parked. Then when I get there I nash in a different direction, following the same familiar path I brought Maria down just the other day, thinking how it seems like months ago now.

I'm soon back at the secret clearing that backs up against the cliff face to form a theatre in which nature's dramas are played out. It looks even more overgrown and green and wild today, like all the seeds that have been lying in the topsoil since they were scattered by the breeze last summer have suddenly sprung into life. It's turned into a perfumed jungle that's never been corrupted by a single human footprint. It's like consecrated ground. A holy place.

Water is still running down the rock and trickling down into a boggy corner. I walk over to it and scoop mesel a handful to wipe my teary face and rinse me mouth out. It's brackish. It has the faintest trace of summat coppery in it. Metallic and tangy. The water makes us feel better though so I drink more and as I do I feel me mood lifting.

It's funny how it's the simplest of things that can make you happy.

I walk up the little bank up to the bottom of the rock where me and Maria lay down and did the business. I chuck my coat down and lie down on it and stuff the kit bag behind me head as a pillow. It's still nice and warm and sunny but there's this light through-breeze blowing crossways, a faint movement that's like hollow fingers brushing the damp hair from me brow and gently pulling down me eyelids as if to urge us to go to sleep for a bit. Yawning, that's what I do.

I must have had a proper deep sleep because when I wake up it seems like maybe a few hours have passed and though it's not yet dark I know it's in the post. I don't much feel like moving so I lie on the ground for a while, searching the sky for shapes and patterns and listening to the trickle of the water down the rock, and it's so still and peaceful it's like I've not got a trouble in the world. As I lay flat, clinging to the earth, a big shudder runs right through us. A big pleasurable shudder, right down from me head to me toe.

But then a voice speaks to us again. It's him. Mithering us again. Me Dad. He says: *they're coming for you, you know. They're coming for you tonight and you're just bloody laying there daydreaming.*

Aye, I say. They probably are.

And what are you gonna do about it?

I dunno.

Well you better think on, hadn't you lad?.

What do you care? I say out loud, my voice hanging there in the clearing in the woods, but there's nee reply, and I'm pretty sure I've just imagined it all, this conversation, and mebbe I'm going a bit mental, or have been spending too much time on me own. A lifetime on me own, in fact.

And then I think, OK shite-arse. Mebbe you're right. Mebbe they are coming. And when they do I'll show you. I'll bloody show all of you. I'll be waiting for them. There'll be nee more daydreaming. I'll surprise the lot of you. Guaranteed.

Good, says a voice. *Good lad. That's my boy.*

Get fugged, I say. I'm not your boy.

*

You'll not remember but Bobby resented you right away. From day one. Because your brother had already set about making himself hard and cruel and detached just like his father. He'd not been to school in years and was working on the markets with Eddie from eight or nine year old. They sold cleaning products, dusters, rags, batteries. Bits and bats that people always need. He was up at five and off to a different market every day. Always changing. Chester one day then Birtley or Washington or Darlo the next.

And you grew. Baby John-John. You learned to walk and talk and you were a tiny wee thing with black hair and sticky-out ears just like your Dad. And I called you me own.

Because Charmaine was to be sent away to work. Your Dad said she should go somewhere where they didn't know her, so he got her up on the fish-packing plant line in Newcastle. Mac arranged it for her to stop in a van on a site run by his cousin Johnny Wisdom, a grassless patch of concrete over in the corner of an industrial estate out past Benwell way.

And time rolled on and the seasons came around and I buried the darkness of what had happened as best I could.

It was the accident what done him. That's what I told mesel. He's not been right since, I said. They wired him all wrong.

The limp and the stutter were there and Mac was not the man anyone remembered, but he was still strong enough to knock you about. His own son.

"He's a mis-shape, that one," he'd say.

Do you remember?

You must do. You must remember some of it.

Then Charmaine started seeing someone. A gorger lad with a house and a car. And she said she loved him and she wanted to marry him one day soon. Mac told her no daughter of his was marrying a gorger and she should stop coming around. So she stopped coming around.

"I'll be back for the bairn," she said. "As soon as we're wed I'll be back for my John-John."

And that's why we raised you as our own, the last child of Mac and Vancy Wisdom.

*

When they finally turn up I'm waiting for them. I hear them a mile off, crashing through the undergrowth and snapping branches.

I telt you they'd come, didn't I.

I know Da. I know.

I see them soon enough too because the silly numpties are waving torches about and burning big biffters and acting like a right bunch of sackless gets. They sound pissed mortal and high an all, judging by the way they're carrying on. I count at least three of them because there's three torch beams fanning about down the hill. There'll be more though. Loads more.

And I knew they'd come after sundown. Twats like that are too lazy to do much in the day-time. Too sober. It takes the curtain of darkness to drop before they can begin to feel brave. Because in the daylight the truth of themsels is laid bare. In the daylight they're forced to face who or what they really are; and when they do all they see is fear and loneliness. That's why they're children of the night.

I'm sat in the tree that's up the hill from where I left Arty's ice cream van. I'm perched on the right-angled alder branch that extends straight out from the trunk sideways. It's a good vantage point.

I've got me coat on and me hood up and I'm smoking a tab which I stub out then flick into the darkness at the first sign of them.

Flecks of burning tab ash fall, a mini shower of dying fireflies.

And that's when I know that Maria has sold us out again. Grassed us. Snitched us out and stitched me up like a Craster bloody kipper.

They've probably been driving round for hours trying to find us before she's remembered this place. I bet they've been to me flat again, then round the town and down the river and that. They might have paid Arty a visit for all I know. Roughed him up a bit or summat. He's not a bad auld lad is Arty, but he probably deserves summat for getting into bed with the likes of them in the first place.

Sleep with dogs and you wake up with fleas.

She's a smart lass, Maria, I'll give her that, because it's not an easy spot to find when there's nee signs about and nowt in the way of street lights. It's a proper remote spot, so she must have a good memory.

I still can't quite believe she'd do that though. Na. Not after them tender moments we shared together.

Of course she grassed you up.

Anyroad, I don't suppose it matters now. Because we'll not share any tender moments again. I'll not be opening me heart to her. There'll be nee more *living la vida loca*. At least I know whose side she's on now anyway.

Your problem is you've nee gumption. Letting some lass in like that. You deserve owt coming to you if you ask me.

Aye, well. I'm not asking you am I.

Mind, I've been busy. I've not been scratting me nadgers up this tree all evening. I've been preparing. I've been doing stuff. Getting ready to finish this once and for all.

Good lad. Do us proud. Mebbes you're not as soft as I thought.

So I've got mesel ready. The green cathedral is my house and them coming at us like this, it's nee different to poaching is it. All you've go to do is understand the landscape and understand your prey. You set and bait your traps, and you let them come. And when there's bait in them traps they just cannot resist. Every time. Because all animals are creatures of habit. And this lot are just a bunch of beasts.

So I've been doing stuff. Putting what little me Dad learnt us as a bairn to good use. Doing old Robinson Crusoe proud.

I've been sharpening sticks. The knife is a good one so it's not took us long to get a good collection of spears and spikes on the go. Then just as it was getting dark I went and put them around and about. Three I dug in deep on the main path at an angle. The path up from the van to the clearing. Dug in about so high. Knee height.

Then I went off into the woods and stabbed the rest of them into the soil in a large semi circle ower a hundred yards or more, and stashed the rest up trees and that. I made sure to memorise me steps an all, picking out trees with big knots on their trunks or strange-shaped branches I'd recognise against the night sky. Anything I could see or touch or smell and use as signposts in the dark.

Nature provides.

What about them boulders?

Aye, I was getting to that

I taught you good. You thought I was hard on you, but I taught you good.

Did you shite. You taught us nowt but hate and violence.

After that I went back up the clearing, where me stuff was stashed. Then I walked round to one side and found a route up round the side of the cliff. It was steep and muddy but there were plenty of hand holds and roots to help pull mesel up with. I scrambled up that bank that had not seen human footprints for years.

From up there you can see across the treetops. It was like being in the whatsit of a sail ship. The crow's nest. And the tree tops looked like a field or mebbes a sea, and the sea was moving and swaying slightly, and over in the distance, through the haze of the summer's evening, you could just make out the spires of the cathedral and the ragged edge of the castle next to it.

The town – out there.

Life – out there.

I sat down for a moment and treated mesel to a tab while I looked around us. I saw what I needed. Boulders. A few of them scattered about. Half sunk in the soil like the earth was trying to swallow them whole.

They were too big to lift, but small enough to roll. One of them took a git thick branch to help jimmy it, but then I was able to roll it close enough to the edge of the rock face. Then I left them there, ten yards apart, ready for toppling, like. Well medieval.

When I'd done that, I half slid and half fell down the bank and into the clearing, where I washed me hands under the trickling waterfall and had another drink.

As I scarfed another Mars bar I thought of summat else. Summat important. I went into me kit bag and pulled out one of my T-shirts. One of them green army ones.

I went downhill through the trees to the van. I rolled up the T-shirt then unlocked the petrol cap and dangled it in there until it were nice and soaked. Then I left it there, with only a tiny bit of cloth sticking out.

Nee turning back now. Arty'll be insured. He owes us anyway, trying to stitch us up like that. Dropping us into the Nook mess like that.

Never go on the back foot.

Aye. That's right.

So I've been busy. I've been doing stuff.

And I'm alright, me. I'm alright. I'm not scared, me.

No.

Not scared.

Not a bit.

I'm tired and a bit wired and a bit sweaty in me army clobber but I've not been scared of the trees and the night noises for a long time, not since I turned the woods into a green cathedral when my auld man left us out all night when I was a youngster.

A valuable lesson that, lad. It all worked out in the end.

Sherrup did it.

I'm at home here. I'm in me element. More than in any prison cell or caravan park or povvy council-owned halfway house for halfwits. I'm up the tree and nee-one can touch us here. Only now someone wants to come into me special place and desecrate it with their noise and their mess and their violence. Wants to destroy the last pure thing I've got left.

And I'm not having it.

No. No way.

I'm not having that.

I'm not having *them* come in *here*.

Na.

No.

Over my dead body. Or theirs.

*

The stump-ended branch of the family tree, was how he called you, may God rest his soul.

But it wasn't him talking. You never saw that dark sparkle. You never knew what he was, what he had been. He was a shadow now, a half-mad mystery; a strange stuttering demon doing weird and wild acts. He was a beast to you from the moment you were born.

I remember how you told me about that night in the woods. You can't have been more than six.

Pheasants, you were after. Fat roosting pheasants that your Dad had staked. He knew all their runs and roosting branches and needed nowt but a fishing line and hook to get them.

So he took you down there, slipping in the mud and stifling your breathing in case the keeper was close by.

It was dark as tar pitch in there. Must have been. Too dark to see the ground or your hands in front of their faces.

Sit down by this tree trunk and sherrup, he'd said.

Sit down here, he'd said. Don't say a word. Don't even breathe. He'd be back in a minute.

So you sat there in the leaves holding your breath. Every sound of the woodland was amplified: the snap of a twig or a rustle in the undergrowth, an owl's hoot. Something screaming.

And time passed. More than the minute your father had promised. Much, much more than a minute. Your eyes adjusted to the darkness but all you could see were shapes. Great towering things. Monstrous, they were. And they were looking for you.

Waiting for you. Waiting for you to make a noise so they could pounce and tear your young throat out.

You sat there as still as a statue, shivering, your eyes closed tight with fear, all alone, and you needed to piss really badly, but you couldn't move so you went right there in your trousers, a warm trickle stinging your crotch. And after a while the piss stain turned cold and you shivered and tried to sniff up the snot that was running from your nose but it made too much noise so you let it hang there suspended. And still your father never came back.

Gradually the blackness began to change. It lightened, turned blue, then merged into a whole range of blues as a new day started to filter through. The monsters turned into trees and the ghosts became the spaces between them and the fear began to wane.

When it was light enough to move you stood and stretched and brushed yourself down, then you turned and re-traced your steps back through the woods, then out across the fields, finally returning to the site.

I can see you now, running across the grass as I pegged out the washing.

You opened the door and entered and there sat your Dad, laughing as he scooped an egg into his mouth with a fried slice. Yellow from the yolk stained his mouth and he laughed long and hard.

You said nowt and he said nowt. He just laughed some more and then sighed and carried on eating.

*

And then they're here and the calm of the woods is broken and I'm dropping down from the alder.

I move through the trees like a will o' the wisp, light on me silent toes and making sure I know where they are at all times, which isn't hard given the fuss they're making. It's like I'm floating.

I'm ready for them.

I'm prepared.

The only thing that scares us is the possibility that I may actually enjoy this.

It's summer-dark again. August dark. I let me ears do the work for us. I can hear car doors and voices, then someone going *shhhh* dead loud, as if by shushing rather than speaking they think they'll not be heard. I take a wide arc down the hill keeping me ears peeled. There's two cars down there, further back on the main track.

I move quicker now, brushing past branches and leaping ower gnarled roots that stretch out like trip wires. Me senses are guiding us. I feel good. Like I could do all this blindfold. Like summat is watching over us, willing us to win.

Then I'm at the passing place where me ice cream van is parked, further down the track from them, and I know they're close.

I can hear hushed voices but the daft bastards have still got a torch on. There's plenty of time. I crouch down with the lighter in me hand. I unscrew the petrol cap. Then I wait until the torch beam is closer.

And still I wait.

From round the bend of the track the beam slowly sweeps round in my direction, then I hear a voice, raised this time. A voice of acknowledgement, of whatsit. Recognition.

I pull out the soaking t-shirt, flip open me Zippo, touch the flame to it and by the time it takes I'm already back into the woods heading uphill again. Up the hill to me tree. To me branch.

It takes longer than I thought it would. I'm just starting to think mebbes the flame's gone out and I've banjaxed it when there's a flash. There's nee noise – just a beautiful orange flash. Like, *whoooof.*

Then comes the explosion, a short sharp bang as the van and all that's in it goes up. It is spectacular, but it feels wrong doing this here in the green cathedral. Creating like this. But it's sink or swim time and if that lot get a hold of us I might not make it out of here alive.

And I'm not having that.

Na.

No way.

Aye. Smash em son. Smash their cunts in. Do it for the Wisdoms.

After the git big bang and the roar of the fireball that lights the sky up for a second there's a yell, a howl of pain, and there's voices echoing about the trees and shouts of shock and panic and confusion, like what the fuck and he's here, the pikey's here, then someone else shouting get the dirty little inbred fucking bastard, and the beams of torches are flicking this way and that like the eyes of deranged robots. I hear more branches snapping, the sound of stumbling. Chaos. They don't know what's going on, the sackless, feckless, fugless twats.

What are you waiting for? Get down there, get your top off and fight them like a bloody man.

Aye, but it doesn't work like that any more, does it Dad.

It sounds like there's bloody loads of them running this way and that. Like a small army or summat. And you don't send that many people just to pop by and say hello. I can hear voices of lasses too, more than one, and the sound of bodies crashing through twigs and branches and that.

Then through the dark I can hear someone coming close. It's a lad and he's breathing heavy and I can see he has summat in his hand. It's a sword. A bloody martial arts sword with a big fug-off blade gleaming in the moonlight, its edge the thinnest line of silver.

He's run up the hill, and there's panic in his breathing, and he's even closer to me now, so close I can smell him – a mixture of tabs and sweat – and the sword is dangling by his side, and it's meant for me, and that's when I drop down on him, just like I did on that doss twat in the alley; down from above like a toppled angel.

I'm right onto him, feet first, cracking his back, mebbes even breaking summat by the sound it makes – like a series of clicks. It's like jumping on a rotten xylophone or summat.

There's nee noise from him at all except for the air vacating his body as he flops forward like a ragdoll.

He groans then goes to make a move but I bend down and pick up the sword and in one quick move slam it down on his arm and it must be sharp because I damn near chop his hand off at the wrist. It feels like nowt. Like a warm knife cutting through a pat of butter.

Fucking get in. Now stamp on his head. Stamp on his bollocks.

And then he's making a noise. Oh, he's kicking up a right stink now, screaming like a bloody banshee, and there's shouts from around me in the wood, but they're not close. Even I'm surprised by what's just happened – and it was me that bloody did it.

I bend down and between his hand and the rest of him I can see a gap. I can see dirt. There's a moment where everything goes still, the wood falls silent and even the lad says nowt for a moment, and I say nowt, and then the gap fills up with blood that spreads and seeps into the mud and I boot the hand and it tears that last inch of flesh that's joining his hand to his wrist, and the hand lolls off into the darkness like an injured animal, and the lad screams some more, and then I'm gone.

*

Another incident.

Later, when you were seven or eight, your father placed a bet on a horse. Remember?

Do you remember that?

He reckoned he could knock it out with one punch – the famous Mackie bullhammer.

267

He was back drinking again. The lads were round again. Round the fire after closing time at The Bluebell, ruddy-faced and grubby-handed.

That's how I knew he was on the mend. Because in the drink Mac was back to being his boastful self. But he was older now, different. As I said: re-wired wrong.

Simey Samways was there and Jim Brazil was there and others too, like Kenny Cutmore, a non-traveller. And once the boast was made there was no going back – not among betting men like these.

"No way you can knock out a hoss," said Simey Samways.

"Knock it out? One of my uppercuts'll turn it into a bloody giraffe. I'd bet a ton on it."

"You're on."

"What about you, Ken?"

"Why not. But where are we going to get a hoss from?"

"I know of one," said Eddie. "A nasty little colt up at Rogergate estate. Fucker bit me a month back. Took a chunk right out me arm."

"I'll fetch the little un," your Dad said. "He needs to learn how to throw a punch. Howay."

"What – now?" said Simey.

"No time like the present."

You were under the blankets when Mac bundled you into the front of Simey's pick-up. I tried to stop him. I tried to tell him. But he pushed me aside.

The others climbed on the back and they did break the seal on another bottle of whisky as they drove down darkened country roads.

They parked down a lane and then vaulted a wall. Eddie went on ahead to the paddock where he knew the horse would be. He found it there on a short tether, snorting in the dark, framed by the night. It was a skewbald cob; white, with only the smallest patch of brown on its flank.

He whistled for the others to follow.

"Right, watch and learn," said Mac, taking his coat off and passing it to Jim. "One punch."

You were stood next to your uncle, tugging at his sleeve.

"He's not going to hit the hoss is he Uncle Eddie?"

"A bet's a bet, lad. And anyway he's Mac Wisdom. He's hardly going to back out now, is he."

Mac rolled his neck and swung his arms and felt the old adrenaline surge come back again; that need to punch his way through flesh and blood. He walked up to the cob, which snorted back at him. The men could tell it was rattled by this unexpected nocturnal intrusion. All it could see were shapes, but it sensed the tension.

"Reet," said Mac. "Watch and learn. Watch and learn. Bullhammer time."

"Don't Da," you said. "Don't hit the hoss."

Mac ignored you, stepped toward it and threw a big, loping overhand right onto the smooth convex slope of the horse's nose. The sound was an unforgettable crunch of bone on bone.

The shock caused the horse's eyes to widen with fear. They looked like headlamps in the dark. It reared up onto its hind legs like a creature rising from the deep, and went to bolt. The noise it made was like nowt any of them had heard before. It was a scream of pure pain and a cry of shock rolled into one. Its howl cut through the night: why me?

Mac stepped back as it made to run off into the night, a rearing, snorting hysterical blur clawing at the air.

But the tether was too short and the tether was too tight.

The rope pulled it sideways and the horses legs went from under it. It fell crashing to the ground. Its heavy torso flopped in the mud.

The horse screamed like a child. Like a baby. Its legs thrashed in the air.

And you, John-John. You screamed too.

"Help it," you said through tears. "Somebody help it."

"Christ almighty," said one of the men.

The horse writhed and kicked some more and the men jumped back out of harm's way, and then it was kicking no more. It was still, its legs sticking upwards like a crude pastiche of death. The horse's heart had stopped and you were crying uncontrollably.

"Right," said your Dad. "That's a ton each of you cunts owes us."

*

The sword's in me hand and I'm feeling sickly and sweaty. Me stomach's lurching so much I feel like I might gip at any moment and there's droplets of sweat turning to tiny ice cubes on me spine.

I stop and look at the weapon. The blade edge has been hammered and honed and sharpened right down, forged so sharp it cut right through that lad's wrist so swiftly and so silently that there's hardly even a trace of blood on it. It's scary how quickly it happened; my potential scarier still.

The screaming tells us this is all too real. Screams like an animal backed into a corner, coming from down where I did the lad. Screams like an animal caught in a trap. Then there's voices. Shouting. Branches breaking towards the screams.

It's best I keep moving.

It's good this, isn't it.

No. It's not bloody good. It's bloody survival.

I run quickly, pausing every thirty seconds or so to check the bearings of Banny and his lot. So long as I keep moving there's nee way they can catch us in here. I was born for this. They're just a bunch of povs and slags and druggies who belong on the estate where all they've got is the weeds pushing through the paving slabs.

But the green cathedral is my natural habitat. The woods were my education, the hoot of the owl and the scratching of rodents my vocabulary.

I've got me night eyes on now. Turned on and tuned in. Me ears are cocked and me nostrils are proper flared.

As I move I think about that hand lying back there somewhere in the leaves, a solitary hand without a body, all alone in the dark, and the gip rises up into me throat, and I can taste it all bitter, bilious and sicky, but I swallow hard and keep moving.

I half-run up the hill. Up the hill and through the trees. Through the trees and into the warm August night.

I'm not far off the main path that leads up to the clearing where I know Maria will be leading them. It's all plain now: one way or another she's sold us down the river.

Then there's a movement, a shifting of shadows just below us. Voices. Close by. Voices and breaths. Two of them. Lads. And I remember there's them sharpened sticks between us. It's all so perfect.

I jump out into the path and whistle.

Then I gan, *Ower here, you sackless povvy charver Nazi gets*, and I hop back into the trees and gan back, towards them, but unseen because I'm off the beaten track.

There he is, gans one of them, shouting, he's ower here. Lads, he's ower here. I've got the cunt.

He runs up the path and straight onto the spikes. It's too dark to know where he's been impaled but I've staggered them nicely so if one stabs you, you'll fall forwards on to the second one. Good thinking, that.

Ayaz, he yells. Ayaz, yer fucker.

I move closer. I'm floating through the trees, and the moonlight shows us he's face down on the floor and his marrer is tripping over onto him from behind. It's proper whatsit. Proper slapstick. Like Laurel and whatsit.

The first spike is still in the ground, but the second must have stuck in the lad somewhere. And as the second lad falls I'm right on him. I leap out and kick his head like a football. It's a proper kick an all mind, like I'm taking a cup final extra time penalty or summat. I nearly boot it right off his stinking neck and out the bloody stadium.

There's a dull thud like a watermelon's been dropped from a second floor window and right away pain shoots across the top of me foot and up me leg. It bloody knacks. He's out cold though. Sparko. I don't feel good about it, but this is life and death, this is. Survival of the dirtiest.

The first lad is trying to get up but his leg is mashed up from the gouging, and he's trapped under his marrer who has gone all floppy on top of him. I almost feel bad for the pair of them. Almost.

Gan on then – stamp them. Stamp them both. Kick their bleeding jaws off.

I limp off into the trees again with the dead leg that the lad's fat head has given us. I've still got the sword in me hand, dangling by me side.

What you doing, man? Get back there and finish them off. Chop their bloody heads off.

Them two'll not be going anywhere fast so I stop for a moment and try to shake the pain and numbness out me leg. I stand stock-still for a few seconds, thinking, bloody hell this is ridiculous. It's all gone proper mad, this. Like a bloody fillum or summat. It's like when I was a bairn and the few times I'd be allowed out with the gorger kids we'd be playing cowboys and Indians. I was always the Indian – just me, mind – and they'd all be coming after us, hollering and hooting and shooting their imaginary pistols, and them yelping pow, pow, get the Injun would soon turn into get the fucking stinking gyppo, and then they'd pile on us and batter us, and I'm thinking about how it's all exactly the same now, only there's even more bloody cowboys and they divvent have guns made from their fingers nee more, they've got knives and bloody swords and nunchukkas and Christ knows what else. But I'm still the Indian.

You need to toughen up lad. Make your Dad proud.

You shut it you mental stammering peg-legged twat. This isn't about you.

*

*You stopped going to school at eight or nine. The learning was
pointless and all them boys was always picking on you.*

*Of course they sent us social workers. They threatened us with
prison but Bobby, when he was around, was good at sending
them packing. He'd been through it himself.*

*You'd learned your ABCs and your 123s and that was enough.
You were better off in the real world – the one with fields and
woods, trees and leaves, grasses and streams.*

Remember?

*

The woods fall silent again for a moment and then something
weird happens. I need a shit. I properly need to go – like,
desperately. Urgent and that. I've broken into a sweat and I've
got the proper hot tingles. It's like me innards are fighting to
escape.

There's nowt I can do but drop me kecks and undercrackers
and squat where I stand. It comes out straight away in a git big
fiery gush and splatters noisily onto the ground. Oh Christ. I'm
reminded of landslides and liquidisers and lorries tipping out
five ton of gravel.

I do a couple of trumps and then there's another load, just
as heavy. Sweet bloody relief. I let out a tiny groan of pleasure.

I feel light-headed, like I've just halved me bloody body
weight. It stinks summat rotten like a creature has crawled up
inside there and died, but I feel good with it, cleaned out, like.
I feel like laughing at the ridiculousness of getting caught short
like this.

And that's when the torch beam falls upon us. It comes from
nowhere. It swings around and illuminates us crouched there
with my hands on me waist band and me junk dangling like
bloody conkers. I've not even had a chance to find a leaf to
wipe me scut with.

I squint into the light, but I can't see who's behind it. Don't
need to though. I know who it is.

Got you, you dirty little pikey bastard says a voice from behind the beam.

You divvy little prick. You couldn't even wait for a bloody shite. You're still a little babby, you. Did they learn you nowt when you were away? Looks like you need another lesson, boy.

Then another voice goes what the fuck's he doing man? He's bloody shat himsel.

Then another voice, unseen, a girl, pleading. Maria.

Howay, she says. Just leave him Kyle.

The first voice again. A dull flat voice. The voice of Banny.

Get him.

And I'm off again, turning and pulling up me trousers and legging it all in one fluid movement, me cheeks squelching. I can hear them behind us like dogs after a fox, but I'm moving like the wind, me.

I'm still fastening me belt when I burst out of the woods and into the clearing. I divvent pause for breath as I run round the side of the cliffs and scramble straight up the dirt bank in the half-darkness. I'm scrambling and scrabbling hand over foot but I get half way up there like a bloody rocket. I don't need to see because me other senses are guiding us. Feel, smell, sound. I cover thirty, mebbes forty feet in what seems like seconds. I stop, look round and can see the sweep of Banny's torch beam below us still in the trees.

I turn and leg it up the rest of the bank, pulling mesel up by roots and branches and rocks and owt I can get me hands on, praying that none of them come loose and send us falling backwards, down to the baying pack.

Then I'm up near the top of the cliff, above the trees, and it's lighter up here. I'm close to the sky and I'm sweating cobs. The moon is high above us, clear and cold and white and round and clean.

The clearing sits way below us and the shadows of the cliffs creep across it like accusatory fingers. One minute there's grass, the next there's nowt but space. Nowt but a big, big fall onto

274

the rocks. I need to watch me footing. Mebbes this clearing is an auld quarry or summat. I used to think that it was a natural hole in the ground but the way the earth just drops to nothing and the rock face is all jagged and vertical, I reckon maybe all of this is man-made, like mebbes a thousand years or more ago they plundered the earth here for stone to build the cathedral with. They dug it and shaped it and dragged it with ropes and rolled it on logs the many miles through the woods and across the fields to the city, where it was turned into a monument to God on that peninsula formed by the bend of the river.

Aye, I reckon that's it.

All these years of coming here and I've only just realised that this green cathedral of mine was built by man an all, just like the one in town, only this one is the shell of a cathedral; a cathedral-shaped hole. My paradise. And there's this lot that want to spoil it.

So do summat about it then. Do it now.

I bloody will an all.

*

You had to find out the truth sometime, but when you did it came out all wrong.

All it took was an offhand comment and just like that, Mac Wisdom casually destroyed your life.

You were the same age as Charmaine had been when she'd given birth. Given birth to you, the bairn. Charmaine, your real mother. Not me, her. Fourteen she was and fourteen you were too, when you found out about him sticking it to her. Corrupting her. Seeding her. Month after month in the leaves and mud, under the trees and sky, in the woods. Her own father, the glass-eyed broken man. My husband, your Dad. Him that gave you a grandmother for a mother. A mother for a sister. An uncle for a brother. Him that made it all twisted and confusing and wrong and destroyed your life before it even began, then destroyed it all over again fourteen years later.

Just like that Mac told you who you really are and where you came from, and why exactly he thought you were nature's aberration, and the worst thing was I think he enjoyed it.

*

And then they're here in the clearing.

Some lad I can't make out comes out the trees first. He's holding the torch and carrying a bag, then there's Banny, dragging Maria behind him by the hand. My Maria. Maria with a bairn in her belly.

Is this it? says the lad.

His voice carries up to me like he's stood six foot away.

Shhh says Banny. Button it, you.

I'm up there on the cliff edge, the moon lighting the way. Lighting the clearing. I find where I perched the first boulder and I crouch down beside it. I keep low so me silhouette doesn't give us away.

Banny turns to Maria and says summat I cannot hear. She says summat back and then he smacks her one. Properly backhands her. The cracking noise echoes round the clearing.

Banny's got summat in his hand. It looks like a stick, but then I realise by the way he's holding it that it's not a stick. It's a bloody air rifle. Me guts gan cold. What's he need a bloody gun for?

Your thick head, that's what.

Then he spots something and nods with his head. The torch beams moves round and I follow it as best I can across the clearing. It stops on something. Summat heaped on the ground.

Shite, shite, shite. I've left me bloody kit bag out haven't I. Left it right there where I lay, at the bottom of the crack in the cliff. At the bottom of that little gully, right where Maria and I lay that time and all. Right where anyone could see if they were looking for it. Bollards. Big bloody bollards.

Some soldier you'd make. You bloody inbred.

I've got me glass eye in me hand and I'm rubbing it and squeezing it hard. So hard it feels like I could crush it. Then Banny does summat I divvent expect. He nods backwards with his head, moves the rifle from one hand to the other, then turns and heads back into the trees. And just like that they're gone again.

That's it then. He knows I'm here. He must do. He knows I'm close and he doesn't want to be exposed, not when I'm picking them off with nowt but sharpened sticks.

His eyes are probably on us now. He's probably sent the lad back to get the rest of them and now he's waiting. Mebbes he knows I'm up this bloody cliff with nowt but a glass bloody eye and moonlight for company. Mebbes he thinks he'll flush us out like a cornered rat. And mebbes he's right because in front of us is the drop, round the sides the steep dirt banks that lead down the way I came up and behind us there's just a thick tangle of brambles, then beyond that – fug knows.

I want a tab but I daresn't spark up in case someone sees the flame. I take a couple of steps back and sit mesel down. Then I lay, me chin more or less on the edge of the drop that dips and slopes away into the night.

I fix me night eye on the woods as it all gans quiet. There's nee voices or torch beams, just a spiral of smoke from the smouldering ice cream van off in the distance. I can see easy enough because over that way, out to the east, the sky is already lightening.

I wonder what Maria's doing, what they're planning, what her involvement in all this is and it's sort of doing me head in, but at the same time I now know we can never go back to those moments riding round in the van living the *vida* bloody *loca*, or down there in the clearing, with our kecks off, writhing and moaning and listening to woodpeckers and that. Even a daft twat like me can see that.

Even stupid inbred povvy gyppo John-John Wisdom can see there's no going backwards now.

Amazing really, how quickly it's all turned to shite. And now I've got nowt to lose but me freedom.

What bloody freedom?

Exactly. What bloody freedom.

So you're just going to lie here blubbing again are you, son?

Am I bloody bollards.

What are you going to do then? Hunt them and kill them, the lot of them. Aye, that's exactly what I'd do. And that's exactly what you'll do if you're a true Wisdom.

I'm not though, am I. A true Wisdom. And I never bloody have been. I'm the little bastard secret Wisdom and that's the bloody problem. That's why all of this started. All of this – everything that's happened, right from day one. It's all your fault, Dad.

It's all your fucking fault.

*

And when Mac told you, sneering and stuttering, drunk and laughing with spittle on his lips, you wouldn't believe him. Not at first.

"I done her and I seeded her and that's all there is to it."

You said nowt.

"Do you hear me? Your sister. It's your fucking sister that's your real mother. Not your mother. That's why you come out all wrong."

Then all them things that had troubled you, like why you were born small and puny, like why Charmaine was sent away, and why Bobby beat you, and why you had never felt a part of it, this thing of ours – being a traveller – and why it was you felt no attachment to any of us, except maybe your sister who always looked upon you with sad wide eyes and hugged you tight when she left, all of that suddenly fell into place. It all made some sort of horrific sense to you.

And now your father was a far greater beast than you had even imagined. And now your entire life was a mistake. So you

278

did what you had dreamed of doing every day as far back as you could remember.

"You're a bloody stillborn," he said. "You're the stump in the family tree," he said, and that was when you took the poker and you brayed him. Brayed him and flayed him. Your Dad. Battered him right there in the rotting, stinking van on that cold and lonely site where we'd all festered for years and years.

You took the poker and you struck the man who was your father and grandfather.

You took the poker and smashed the skull of this once feared man.

You hit him so hard his glass eye popped out and rolled across the floor but you didn't even notice because you were panelling his arms and legs too.

And then you stopped and Mac was over, your Dad was over, all of it was over, and you threw the poker aside and you sat down and waited and watched.

Then you noticed his glass eye and you picked it up and looked at it in your hand. You stared at it.

Sweat matted your hair. You closed your eyes and let yourself go, like you were drifting high above the van, a beautiful ascending angel, so high you were looking down on the field and it didn't look so big from up there, just a small insignificant rectangle, nowt special, and mebbes you could see the lane and the road too, and then you were floating higher, up above the patchwork landscape. You'll have seen the woods and the river, the village and the abbey, and over in the distance, in a hollow in the earth, the city gleaming and shimmering and twinkling. It was all you had ever known, but for the first time you could see what lay beyond it. You had done an evil thing my son, you had committed the ultimate sin and in that moment I knew that the life we had known was over, and by the time your Dad was in the soil they'd have sent you away and nothing could ever be the same again, that I'd have to turn my shoulder away from you and finally leave this place forever, turn you out into the world and let you find your own way because in the end, somehow, I knew you would make it.

*

It's getting light now.

The short night is ending and it's at that stage where everything softens. It's like watching an auld fillum. The air is grainy. The grass is rustling and the daisies are stretching and yawning.

I'm thinking about elephants' bones and me Dad and I'm just about nodding off when I see a movement in the trees over to one side of the clearing. A lad emerges. I can't make out which one. He crouches down then looks to his left. I follow his eyes and see someone else step out of the trees at the other side. They crouch low down, but they look out of place in their brightly-coloured street clothes. I can see them a mile off. They need some khaki on, this lot. A nice bit of cammo like me, the bloody great numpties.

I watch them. They sit like that for a bit, then someone else walks out into the clearing between them. It's Banny. He's got a bin bag and the gun is in his hand. He opens the bag and pulls something out of it and sets it on the ground in front of him. It's one of them whatsits. One of them tape player things. One of the git big ones. Ghetto blasters.

He fiddles about with it for a moment then a noise echoes out around the clearing. It's like nowt I've heard before. Like a howl or moan or a cry of pain, but high-pitched and sort of stretched out. It's the worst sound in the world. There's another one, and there's a wash of noise behind it too, a swirl of crackling, distorted laughter. Banny turns the volume up and I hear it again. Louder this time. That tortured howl again, followed by a strangulated yap.

It's a bark. The bark of a dog. My dog. It's Coughdrop. Me Man Friday.

The bastards. They've got him on tape being taken apart in me own bloody living room and they're laughing as they do it. Bloody laughing.

I go to stand. I go to stand and shout come on then you spineless bloody bastards, I'll take the lot of you on right now with me own bare hands, I'll bite your fugging noses off, I'll cut your bollards off and stuff them down your throats.

I go to stand up and shout this from the cliff top. I go to shout it loud across the clearing and over the tree-tops, scream and bellow it all the bloody way to town.

But summat stops us. Summat pulls us back. A force, like gravity gone mental.

No son. Stay where you are. Stay where you are.

It's the force of me Dad. The voice of me Dad an all. Mac bloody Wisdom.

I'll bloody murder them.

No John-John. It's what they want. You stand up and you'll have a bullet in you two seconds from now. You watch.

As he says this I realise it's the first time I can remember him calling us by me proper name. No Little Runt, no Black Sheep. No Little Fucker. Or Inbred. Just John-John.

So what do I do, I whisper.

Well now. That's for you to decide.

But I need to know what to do.

You'll do the right thing, son. Because despite what you think, and despite what they tell you, you always have done.

So I do nowt.

Instead I stay down and all the while Banny's rifle is pointed up here. Trained on us, like. Pointed to where he reckons I might be. I stay down and I listen to him rewind that tape over and over and hear the horrible sound of me little pup being killed by that gang of bloody twats.

Them soft twats.

Them cowardly twats.

Twats who'll go nowhere and do nowt with their worthless lives.

Me, I'm not going to be a part of that. I'm not killing nee-one else and I'm not going back to prison neither. I'm not going back anywhere. I'm going forward, me. I'm going to do things differently, me. I'm never going on the back foot.

Nor.

Never.

I look down once more and there in the still silence of dawn I can see a movement. A tiny movement. It's one leaf trembling on a tree. One leaf among thousands. Among millions. An individual, doing his own thing.

Then I know what to do. Then it all becomes clear.

I take the glass eye from me pocket and place it on the grass, on the edge of the cliff so that it's looking out over the land, right the way across the north-east like a periscope that's popped up deep from within the soil, then I push mesel backwards in a silent retreat.

I work me way back until I can nee longer see the clearing or any of them lot in it. I button up me coat and pull me beanie down and I turn and run toward the thick tangle of brambles behind us, the back wall of the green cathedral. When I reach it I drop down again onto me belly and scurry forward.

I burrow in and the thorns slice at us, at me bare hands and me face. They grab and scratch but after a while it's not so bad and after what seems like a long time I can see light. I push through the thicket towards it and then suddenly I'm out the other side and there's nowt but an open field there. A wide open field, that's been furrowed and ploughed and planted with corn that's come up nicely. There's a whole sea of corn, just swaying gently in the soft early minutes of a beautiful English summer's day.

I run into it, into that golden shimmering sea, up to me hips, and I keep running and the big orange sun that sits behind it all is going come on lad, come to me.

I'll show you the way.

ALSO AVAILABLE BY BENJAMIN MYERS

THE OFFING

An *Observer* Pick for 2019

One summer following the Second World War, Robert Appleyard sets out on foot from his Durham village. Sixteen and the son of a coal miner, he makes his way across the northern countryside until he reaches the former smuggling village of Robin Hood's Bay. There he meets Dulcie, an eccentric, worldly, older woman who lives in a ramshackle cottage facing out to sea.

Staying with Dulcie, Robert's life opens into one of rich food, sea-swimming, sunburn and poetry. The two come from different worlds, yet as the summer months pass, they form an unlikely friendship that will profoundly alter their futures.

'Deeply tender, timely and necessary' Luke Turner

'Both beautiful and beautifully told ... Reaffirms the values and riches of human connection, freedom and the joy of living on your own terms' Rob Cowen

'Dulcie Piper is one of the best characters I've read in ages' Jenn Ashworth

ORDER YOUR COPY:

BY PHONE: +44 (0) 1256 302 699; **BY EMAIL:** DIRECT@MACMILLAN.CO.UK
DELIVERY IS USUALLY 3–5 WORKING DAYS. FREE POSTAGE AND PACKAGING FOR ORDERS OVER £20.
ONLINE: WWW.BLOOMSBURY.COM/BOOKSHOP
PRICES AND AVAILABILITY SUBJECT TO CHANGE WITHOUT NOTICE.

WWW.BLOOMSBURY.COM/AUTHOR/BENJAMIN-MYERS

BLOOMSBURY PUBLISHING

THE GALLOWS POLE

Winner of the 2018 Walter Scott Prize and a Roger Deakin Award

From his remote moorland home, David Hartley assembles a gang of weavers and land-workers to embark upon a criminal enterprise that will capsize the economy and become the biggest fraud in British history. They are the Cragg Vale Coiners and their business is 'clipping' – the forging of coins, a treasonous offence punishable by death. When an excise officer vows to bring them down and with the industrial age set to change the face of England forever, Hartley's empire begins to crumble. Forensically assembled, The Gallows Pole is a true story of resistance and a rarely told alternative history of the North.

'One of my books of the year ... It's the best thing Myers has done' Robert Macfarlane, *Big Issue* Books of the Year

'A windswept, brutal tale of eighteenth-century Yorkshire told in starkly beautiful prose' *Guardian*

'A brutal tale told with an original, muscular voice' *The Times*

ORDER YOUR COPY:

BY PHONE: +44 (0) 1256 302 699; **BY EMAIL:** DIRECT@MACMILLAN.CO.UK

DELIVERY IS USUALLY 3–5 WORKING DAYS. FREE POSTAGE AND PACKAGING FOR ORDERS OVER £20.

ONLINE: WWW.BLOOMSBURY.COM/BOOKSHOP

PRICES AND AVAILABILITY SUBJECT TO CHANGE WITHOUT NOTICE.

WWW.BLOOMSBURY.COM/AUTHOR/BENJAMIN-MYERS

BLOOMSBURY PUBLISHING

BEASTINGS

Winner of the Portico Prize for Literature and the Northern Writers' Award

A girl and a baby. A priest and a poacher. A savage pursuit through the landscape of a changing rural England.

When a teenage girl leaves the workhouse and abducts a child placed in her care, the local priest is called upon to retrieve them. Chased through the Cumbrian mountains of a distant past, the girl fights starvation and the elements, encountering the hermits, farmers and hunters who occupy the remote hillside communities. An American Southern Gothic tale set against the violent beauty of Northern England, *Beastings* is a sparse and poetic novel about morality, motherhood and corruption.

'Intimate and elemental ... Myers has the potential to become a true tragedian of the fells' *Guardian*

'This bitter, alarming, occasionally visionary novel of the British wilderness is likely to linger in the mind for some time' *New Statesman*

'Myers is quite simply an excellent and already accomplished writer. His prose is taut, confident, professionally polished but at the same time maintaining a sense of rustic and unrefined authenticity, that which is truly hewn' Sarah Hall